THE SILENT CHASE

Also by Cap Daniels

The Chase Fulton Novels Series

Book One: *The Opening Chase*
Book Two: *The Broken Chase*
Book Three: *The Stronger Chase*
Book Four: *The Unending Chase*
Book Five: *The Distant Chase*
Book Six: *The Entangled Chase*
Book Seven: *The Devil's Chase*
Book Eight: *The Angel's Chase*
Book Nine: *The Forgotten Chase*
Book Ten: *The Emerald Chase*
Book Eleven: *The Polar Chase*
Book Twelve: *The Burning Chase*
Book Thirteen: *The Poison Chase*
Book Fourteen: *The Bitter Chase*
Book Fifteen: *The Blind Chase*
Book Sixteen: *The Smuggler's Chase*
Book Seventeen: *The Hollow Chase*
Book Eighteen: *The Sunken Chase*
Book Nineteen: *The Darker Chase*
Book Twenty: *The Abandoned Chase*
Book Twenty-One: *The Gambler's Chase*
Book Twenty-Two: *The Arctic Chase*
Book Twenty-Three: *The Diamond Chase*
Book Twenty-Four: *The Phantom Chase*
Book Twenty-Five: *The Crimson Chase*
Book Twenty-Six: *The Silent Chase*
Book Twenty-Seven: *The Shepherd's Chase*

The Avenging Angel – Seven Deadly Sins Series
Book One: *The Russian's Pride*
Book Two: *The Russian's Greed*
Book Three: *The Russian's Gluttony*
Book Four: *The Russian's Lust*
Book Five: *The Russian's Sloth*
Book Six: *The Russian's Envy* (2024)
Book Seven: *The Russian's Wrath* (TBA)

Stand-Alone Novels
We Were Brave
Singer – Memoir of a Christian Sniper

Novellas
The Chase Is On
I Am Gypsy

THE
SILENT
CHASE

CHASE FULTON NOVEL #26

CAP DANIELS

ANCHOR WATCH
PUBLISHING
** USA **

The Silent Chase
Chase Fulton Novel #26
Cap Daniels

This is a work of fiction. Names, characters, places, historical events, and incidents are the product of the author's imagination or have been used fictitiously. Although many locations such as marinas, airports, hotels, restaurants, etc. used in this work actually exist, they are used fictitiously and may have been relocated, exaggerated, or otherwise modified by creative license for the purpose of this work. Although many characters are based on personalities, physical attributes, skills, or intellect of actual individuals, all the characters in this work are products of the author's imagination.

Published by:

ANCHOR WATCH
PUBLISHING
** USA **

13 Digit ISBN: 978-1-951021-57-3
Library of Congress Control Number: 2024934609

Cover Design: German Creative

Printed in the United States of America

The Silent Chase

CAP DANIELS

Chapter 1
Pity for the Enemy

Autumn 2011

My objective lay less than twenty yards ahead, and from my position of partial cover and concealment, there was only one viable route to it. I could cover the distance in less than five seconds, but doing so would expose me to the well-armed, even if poorly trained, gunmen lying in wait for me to make the move they anticipated. Surviving the sprint to the objective might be possible, but freeing the treasure and escaping the kill zone would likely spell my demise.

My heart pounded, and I fed my mind and body the oxygen they required in deliberate cycles of combat breathing: inhale five seconds . . . hold five seconds . . . exhale five seconds . . . hold five seconds. The pattern supplied more-than-sufficient oxygen, but it did something at least equally as important. It gave my mind a course and rhythm, like the bass guitar in a band. Everything, especially combat, needs a rhythm, and my situation in that moment was no exception. Achieving my objective wasn't optional. I *would* claim the treasure, and nothing would stop me.

I was far from alone. Behind and beside me stood, knelt, and lay some of the fiercest and most devoted warriors the world has ever known. Through the decade we'd spent together, we'd grown to move as one body and think as one collective mind. I had lain my life in their hands in countless conflicts on five continents, and they'd never failed me. Just as I trusted them to keep me alive, every man on the team trusted every other as if we were the same blood, the same soul. No force and no foe could shatter the bond my team had forged, nor could they plant the seed of doubt in our thoughts. Failure was not only not an option; it was an impossibility. As surely as my heart beat and my lungs breathed, defeat would not consume us, and failure would not define us.

"Alpha One, Alpha Six."

The confident baritone of Jimmy "Singer" Grossmann, the deadliest sniper I'd ever known, sounded inside my skull as if the voice were my own.

"Go for Alpha One."

Singer said, "Countersniper at three o'clock high."

I subconsciously glanced up and right in a wasted effort to spot the well-concealed marksman. From my vantage point low in the environment, the killer was out of sight, but few, if any, fighters could hide from the eyes of our sniper. Even though I couldn't see Singer's adversary, I didn't need eyes on the target to know the assassin was the greatest threat to my successful rescue of the objective.

"Eliminate the countersniper."

I gave the order as if the tiny movement of Singer's trigger finger wouldn't actually erase another life from the planet. Pity for the enemy could lead only to my demise, so I couldn't allow the humanity—or inhumanity—of my order to enter my conscious thought. Paving the road both in and out of the objective would be done with one press of the trigger and one felled enemy at a time. Patience equals prudence on the field of battle, and patience would keep us alive while our enemies fell.

The shot was barely more than silent as Singer's rifle breathed its deadly hiss. Although Singer's mortal application of his skill was never in question, I waited for his declaration.

"Countersniper eliminated."

I clicked my tongue against the floor of my mouth, sending a ringing vibration through the bone conduction device cemented to my jawbone and then to the transceiver that would send an invisible message hundreds of miles through space and time. The satellites overhead would receive, decipher, transmit, and relay the simple message to the sat-com at my sniper's side and through the tiny device, identical to mine, implanted beneath the flesh of his jaw.

Dr. Celeste Mankiller had been a brilliant technical services officer with the Department of Justice before joining tactical Team Twenty-One, our team of covert operatives. With a bountiful research and development budget and a laboratory any mad scientist would kill to own, Dr. Mankiller was free to unleash her boundless imagination to hone the cutting edge of clandestine gadgetry exclusively for me and the warriors I proudly led.

"Alpha One, Alpha Two."

Marvin "Mongo" Malloy, the giant brain of our team, whose physical size more than matched his intellectual prowess, said, "I'm hit."

I swallowed the bitter taste hanging in my throat as the thought of losing Mongo became a reality.

I said, "Medic is en route."

Mongo answered almost instantly. "Negative. I'm out of the fight, and there's no ingress for the medic. It's done, but Chase, don't let them beat us. Don't let this be in vain."

The nobility of the man who bore the burden of second-in-command was beyond question, and carrying on without him at my side was almost unthinkable. But letting his end come un-avenged was more than I or my team would allow.

Pressing on when brothers-in-arms fall in the fiery pit of bat-tle is the darkest of all demands on the soul of the surviving war-rior. The bodies of our dead and wounded would be claimed, but not before the objective—the mission—was accomplished.

Clint "Gator" Barrow, the newest member of our team, crawled into position five yards to my right and surveyed the open killing field in front of him. His eye caught mine, and I didn't have to guess what he was thinking.

I whispered, "Don't do it, Alpha Eight."

He continued studying the void between us and our goal. "It's the only way."

"No," I demanded. "There has to be another option."

Gator said, "I'm going. We're pinned down, and none of us will make it out of here if I don't. I'll draw their attention and their fire while you make the rescue."

Sacrifice is the hallmark of the patriot, and every warrior un-der my command was the epitome thereof. Jesus Himself said, "Greater love hath no man than this, that a man lay down his life for his friends."

Every soul on our team—our family—would, without hesita-tion, sacrifice himself not only for the lives of his team, but also for the life of anyone reaching in desperation for the flag of free-dom. Bravery, strength, and sacrifice were more than mere words. They were the standards under which my team marched and lived every day of their lives.

I reissued the command, but it fell on deaf ears. "Stand down, Alpha Eight."

As if I'd never spoken at all, Gator drew his boots beneath his body and sprang from his position so close yet so distant. The sacrifice was made. He was committed, and I wouldn't allow his valiant effort to wither on the vine. The fire came, and rounds filled the air, riddling Gator's body with the crimson stains of war.

Singer said, "Three down, Alpha One. Go, go, go!"

The three rounds our sniper put in the air while Gator made the ultimate sacrifice found their marks on the exposed enemy shooters, and the door was open. I lunged from my position and willed my legs to carry my body across the battlefield that had become my entire world in only seconds. Almost before my mind could realize the victory, the prize was in my grasp, and I was turning on a heel to escape the slaughterhouse in which I'd risked everything to achieve the ultimate victory.

Three strides into my egress, I was at full speed and more determined than ever to make my escape. My rifle bounced against my chest at the ends of the sling around my neck and shoulder. My breath came hard, my mind no longer counting seconds between inhalation and exhalations. I was running for my life, and victory lay only feet away . . . until it happened.

The foe I could've never expected stepped into my path, rifle raised, ultimate determination beaming from dark eyes, and I faltered. Instead of raising my weapon in a desperate effort to beat my adversary to the trigger, I staggered sideways and grabbed my chest in disbelief as the bullets of my enemy found their mark and the pink mist of what had been life sprayed in every direction from the impact.

With the mission a failure and the battle lost, I fell to my knees and stared up into the dark eyes that had been my undoing, my ultimate weakness, and my greatest joy.

My beautiful, captivating wife, Penny Fulton, stood over me, her paintball gun held at the ready and glee exploding from her face. She spun and laughed. "Girls win! We beat the super spies!"

The women we loved showed themselves from behind inflated barricades and makeshift hiding holes, leaping and dancing like excited children, and my embarrassed team ambled from their positions, heads held low.

I stood. "Would you believe me if I told you that we *let* you win?"

Chapter 2
Recess to Excess

If ever there was an island of misfit toys, it was Bonaventure Plantation, my family's ancestral home nestled on the west bank of the North River in Saint Marys, Georgia, where my team lived, worked, played, trained, and grew into a family like no other. Recess was everybody's favorite part of the day, and when we weren't on a mission, life for the family was an ongoing state of recess to excess, but when someone pulled our pin and tossed the grenade, we were into the fray, and the resulting explosion was anything but child's play.

Our enormous table made for the perfect setting when dinner was served family-style. Clark's wife, Maebelle, was a world-renowned chef and just happened to be my cousin. When our great uncle, Judge Bernard Henry Huntsinger, passed away, Bonaventure became mine, and Maebelle's inheritance became El Juez, the hottest new restaurant on South Beach. When the whole gang was home, Maebelle loved nothing more than seeing all of us devour her latest creation and come running back for seconds.

With dessert astern and steaming cups of coffee lining the table, I said, "I want a rematch."

Penny laughed. "Okay, fine. But this time, I'm calling your little Russian girlfriend to join us. With her on our side, we'll beat you boys in record time."

"She's not my girlfriend," I said.

Penny lowered her gaze. "That may be your position, but that's not how she sees it. If I were out of the picture, she'd move in here tomorrow."

"Come on. If that's really what she wanted, why did she give you part of her liver?"

"I've been thinking a lot about that," she said. "I'd really like to ask her that question face-to-face."

"Why?"

She chewed her lip for a moment. "I'd really like to know. I'm sure she had some ulterior motive. Nobody gives their ex-boyfriend's wife an organ purely out of the goodness of their heart."

"What ulterior motive could she have?"

"I don't know. But why don't you give her a call and make up some reason to ask her to come to Bonaventure for a few days?"

"That's crazy. What kind of reason?"

"Why's it crazy?" Penny asked. "What are you afraid of?"

I stared down the table, hoping someone would come to my rescue, and Mongo volunteered. I only thought he was on my side.

The big man said, "Don't get me wrong. I love watching Chase sweat, but I've got a better idea than inviting Anya to come to Bonaventure."

The look on Penny's face said she was intrigued. The look on mine probably said I was still way too uncomfortable with the whole ordeal.

Mongo said, "Tatiana is dancing as Odette and Odile in Swan Lake at the Metropolitan Opera House in New York on Saturday and Sunday. Irina and I are going, of course, and Anya will be there to see Little Anya in her first principal performance."

My heart sank. *That's what I need in my life. Sitting through two days of ballet I don't understand and my wife communing with*

Anya, the woman Penny thinks wants to be back in my bed more than anything else in the world.

Before I could protest, Penny's eyes lit up like a Christmas tree. "That's perfect. I'm in." She grabbed my hand. "You can come, too, if you want."

"Oh, I wouldn't miss it for the world." Those were the words that came from my lips, but the look I shot Mongo carried quite a different message.

In addition to being the strongest man I'd ever met, Mongo had a soft side no one would ever suspect. When he married Irina Volkovna, he got a Russian two-for-one deal that changed his life forever. Irina's daughter, Tatiana, had wrapped the big man around her little finger in an instant. She studied at the Bolshoi prior to defecting to the States with her mother. Tatiana was a prodigy by any definition. Ballet ran in her veins where blood should've been, and she became the shining star of Juilliard and the most highly sought-after ballerina in the country.

"It is date," Irina said. "We will have wonderful time in New York." Apparently, the Russian accent is impossible to shed, but Irina was trying.

Since misery loves company, I said, "Let's all go. It's on me."

Skipper, our brilliant analyst and practically my little sister, leapt to her feet. "I'll make the reservations."

A few groans escaped the lips of my brothers-in-arms, but if I was going to suffer through it, I wasn't going to do it alone.

Gator stared around the room as if begging anyone to tell him what just happened.

Singer threw an arm around his understudy. "Do you like the ballet, kid?"

He shrugged. "I like ballerinas. Does that count?" That got a chuckle, and he cocked his head. "Anya is Chase's Russian girl-friend . . . The hot blonde, right?"

I lifted a knife from the table and pointed it straight at Gator. "You're fired, and I'm trying to talk myself out of killing you right now."

Penny pulled the knife from my hand and held it to my neck. "Don't worry, Gator. You're not fired, and no one is going to kill you."

I croaked out, "She's not my girlfriend, and she's way less hot than Penny. *Way* less."

My wife dropped the knife. "Good answer. And for the record, nobody has to go who doesn't want to go . . . except Chase."

"Oh, no," I said. "Skipper's already made the reservations. We're committed. All of us."

* * *

Friday arrived, and the whole family climbed aboard the *Grey Ghost*, our Gulfstream IV, that would whisk us away to the Big Apple. We touched down at Teterboro two hours later, and the bite of the cool autumn air was only the first sting I'd endure for the weekend.

Skipper, as usual, knocked it out of the park as the team's travel agent. Our hotel just off Columbus Circle, overlooking Central Park, was five-star, from the doorman to the penthouse, but ultra-luxury is often wasted on knuckle-draggers like my team and me. The warm, damp towels on little silver platters made us look like savages. I'll admit that I was neither sophisticated enough nor smart enough to understand why we needed fancy wet washcloths in the lobby of a hotel, but one of the bellmen leaned in and whispered, "Don't worry. Ain't nobody needs one of them pretentious towels. Come on. I'll take you up."

It took all three elevators and four bellmen to haul us and our bags to the suite of rooms on the fifteenth floor. My new best friend, the bellman, accepted the pair of folded bills I pressed into his palm, and he said, "You guys have got the whole floor. It's all yours, and I promise ain't nobody gonna bring you no more of them goofy towels. The only thing on silver trays up here is some of the best chocolate in the city."

He shot a glance into his palm and pocketed the tip. "Thank you, sir. What brings you guys to the city?"

I chuckled at the words that were about to come out of my mouth. "We're going to the ballet."

He recoiled. "You don't say. Which one?"

"There's more than one?"

He waved his arms. "This is New York. There's more than one of everything and too many of a lot of things, if you ask me."

I pointed down the hall. "Did you see that huge dude with us?"

"Yeah, sure, Goliath. How could I miss him?"

"His daughter is the principal dancer in Swan Lake at the Metropolitan Opera House."

"No way," he said. "The wife and me seen that one last week." He palmed his chest. "I know, I know . . . I don't look like no patron of the arts neither, but I gots this little niece, and she's a little ballerina or whatever. You know how it is."

I held up a finger. "Wait right here."

I was back in sixty seconds with Mongo at my side. I said, "Mongo, meet my new buddy."

The bellman stuck out his hand. "Charles. Not Chuck or Charlie, but Charles, at your service."

Charles's hand disappeared into the big man's.

"Call me Mongo. Nice to meet you, Charles."

"Mongo, it is. Mother of God, you're a giant up in here."

The big man shrugged, and I said, "Charles's niece is a ballerina, and they saw Swan Lake last week. I thought maybe we could ask Tatiana if she could do something for the little girl."

Mongo grinned. "Give me your number, and I'll have my daughter set up a backstage visit for your niece."

"Oh, no way," Charles said. "Get outta here."

Mongo produced a pen, and Charles pulled a card from his pocket. He wrote a number on the back and handed it to Mongo.

"What's her name?" Mongo asked.

"Tiffany Pagliano."

Mongo said, "My daughter is Tatiana Volkovna. We're having dinner with her tonight, and I'll have her give you a call to set it up."

Charles shook his head. "Really, this is all too much. Little Tiffany is going to freak out when she hears about this. My wife, too. She was a dancer a long time ago, but not no more. She's packed on more than a few pounds since them days. You know what I'm saying?"

Mongo patted his stomach. "There's nothing wrong with a few extra pounds."

"Whatever you say. You're the one with the Russian ballerina for a daughter. At least she sounds like a Russian."

"She was, but she's red, white, and blue through and through now."

Charles said, "I don't know what to say. Thanks again, you guys."

Mongo said, "Don't mention it. Tatiana will be glad to do it."

* * *

Neckties should've been outlawed before they were invented, and whoever came up with the idea for the bowtie should've been choked out with a shoelace and drawn and quartered. I'd never seen a team of warriors look more dapper or uncomfortable than we did in our black tuxedoes.

Clark said, "If I had a monocle and a top hat, I could be Mr. Peanut."

I laughed. "We should've brought Earl and Kenny. They would've fit right in."

Earl was Earline Pendergrass Buck, a certified boat bum and the best diesel mechanic on Earth. And she was the same height lying down as she was standing up. Kenny was the person Earl called "her man." To the rest of the world, he was Cajun Kenny LePine, owner and operator of the most honest and hardworking heavy equipment company in coastal Georgia. They made quite a pair, but I'd put money and good odds on the fact that Kenny would never be caught dead in a tux, and Earl probably didn't own a dress.

A fleet of black SUVs carried us the five blocks to the compound that housed the Metropolitan Opera House between Columbus Avenue and Amsterdam.

As we turned onto a street north of our hotel, Clark's eyes lit up. "Look at that! Sesame Street is a real street. Who knew?"

I tried to pretend I was worldly enough to know New York like the back of my hand, but I was just as surprised as Clark.

The opera house wasn't the only prestigious structure in the neighborhood. The massive compound housed the Lincoln Center, the Guggenheim Bandshell, the Koch Theater, and the New York Philharmonic. I could step onto any battlefield in the world and feel confident I'd survive whatever the enemy threw at me, but the Upper West Side was a battleground I hoped I'd never have to defend. Urban warfare in that arena was for someone else. Give me a muddy hole in a rainforest any day, but keep me out of the concrete jungle.

As good as Skipper was at arranging everything, even she couldn't arrange for all of us to sit together. There were no bad seats in the opera house, but the tickets I held placed Penny and me in row five at center stage, right beside Mongo and Irina.

Gator's odd-man-out ticket planted him in the row with us, so he tagged along until we stepped into the aisle leading down to our seats. And that's when it happened.

A breathtaking blonde in the most elegant black gown imaginable slipped her gloved hand inside Gator's elbow, and in her undeniable Russian accent, said, "You are new person who I do not know yet. I will be for you date for ballet, yes?"

Gator froze in disbelief and stared at Anastasia Robertovna Burinkova.

I was thankful beyond words that she'd taken his arm instead of mine, and I said, "Gator, meet Anya. Anya, he's the new guy, Gator."

She cooed. "Is pleasure for me. You are beautiful man, and I am lucky girl."

Gator's eyes flew back and forth between Penny and Anya. "Uh, you're *the* Anya?"

She said, "I am only Anya. Why would there be another?"

Chapter 3
Tears of a Giant

We made our way to our seats, with Gator unable to take his eyes off the Russian on his arm.

Penny brushed past him and whispered, "Watch out. She'll cut off your tongue while you're sleeping."

Gator made a show of wiggling his tongue inside his mouth and whispered back, "It might be worth it."

No one could deny Anya's physical beauty, but with her and Penny standing side by side, I had no doubt in my head or in my heart that I made the best decision any man could make. I wouldn't trade my North Texas beauty for a thousand Russian Anyas.

The house lights went down, and the curtain went up only minutes after we settled into our seats. I can't say I was excited about the coming two hours—or more—of my life, but I was intrigued by the sideshow to my left, with Penny and Anya sitting next to each other in the dark.

A powerful wave of sound poured from the pit as the orchestra came alive. It was as if the music flowed through me and became part of me rather than simply processing through my hearing aids and into my skull. I was immediately drawn into the performance before anyone stepped onto the stage. Everything around me was still happening, but all of it seemed, somehow, trivial as the performance consumed the room.

A man in tights—exactly what I *wasn't* looking forward to seeing—flitted across the stage, leaping, spinning, and posturing. He was obviously physically fit, but so were the men and women sitting around me. None of us could dance like him, but I laughed quietly to myself when I thought of him going fisticuffs with Hunter or Gator. The guy may have had impressive calves, but I doubted he could take a punch.

Then, everything changed. The stage filled with more dancers than I could count, all dressed perfectly in white, with their flared skirts cutting through the air as they spun, leapt, and danced en pointe. I grimaced as I thought of the thousands of hours they must've spent with their feet extended and their full weight on their toes, one foot at a time. I'd spent years with a combat boot strapped to my one remaining foot, but the discomfort I experienced was pure luxury compared to the agony those young women must've endured every day.

The corps de ballet, as I later learned the mass of dancers was called, moved with such graceful power, it was almost like watching elite soldiers moving in unison and silence. I couldn't look away as the music, combined with the choreography, demanded my attention. I'd never experienced anything that filled my senses and demanded my focus more powerfully than what I was witnessing.

The mesmerizing story played out before my eyes, and practically at my fingertips, in the traditional Russian arrangement of three acts of four scenes, and within moments of its beginning, I never wanted it to end. Time seemed to stand still and pass too quickly to measure it all in the same instant, yet, somehow, I found the ability to look away from the stage for only a moment.

In that instant, with my eyes cast to the side, I saw Irina's small hands wrapped lovingly around Mongo's massive forearms and

tears streaming down the big man's face. Just as I'd been mesmer-
ized by the whole performance, Mongo, my brother-in-arms, was
focused with laser-like attention on Tatiana, the child who'd captured his heart and then grown to become the master of the stage
before us. She danced with such beauty and elegance, making every pose appear effortless as she floated to every note of the music
blooming from beneath the stage. I'd seen my brother tear men
apart with his empty hands. I'd seen him crush enemies as if they
were nothing more than trash beneath his feet. I'd seen him per-
form acts of strength that saved countless lives on battlefields all
over the world. I'd witnessed his strength at its indescribable apex,
but I'd never seen his heart and soul as I saw them that night. Every tear spoke of love for a child he hadn't fathered, but who he
treasured above all else. As moving as the dancers and musicians
were, the one thing above all else that I'll never forget that night
was how strong the unseeable force of true love can be in a moment so public, yet so personal, for one of the mightiest warriors
I've ever known.

Still in disbelief, I glanced to my left to see Penny entranced at
the spectacle before us, and just beyond the woman I adored,
Anya pressed a finger to the corner of her eye, stifling the tear that
was desperately yearning to escape. In that moment, in that place,
something more than emotion and fascination overtook me. It
was the realization of how our minds and bodies can react and
succumb to the ultimate amalgamation of true grace, beauty, and
precision.

Our hearts thundered in our chests as if the hundreds of us inside the opera house were one body swirling and living the story
before us. We gasped in unison. We cheered as one. And when the
final dramatic scene unfolded and Tatiana as Odette threw herself
into Swan Lake, followed by her lover, Siegfried, we shared a moment of disbelief and emptiness until the masterful scene revealed

the expression of Siegfried's and Odette's boundless love for each other and broke the spell of the enchanter, killing Von Rothbart at center stage, and the lovers' spirits reunited for eternity.

As the story closed, the audience exploded from their seats, pouring uproarious applause and cries of praise for the dancers, the orchestra, and especially for the principal ballerina, Tatiana Volkovna. As she took her bows with roses falling like raindrops at her feet, she pressed her hands to her chest in sincerest appreciation for the admiration. Just as I'd known the fury of battle was where I was meant to be, Tatiana had found her home, her purpose, on the stage before throngs of adoring fans—especially the ones who belonged in body armor and boots instead of tuxedoes and tails.

Mongo dried his face and held Irina in his arms, consumed by emotion and pride. Anya stood with her face held in the stoic expression of the proper Russian woman and clapped her hands, never taking her eyes off the beautiful woman on stage who'd once been called Little Anya by her ruthless uncle, a Russian mafia boss who met his fate at the deadly hand of Anastasia Burinkova.

As the lights came up and the awestricken audience made its way from the opera house, Mongo and Irina moved against the crowd to get closer to their daughter, whose lifelong dreams had just come true. They disappeared behind the stage, and I caught a glimpse of Charles, our doorman, and the girl who must've been his niece slipping behind the curtains for their promised backstage experience with the principal ballerina.

Outside the opera house, most of our family was reunited, with the exception of Mongo and Irina, who were no doubt still reveling in the moment with Irina. Our black SUVs returned and parked in a neat row that was reminiscent of convoy procedures we'd used around the world. The vehicles weren't hardened with armor plating and bullet-resistant glass, but with a few thousand dollars and a few days of work, they could've been battle-ready, just like my team.

I watched a scene play out before my eyes that could've harbored the same drama and emotion we'd witnessed inside on the stage. The stage for the act I was watching was destined to be the back seat of the lead SUV. Penny took Anya's hand and led her toward the vehicle. A knot the size of Times Square formed in the pit of my stomach as the two slipped onto the seat and closed the door.

Skipper slipped her hand inside my elbow and leaned close. "Want to hear what they're saying?"

I glanced down into the mischievous eyes of our analyst. "How?"

She pulled a credit card–sized receiver from her purse, squeezed a corner, and slipped it into my jacket pocket. "Enjoy."

My ears were only the most recent sacrifice I'd made in my life's work of pressing back when bad guys targeted the country and the people I loved. Thanks to the miracle of modern audiology, I could hear better than a twenty-year-old through the electronic devices that had become part of my body. I stepped away from the crowd and listened as Penny opened the conversation.

"That was really something, wasn't it?"

Anya said, "Yes, it was beautiful. Tatiana is already master. Did you know I was to be figure skater for Soviet Union when I was child?"

I could almost see Penny cocking her head. "No, I didn't know that. What happened?"

"I was strongheaded person, even when I was child. I hated cold, and skates hurt my feet. I refused to learn because of this. I was also strong in body, not only in will of mind. This is why I was next chosen to become gymnast. This was very good for me, and I learned quickly and grew stronger every day until . . ."

A moment of silence came, and I tapped the receiver to make sure it was still working.

Finally, Penny asked, "Until what?"

"Until I grew too tall. My legs were too long for gymnastics, and I was too strong for Soviet Union to waste. This is when I became student of KGB before SVR."

Another moment passed, and Penny spoke softly. "I'm sorry, Anya. I didn't know."

"Is okay. I am now living comfortable life inside USA most of time, and is maybe better than life of former gymnast inside Russia would have been."

The tone of the conversation changed when Penny cleared her throat. "Listen, Anya. I never got the chance to—"

"Do not give to me thanks."

"But I have to. You saved my life. Without the partial liver transplant, I would've died. You didn't have to do what you did. It was the greatest gift anyone could've ever given me."

Anya's cold tone, a tone only Russian women seem to have mastered, filled my ears. "I did not give to you gift. I gave to Chase. He saved my life many times, and was only right for me to give to him gift of your life when I had power to do this."

Penny sighed. "You'll always love him, won't you?"

"This is terrible thing for you to hear from me. I will not be cruel to you."

Penny continued. "It's not cruel to love somebody, Anya. Cruelty is *not* loving those we should."

"This is for me hard to understand."

Penny asked, "Why didn't you let me die? Then you could've had Chase."

The Russian said, "I am sad you think I would do something like that."

"Are you saying you wouldn't want Chase if something were to happen to me?"

Anya said, "Now, I believe maybe you do not understand. Loving someone for me means giving that person what he wants most of all, and you are what Chase wants more than anything in all of world."

"I'm not sure that's always true. Sometimes, it feels like he needs the thrill or rush or whatever he gets from doing, you know, what he does with the team more than he needs me."

Anya said, "English for me is second language, but even I know difference between *want* and *need*. We need to breathe air for our body to be alive, but we want to feel love and respect and security with someone so our mind and heart can be alive. This is what you are for Chase. You are person he loves most of all, and also person he most wants to keep him alive inside soul."

I'd never heard such sincerity from Anya, and I was astonished at how thoroughly she understood the man I am. She was right. I needed the bullets in the air and the blood and sweat on my skin, but I wanted Penny more than I'd ever wanted anything.

Anya said, "I do not say this to hurt you. Is simply truth. I gave part of my body to you so you could be alive and Chase could have what he wants most of all. This is only way I have to tell him I love him."

Silence ruled the air for another long break until Penny said, "That's the most warped, screwed-up reason I've ever heard for doing anything, but from you, for some reason, it makes sense."

She laughed, and Anya joined her. Hearing the two of them laughing together wasn't something I ever imagined possible, and to be honest, it scared me to death.

I heard some shuffling coming through the transmitter, so I stepped back toward the crowd. I didn't want either woman to believe I'd been eavesdropping when they stepped from the SUV, but my assessment had been a mistake. They weren't getting out.

It must've been Anya repositioning herself for what came next. "I want to tell to you something you can never tell anyone. You can do this, yes?"

Penny said, "What is it?"

"You must first give to me vow you will never tell anyone."

"Yeah, okay. I won't tell. What is it?"

Anya said, "This includes Chase . . . especially Chase. You can never tell this to him."

Penny didn't hesitate. "No, that's not how this works. I tell Chase everything. I don't keep anything from him. Omission is the worst lie."

Anya asked, "Even when telling him will only hurt him, you still tell everything?"

"We don't keep secrets, Anya. It's not what we do. I know he can't always tell me where he's going or what he's doing, but there are good reasons for that. I can understand and deal with that, but if you're going to tell me some secret I'm supposed to keep from Chase, don't waste your breath. I don't want to hear it."

Both rear doors of the SUV opened simultaneously, and Penny stepped onto the sidewalk. The doors closed, and I caught a glimpse of blonde hair in the wind on the opposite side of the vehicle. Anya was gone again, and Penny was stepping to my side, precisely where I wanted—and needed—her to be.

Chapter 4
Tell Her

One of the golden rules of covert operations is never tell everything you know. Often, confidential knowledge can mean the difference between completing the mission and failing to stay alive. Little did I know how important that rule would become in the coming days and weeks of my life.

As I stepped into the waiting SUV, Skipper pressed her hip against my door, pinning it open, and she took me by the wrist. "Tell her."

"Tell who what?"

She rolled her eyes. "You're smarter than that, Chase. Tell Penny you heard the conversation with Anya."

I threw up a little. Or at least I wanted to. "You can't be serious."

Skipper lowered her chin. "Trust me on this one. You don't have to tell her you planted a bug in the vehicle, but you have to tell her you heard the conversation."

"I didn't plant the bug. *You* did."

She shrugged. "Semantics. Just tell her."

Back inside the hotel suite, my mind was still reeling from three different angles. The ballet was one of the most incredible things I'd ever seen, and it wouldn't leave my mind's eye. Penny's conversation with Anya, and especially the secret she wasn't willing to keep, kept ricocheting inside my skull.

What was Anya going to tell my wife? What could she possibly want Penny to know that had to be kept from me?

Finally, Skipper's admonition tugged at the logic inside my head. Telling Penny I listened in on her conversation almost felt like admitting betrayal. I could wait and let her bring it up, but delaying the conversation felt a lot like the lie of omission Penny hated above all else.

The woman I loved dropped her gown onto the floor beside the bed and slid beneath the cover beside me. "Wasn't Tatiana amazing tonight?"

"I've never seen anything like it," I said. "And I have a confession to make."

She propped up on an elbow, obviously intrigued.

I said, "I wasn't looking forward to the ballet. I had a headful of preconceived notions about how it would be a live-action chick flick."

She raised an eyebrow. "And now that you've seen it?"

"I want to go back tomorrow."

She frowned. "Back home?"

"No, back to see Swan Lake again. I may have to give up my man card, but it was one of the most impressive things I've ever seen."

Penny laid her head on my shoulder and slid her body against mine. "I'm glad you enjoyed it. If you really want to see it again, I'm up for it."

"There's something else I need to tell you," I said.

"Is it another mission?"

Her question almost made my coming confession a relief. "No, it's nothing like that. As far as I know, I'm not going anywhere soon."

She slid a leg across mine, and my caveman brain told my body to forget about the sabertoothed tiger outside and devour my wife.

Skipper's insistence beat the caveman back into his hole, and I said, "I overheard your conversation with Anya."

She hooked her heel behind my calf and pulled our bodies even closer. "Good. I was hoping you had."

"Really? Why?"

She brushed a strand of hair out of her face. "I don't have anything to hide from you. That's the reason I cracked the window. I didn't know how the conversation would go, so I thought it might be a good idea to have a loving ear tuned in."

"You're an astonishing woman, Penny Fulton."

"And you're still a caveman, Chase Fulton. Now, let's stop talking about Anya, and I'll show you just how astonishing your wife can be."

"I like the sound of that."

She abruptly pulled away and wagged a finger. "And so help me, Chase. If you think about Anya once tonight, I'm going to do something far worse than cutting your tongue in half."

I asked, "Who's Anya?"

* * *

I must've slept through Penny's escape from the bed and her shower because I was awakened by the feel of her wet hair dangling in my face. When I opened my eyes to see her only inches above me, I grabbed one shoulder and the opposite hip and flipped her across my body and onto the bed. "Good morning. What's your name again?"

She drove a thumb into my ribs. "You'll pay for that one, mister. How'd you sleep?"

I stretched and yawned. "Apparently, I slept like the dead. What time is it?"

"Almost eight. Are you hungry?"

I slid a hand around her waist and pulled her to me.

She pushed away. "Not that kind of hungry, you dog."

"I could go for some eggs."

She hopped up and pulled on her robe. "Good, because I ordered room service. It should be here any minute."

I dragged myself from the best hotel bed I'd ever slept on and climbed into the shower. By the time I was dry, dressed in shorts and a T-shirt, and had my prosthetic attached to my knee, a waiter had delivered our breakfast. We ate while watching the sun climb above Central Park, and it was spectacular.

When I'd swallowed the last bite of French toast and wiped my mouth, I asked, "How much did this cost us?"

Penny smiled. "It doesn't matter."

"Of course it matters. If I had to guess, I'd say it was at least two hundred bucks."

She kissed the tip of her finger and pressed it to my lips. "I don't care how much it costs because I just sold another screenplay, and that means, for the first time ever, I made more money than you did this year."

I laced my fingers together behind my head and leaned back. "I could get used to being a kept man."

She choked on her orange juice. "Who do you think you're fooling? You'd lose your mind if you weren't working."

I rubbed my stomach. "I don't know. I think I could get fat and lazy and learn to love afternoon soap operas."

"What'll it be? *The Young and the Restless* or *General Hospital*?"

"Maybe both. We've got a DVR."

She crushed a napkin into a golf ball–sized weapon and hurled it at me. "Put on some real clothes, kept man. We're doing a private tour of Manhattan this morning."

I batted the napkin from the air. "Oh, we are? What if I had other plans?"

She grinned. "Cancel them. I'm more important."

I laughed. "Yes, you are."

I pulled on a pair of jeans and layers for my upper body.

Penny patted my pistol tucked beneath a couple of layers. "You can't carry that in New York City. It's against the law."

I produced my Secret Service credentials. "I've got a waiver."

"That's not a real badge."

"Oh, it's real, all right. I just don't have to guard the president while he's galivanting around doing whatever presidents do."

She placed her palm against my chest. "Speaking of doing whatever they do . . . What do you think Anya's secret is?"

"I don't know or care."

She rolled her eyes. "That's not true. You may not know, but you care. Sometimes you care too much, and that's one of the things I love about you."

"Seriously," I said. "No matter what her secret is, it doesn't affect my life. She probably caught a man in her web, and she's going to marry him or something like that. But again, it doesn't matter. I want her to be happy and safe, but other than working together occasionally, nothing in her life has any connection to mine."

"Okay, Mr. Say-The-Right-Thing. Nicely done. I doubt it's a man, though."

"What are you talking about?"

"I don't think she was going to tell me about a man in her life."

"How could you possibly know?"

"I'm a woman, and sometimes, women just know. She didn't have that gleam in her eye that women get when they're in love."

I shook my head. "Whatever it was, it was a mind game. That's what she does. She plays with people's heads and watches their reactions. That's what she's trained to do."

She hooked a finger behind my belt buckle. "From what I hear, that's not all she's trained to do."

I stepped back. "We're not having that discussion. Now, tell me about this private tour."

"We're playing tourists for the day. Skipper and I arranged for a private motor coach and tour guide. We're doing all the must-sees in the city, including the Statue of Liberty."

"I've seen her up close and personal," I said.

"Yeah, but this time, there won't be anybody shooting at you."

"I like the sound of that. So, the tour is for all of us? Not just you and me?"

"Yep, that's right. The whole big, happy family, including Tatiana and Grayson."

"Do you think she'll let me see her feet?"

"What kind of question is that, you freak? Why would you want to see Tatiana's feet?"

"You saw those dancers last night dancing en pointe. I want to know what that does to a person's feet."

"Look at you, all sophisticated and stuff. Who knew you knew terms like *en pointe*? I'm impressed."

"I'm not an ignorant wretch," I said. "I have some culture."

"Yeah, well, so does bacteria, and no, you cannot ask to see her feet. That's weird."

The motor coach Penny and Skipper arranged was no ordinary tour bus. It was an ultra-luxury coach with leather seats, individual climate-controlled zones, and refreshments. We saw the Empire State Building and even went to the top of Rockefeller Center. The view was magnificent, and Singer spent half an hour teaching Gator how to select the perfect sniper position. The new guy listened and learned under the master's tutelage, but I was on vacation. Playing tourist was absolutely the opposite of the real world for me, and I savored every second of it.

On our way downtown, toward the Financial District, we had high tea on the bus. My team of knuckle-draggers argued over why rich people held out their pinky fingers when they drank their tea.

I listened and laughed as long as I could, and when it had gone too far, I said, "Hey, guys. While you're arguing over the stuff rich people do, take a look at your bank accounts."

Clark held up his teacup in a toast. "And that's exactly why I'll drink my tea any way I want. Sweet, on ice, with a splash of bourbon is my preference."

We stopped to see the Charging Bull statue on Broadway, and Gator decided he needed to ride the iconic creature.

Hunter gave me an elbow. "The kid fits right in, doesn't he?"

"I'm afraid so," I said.

I crossed the street, leaned against the Cipriani Club building, and watched my family take each other's pictures with the bull. I'd seen them lie in the mud and sand and frozen earth, with bullets flying over their heads, and then return the wall of fire. I'd seen them sweat and bleed and fall, only to climb back to their feet and keep fighting. I'd seen the warriors they were, and I'd put that team up against any other tactical team on the planet, knowing we'd come out on top. I'd seen them at their hardest, and watching them misbehave like tourists reminded me that beneath their body armor, boots, and helmets, they were men, like so many others, who loved and laughed and cried and lived. The difference was simple. We could turn it off and become guardians of a humanity who'd never see them and an enemy's worst nightmare. We were still human, but inside of us was something harder, something hotter, something unwilling to lie down and die.

That's when I heard the voice. "I need to talk with you, Mr. Fulton."

Chapter 5
Unwanted Attention

I was well-trained, highly experienced, and battle-hardened, so a voice calling my name in an unfamiliar city almost a thousand miles from home shouldn't have rattled me, but it did. I flinched and reached for my pistol concealed beneath my jacket, but a gentle hand fell across mine.

"Don't pull your gun, Chase. We don't need that kind of attention."

The woman's tone was confident and relaxed. A thousand wheels churning inside my head assessed the situation to be serious but not threatening. She wore a scarf wrapped around her neck and mouth and a toboggan covering her hairline and ears. A pair of oversized sunglasses rested on her face, reflecting my image back at me.

I didn't draw my Glock, but I didn't release my grip. "Who are you?"

She lifted her hand from mine and pulled off her glasses. The eyes were familiar, but my reeling mind couldn't come up with a name or a reason I should know those eyes. A glance across the street reassured me that even on vacation, my team was never off duty.

Clark stood with one hand tucked beneath his sweater, undoubtedly resting on the pistol he'd selected for the day. Singer was moving north with one eye on me and the other scanning the crowd of civilians. Hunter moved southward with the same posture as our northbound sniper. Mongo strode toward me with ambition in his eye. Since the day we met, Mongo had assumed the role of protector. Perhaps it was his nature, but regardless of the reason, I deeply appreciated his willingness to step between me and any threat.

I wasn't convinced the woman standing only inches away from me was a threat, so I extended four fingers, signaling the giant to keep his distance for now.

The woman said, "Thank you for stopping him. I don't want to fight that one. Your men are good, Chase. That's exactly why I came to you."

The hair on the back of my neck was still standing at attention, but I was on the verge of believing the woman was no immediate threat.

Singer and Hunter crossed the street and took up positions ten yards north and south of where the woman and I stood. Mongo held his ground on the edge of the sidewalk, just across Broadway. Disco stood beside Gator, apparently talking him through the scene. Skipper maneuvered Penny behind the enormous bull statue and pressed her phone to her ear. I wondered who was on the other end of the line, but most of all, I loved that Skipper's first instinct was to protect Penny.

Irina, Mongo's Russian wife, was the wild card. Although not officially a member of the team, she possessed a skill set of her own, making her a dangerous adversary. She brushed past Mongo with her gloved hands curled into fists. Her training as a Russian GRU operative had occurred two decades before, but training of that magnitude endures.

"Who are you?" I asked as I studied every visible inch of the woman's face.

She glanced up at Irina, who was drawing ever nearer, and said, "Stop her before she turns this into a spectacle."

I raised a hand just as I'd done to halt Mongo, but Irina ignored the signal. Horns blared, but she pressed on through the passing cars.

"Stop her, Chase. You don't want this to turn into a scene."

The voice . . . the eyes . . . the posture. The woman wasn't a mere civilian. She was alert, aware, and cautious. Something else lingered behind her eyes. Was it fear?

Irina hip-checked the woman as she forced her way between the two of us. She landed a solid palm strike to the center of my chest, and her face reddened in feigned anger. "Why? Why do you do this to me? Everywhere we go, you find another woman. Why? Am I not enough for you? What more do you want from me?"

She continued striding forward, driving me farther from the mysterious woman with every step. Mongo crossed the street and closed the distance between himself and the woman. I tried to ignore Irina and looked across her shoulder at the scene unfolding in fast forward before my eyes.

The woman forced the sunglasses back onto to her face and spun on a heel. There was no escape. Singer guarded the sidewalk to the north, and Hunter slipped passed Irina and me as he moved in on the woman. And Mongo continued his way across the street. The Cipriani building consumed the escape to the west without a cross street for more than a hundred feet to the north. The woman was trapped, and my team was tightening the noose.

I placed a hand on Irina's shoulder. "We're good. Nice work."

A scolded, errant husband on the streets of Lower Manhattan's Financial District apparently wasn't enough to garner any attention at all. No one seemed to care that I had pushed my make-believe wife to the boiling point with my wandering eye. The ruse worked to separate me from the perceived threat, even though I believed the woman was harmless.

She analyzed her situation in an instant and sprinted from the sidewalk and onto the street. A horn from one of the thousands of yellow taxis in the city blared through the cool afternoon air as its right front fender struck the woman. She collapsed onto the car and performed a perfectly executed roll across the hood, then landed on her feet on the opposite side of the cab and yanked open the driver's door.

The speed of her attack was remarkable as she reached across the driver, unbuckled his seat belt and yanked him from the moving car. Mongo thundered toward the taxi with Disco and Gator only feet behind. Irina pieced it together and bolted for the passenger side of the ubiquitous yellow sedan.

The cabbie yelled in protest in a language I didn't recognize as the woman yanked his cell phone from his hand and leapt across him and onto the driver's seat at the same instant Irina's hand met the door handle on the opposite side. Irina yanked with all her strength, but the locked door wouldn't budge. She threw a thunderous elbow strike to the window as the car picked up speed, but the glass didn't surrender.

Everything inside of me wanted to pour a dozen 9mm rounds into the taxi, but the only possible outcome of that would be an afternoon spent explaining why a fake Secret Service officer discharged his firearm into a crowded street in Lower Manhattan.

The woman roared down Broadway and made a turn onto Battery Place. In seconds, she would disappear into a sea of identical cars on any of the hundreds of streets in the city. She was gone, and I still had no idea who she was.

My team assembled on the sidewalk and compared notes. No one other than Irina and I got close enough to get a decent look at the woman's eyes.

Irina said, "I have never seen her before, but her street craft is very good."

"Yes, it was," I said. "She's obviously more than just a New Yorker on the street."

Hunter said, "It's not cold enough for her to wear a hat and scarf. She was intentionally hiding her face."

I nodded. "Agreed. I know those eyes from somewhere, but it won't come. Is everybody all right?"

"We're good," Clark said. "But the woman took a nasty shot to the hip from that taxi. She's probably going to show up in a hospital somewhere."

I replayed the incident in my mind. "I don't think so. Her feet left the ground an instant before the car hit her. She was already airborne and planning the roll across the hood. She's either an operator or a stunt woman."

Skipper and Penny joined the team.

"What was that?" my wife asked, obviously in disbelief at the scene she'd just witnessed.

I said, "We don't know yet, but we can't stick around here. New York's finest are going to be crawling all over this place in minutes. That cabbie is losing his mind over there."

We made our way through Bowling Green park and across Broadway to Beaver Street, where our motor coach was parked and waiting. The driver activated the pneumatic doors, and we climbed aboard, reclaiming the seats we'd occupied twenty minutes earlier before the craziness on the street.

The doors closed, and the driver accelerated toward the East River.

We came to a stop on Water Street, and our tour guide said, "We've arrived at the New York Vietnam Veterans Memorial. If you'd like to see the memorial, we can spend a few minutes here and enjoy one of the few peaceful spots in this part of the city."

A peaceful spot where we could discuss what just happened sounded exactly like what the doctor ordered, so I stood and motioned toward the door. We walked through the memorial and took a seat on one of the curved benches.

I said, "Okay. Any ideas on what just happened?"

Mongo asked, "What did she say to you?"

"She said, 'I need to talk with you, Mr. Fulton.'"

"So, she knew your name."

"Yeah, she even called me Chase when she saw you guys moving in. She was nonthreatening and perfectly calm throughout the whole thing."

"Why did she touch you?" Penny asked.

"When I reached for my pistol, she laid her hand on my jacket and said, 'Don't pull your gun, Chase. We don't need that kind of attention.'"

"Did she have an accent?" Clark asked.

I replayed the interaction in my head. "No, nothing stood out. She didn't sound like she was from anywhere."

"Do you think she was armed?" Skipper asked.

I shrugged. "I don't know. She was wrapped up, so if she was carrying, I didn't see any imprint of a weapon."

Skipper chewed her lip. "Where did she come from?"

"I don't know," I said. "I was leaning on the building and watching you guys horse around by the bull statue. I was just hanging out and enjoying the day, and I didn't see her coming. I'm ashamed to admit the first time I noticed her was when she spoke."

Clark cocked his head and stared into the sky. "And you said she was concerned about you pulling your gun?"

"No, it didn't sound like concern as much as she just didn't want the attention it would draw."

From somewhere behind us, a voice said, "And I was right. We didn't need that kind of attention. You guys overreacted."

Everyone spun to see the woman standing less than ten feet away and pulling off her scarf. I rose to my feet, and I wasn't alone.

Everyone stood. Skipper pushed Penny behind the team, and Mongo stepped to my side.

The woman let her scarf fall across her arm, and she plucked the toboggan from her head. In the same motion, she pulled the sunglasses away, revealing a face I recognized instantly. I shook my head, completely disappointed in myself for not recognizing her the first time she took off her glasses.

I said, "For those of you who weren't along for our little vacation to Uzbekistan and Turkmenistan, meet CIA Case Officer Teresa Lynn."

Chapter 6
Responsibility

Gator looked like a freshman in senior calculus class, so I broke it down for him. "We met Teresa on a mission in Uzbekistan and Turkmenistan. We were deployed to hunt down a rogue operative." I pointed at Teresa. "Her. But as the ordeal played out, she proved to be anything but rogue. In fact, she saved our lives on more than one occasion over there. By the time it was all over, we'd identified the real bad guys, ended some careers, and maybe even left that part of the world a little cleaner than we found it."

Teresa checked the surroundings. "That's not exactly how it all went down, but it's close. Speaking of close, I could use a ride out of here on a nice, cushy tour bus so I can explain what's going on with all the cloak-and-dagger business."

Skipper said, "Before we harbor a fugitive, we need to know what you did with the taxi."

She laughed. "I left it a hundred yards from where I commandeered it."

"Then that leads to two more questions. How did you get here so fast, and how did you know we'd be here?"

She took a step toward us. "I didn't know you'd be here, but I caught a ride on top of your bus, so finding you wasn't much of a challenge after that."

It was my turn to act as chief inquisitor. "How did you find us in the first place?"

Teresa rolled her eyes. "Really? I'm a career Clandestine Service officer. Finding people who don't want to be found is what I've done for most of my adult life. Now, do you think we could get back on that bus and move this discussion anywhere other than here?"

"Let's go," I said. "It looks like our tour of New York City is over, but the excitement is not."

I followed Penny onto the motor coach, and she said, "I guess this means you've got a mission after all, huh?"

"I don't know yet. We'll see what Teresa has to say. Something tells me this one is out of our league."

"And what league is that?"

I said, "The one where we get our assignments from the Board."

On the ride back to Columbus Circle, we made small talk for the benefit of the tour guide and driver. Their ears weren't ready or authorized for the conversation we'd have back at the hotel.

We pulled to a stop, and the tour guide said, "We can finish your tour tomorrow if you'd like, but we can't refund any of your fee for today."

"It's okay," Penny said. "We'll have to take a rain check. As you can see, something's come up."

Back in the suite on the 15th floor, we settled in to listen to Teresa's story.

"As you probably know, my career with the Agency came to an unceremonious end after certain events in Asia."

I said, "We didn't know, but we suspected."

"Well, you suspected correctly. They did give me a pension, which was nice of them. At least I don't have to wait tables in Tribeca to eat."

"So, you're living in Manhattan?" I asked.

"Retired civil servants can't afford to live in the city. At least not the honest ones. I'm not exactly homeless, but I don't have a permanent address at the moment."

I studied her expression as if a veteran of a lifetime in the trenches would divulge anything with her gaze. "So, what's this about? If you're looking for a job, you're going about it in the worst possible way."

"I don't need a job," she said. "But I do need your help."

No one said a word. Each of us sat, anxiously awaiting the next sentence out of her mouth.

She glanced to the floor as if gathering her courage. "Have you ever heard of Ty Emerson, Glenn Phillips, Pamela Bingham, or Zander McAllister?"

I caught a hint of recognition in Disco's face, and he said, "I knew Zander McAllister twenty years ago, but not by that name."

Teresa eyed our chief pilot. "Were you in The Hague when you knew him?"

Disco turned to me as if asking permission, and I nodded.

He said, "There and a few other places."

Teresa said, "He's dead, and so are the others."

I turned to Disco. "Who was he?"

"I don't really know who or even what he was. It was my job to put him anywhere he wanted to be, any time he wanted to be there, by using any flying machine we could find."

"So, he was a spook," I said.

Teresa seemed to ignore the assumption. "Everybody on that list was rock solid. They didn't make mysterious income from unknown sources. They didn't look the other way when things crossed a line. They were the poster boys and girls for Uncle Sam, and they were all murdered in the past four weeks."

"Murdered?" I asked.

She nodded. "*Assassinated* may be a better word for it."

I held up two fingers. "First, how do you know, and second, who killed them?" Before she could answer, I said, "Wait. There's a more important question. Are you a poster girl, too?"

Instead of answering, her eyes fell back to the floor.

Skipper said, "That's why you're here, isn't it? You're next on the list, and you want us to protect you."

Teresa drew in a long breath and looked up. "Not exactly. I don't know how many people are on the list, but yes, my name is probably on it. I don't have any way to know if I'm next, and I can keep myself alive, but what I can't do is protect the others without some help from people I can trust . . . like you."

I asked, "So, you want us to protect them?"

"Yes, but not directly. I want you to help me find who's killing them and stop them."

I processed everything she said. "If you're coming to us, that means this isn't an agency-sanctioned operation."

Teresa looked directly at me. "Is that a question?"

I shook my head. "No, but this one is. Does the Agency know these four officers have been killed recently?"

"I don't know," she said. "But if I figured it out, surely the analysts in their little cave at Langley have, too."

I grabbed a small notepad from the desk and clicked my pen. "What else do the four people on the list have in common besides being honest and dead? Were they all blue badgers?"

"All of them except one. Pam Bingham was DIA."

"Defense Intelligence," I said. "Were they all active when they were killed?"

"No. Like me, they're all retired."

I leaned back in my chair and sighed. "So, you're telling me that four retired Intelligence officers were murdered in the last month, and you're the only person looking into it. Is that right?"

"I don't have any way of knowing who, if anyone, else is looking into it."

"How did you discover the four dead operators?"

She cast her eyes to the ceiling and took a long breath. "There's sort of a network of retired intel officers. In a way, we look out for each other when our careers come to an end. Most of us have been in some scrapes over the years, and it's nice to have a friend or two who understands the game."

"The game?" I asked.

She slumped in her chair. "Okay, it's like this. In a career like ours, it's impossible to avoid making enemies, and some of those enemies have long memories. Old grudges don't die so easily, and some of us feel like we need to settle those old scores before the Grim Reaper gets us."

It was time to lay the foundation for sending Teresa's request up the chain of command, so I gave Clark an eye.

He played with his beard for a few seconds, checked his watch, and stood. "It looks like it's time for me to be going."

"Oh, no, you don't," I said. "I'm not making this call without you."

He nodded toward the door, and I followed him into the foyer.

Once behind a closed door, Clark asked, "What's your gut telling you?"

I glanced back at the door. "There's a lot more to the story than she's telling us."

"That's why you're still alive," he said. "You're gut's smarter than the average bulb in the drawer. What do you think she's holding back?"

"Bulb in a drawer?"

He waved a hand. "Whatever. Think about it. What's the Board going to say if we run this thing up the flagpole?"

"They'll shoot it down before we finish talking, but that's not exactly what I'm worried about."

Clark said, "I'm listening."

"If she's telling the truth—and I don't see any reason she wouldn't be—the fewer people who know about this, the better."

"Are you seriously considering jumping in the fire with her?"

I considered his question. "Is there any way to verify what she's told us so far?"

He inspected his fingernails and picked at some imaginary speck. "I can ask some questions, but Skipper may be the best resource we've got."

"I think you're right, but what do we do with Ms. Lynn in the meantime?"

"Do you trust her?" he asked.

"She saved my life overseas."

He plucked his toothpick from his mouth and rolled it between his fingertips. "But did she save your life as a self-serving act, or did she do it out of the goodness of her heart?"

The mission had become a blur in my memory, so recalling details was like remembering the day I was born. "I don't know, but let's break this down. If she's playing at something sinister, what could it be?"

"Maybe she had another outcome in mind for the thing in Uzbek. Maybe we screwed up her plan and she wants us to walk into an ambush with our guard down."

"Maybe," I said, "but I'm not getting that vibe."

"Vibes or not, you've got to admit that whole thing on the street was completely unnecessary. She could've just walked up and said, 'Howdy, it's me.'"

"I'll give you that. It was a little weird, but if she thought she was being followed, the covert approach would make sense."

"It wasn't covert, College Boy. It was crazy. Covert would've been sneaking into your hotel room. Approaching *this* team incognito and not identifying herself right away isn't the work of a seasoned operator."

"So, tell me what to do."

"You're a big boy," he said. "You make the call, but I'm not taking this one to the Board. If they order us to stand down and we ignore them, I don't know what they'll do, but it won't be pretty."

"Are we under some moral or legal obligation to inform the Board when we take a mission?"

"Define mission," he said.

"What do you mean?"

"If your neighbor asks you to help him cut down a tree, is that a mission?"

"No," I said. "It's a favor."

"So, when a retired CIA case officer asks for help protecting some friends of hers, is that a mission?"

"Yeah, I'd call that a mission."

He said, "Okay, then tell me where the line is. When does a favor become a mission? If you call this a mission and ask your team to come along, you're responsible for them. You're responsible for everything that happens on that mission. If the tree falls on your neighbor's house, are you responsible?"

"I get it, but to tell you the truth, if she's sincere, I'm honored she picked us. You know she's worked with a bunch of operators in her career, and when it came down to something this important, she came to us first. That says a lot about what she saw in us."

"How do you know?" he asked.

"How do I know what?"

"How do you know she came to us first? Maybe she's running down a whole list and finally made it to our names."

"Maybe you're right, but even if we're number thirty on the list, she thinks enough of us to ask for our help."

"Whatever you say, College Boy. Just remember what I told you about responsibility. And you do know what that word really means, don't you?"

"I know what it means, but I'm looking forward to your definition."

"Responsibility is how you respond to your ability."

I was floored. "I didn't expect anything meaningful to come out of your mouth just then, but for once, you dropped some real wisdom on me."

He threw up both hands. "Hey, it's what I do."

Chapter 7
Switzerland

Back inside the suite, I took a seat beside Teresa Lynn, and she opened her mouth before I could say anything stupid.

"Let me guess. He's your handler, and he's not willing to float this balloon. He says it's up to you, and he doesn't trust me. How am I doing so far?"

"Not bad," I said.

She continued. "He—and probably you—know that whoever directs your operations won't approve of helping a retired spook save the lives of a few other former spooks she just happens to respect. He probably gave you a speech about the sky falling on your head if you get involved and things go south. Shall I keep going?"

"You're doing all right, but I'm not a fan of that phrase."

"Which phrase is that?"

"Going south," I said. "People use that phrase to mean things are going wrong. Look around, Ms. Lynn. Everybody in this room except for Gator is a Southerner, and that hurts our feelings."

For the first time, she cracked a smile. "Does that mean you're going to help me find the people killing my associates?"

"I've got two questions before I answer that question."

She said, "Let's hear them."

"First, how many other people have you approached before you came to us?"

She slid to the edge of her seat and stared directly into my eyes. "None. Yours is the first and only name on the list. If you don't help me, I can't afford to run all over the world and tell this story to operators. You know this community, Chase. Within two weeks, I'd have a target on my back the size of Montana. I'm not stupid enough to shop this around. I want you and your team or nobody. What's your second question?"

I diverted my attention to Clark, and he gave a barely perceptible shrug.

"Question number two is this. What do you plan to do when we find the people killing your friends?"

"I never said they were my friends. I said they were former officers whom I respect."

"Fair enough. Now, go somewhere else so we can talk about you behind your back."

She almost smiled. "I'll be in the bar downstairs."

"That's not necessary," I said. "We have the entire suite of rooms. Make yourself at home in any of them, and one of us will come get you in a few minutes. If you'd like a drink, there's a bar in every room. Feel free to help yourself."

Without another word, she stood, nodded politely, and strode down the hallway.

Every eye left in the room turned immediately to me.

Skipper said, "I'm supposed to research the four names, right?" I nodded, and she snatched her laptop from the table on her left. "I'm on it."

"While Skipper's on that, does anyone have anything to say?"

Hunter was first, of course. "Are you buying it?"

"Part of it," I said.

"Which part? The bull or the sheet?"

"Does that mean you're not buying it?" I asked.

"Not a word of it, but I trust you, so if you say we're helping her, I'm in."

As if sounding off for a head count, every member of the team said, "Me, too," in succession.

"We're not having a vote," I said.

Hunter scoffed. "Of course we're not, 'cause we just did. We're in."

Gator piped up. "I thought this wasn't a democracy."

"It's not!" came the unanimous response from everyone in the room.

I shook my head. "I've clearly lost control of the room. Skipper, what have you found?"

She peered over the screen of her laptop. "Ty Emerson, sixty-one years old, dead of an apparent heart attack in Olongapo, Philippines, six days ago."

"That's one out of four," I said.

Clark tapped on the table beside him. "No, that's *possibly* one out of four. She said apparent heart attack. That doesn't sound much like an assassination to me."

"I'm not finished," Skipper said. "Glenn Phillips, sixty-six years old, dead of apparent suicide, found nine days ago hanging in his garage at his home in Newport News, Virginia."

Clark said, "Yeah, boy. The murders are piling up now. We've got two dead old guys. One from a heart attack, and one from hanging. If I'm not mistaken, those are the two most popular assassination techniques."

"Give me a break," I said. "Was an autopsy done on either of them?"

Skipper struck some keys. "Definitely not in the Philippines, and I'm not seeing one in Virginia, but I'll come back to that. Zander McAllister, sixty-nine, died of a gunshot wound in Montana while hunting pronghorn antelope. Apparently, Disco's buddy caught an accidental, errant bullet from a distant hunter three weeks ago. According to the story, McAllister was hunting with his grandson, and they were set up about half a mile apart. When the elder McAllister didn't return to pick him up, the grandson went searching for him but never found him. Another hunter found Zander's body the next morning, just after daylight."

I said, "Let me guess. They never found the hunter who fired the shot that killed him."

Skipper hit a few more keys. "According to the authorities, the death was ruled an accident, and they're still searching for the hunter who may have fired the round, accidentally killing McAllister."

I turned to Clark, and he said, "Okay, I'll admit it. That one sounds like an assassination by a pro like Singer."

"How about the woman?" I asked. "Pamela something."

Skipper said, "Pamela Bingham. But did you catch how Teresa called her Pam and not Pamela?"

"Yes, I did. Have you found anything on her?"

"That's the weird one. I found a bunch of people named Pamela Bingham, but none of them have gotten themselves killed in the past few weeks."

I said, "Keep looking. And while you're at it, see if you can find any evidence of our girl Teresa being anywhere near the deaths."

"What are you thinking?" she asked.

"I'm not thinking anything yet, but I want to know how Teresa knew about the so-called assassinations."

Skipper screwed up her face. "Hey, wait a minute."

I leaned in. "What?"

She held up a finger and then typed furiously. "There's a discrepancy with McAllister. This says he was found on the Crow Indian Reservation in Montana, so why would Wyoming authorities say anything about a death in Montana and inside an Indian reservation?"

Not directing my question at anyone, I mumbled, "Who investigates murders on Indian reservations?"

Mongo said, "The FBI has jurisdiction to investigate murders on reservations, but if the BIA ruled McAllister's death an accident, the FBI would likely never hear about it."

"What's BIA?" I asked.

Mongo said, "Bureau of Indian Affairs. They have their own tribal police on most reservations."

I waved him off. "We're getting too deep in the weeds here. First, are you sure the ones you pulled up were former CIA officers?"

Skipper said, "Yeah, I double-checked that, first thing. Although there's no direct reference to the Agency, they're all listed as retired civil servants."

I chewed on the information for a moment. "Okay, show of hands. Who thinks we should walk away from this thing and tell Teresa Lynn we're out?" Everyone except Gator raised his hand, and I said, "That's what I thought. Now, also by show of hands, who thinks we should jump all over this thing, figure it out, and stop whoever's killing these people?"

Again, every hand except Gator's went up.

I eyed the new guy. "Why didn't you vote?"

Gator said, "Because this isn't a democracy, and I'm Switzerland."

"You're Switzerland? What does that mean?"

"It means I'm neutral until we know what's really going on."

I chuckled. "Somebody get Teresa back in here before another retired civil servant ends up accidentally dead."

Kodiak trotted down the hall and returned with our favorite former Clandestine Service officer, and she said, "If you guys are as good as I hope you are, you found three of the four names I gave you, and you found out all of their deaths could've been something other than assassinations. Am I right?"

Skipper said, "We found them all except Peggy Bingham."

"Pamela," Teresa said.

I said, "You called her Pam earlier. Did you know her well?"

She bit her lip. "We went through the Farm together. You know they rarely put classmates from the Farm on the same assignment, so we never worked directly together, but we kept in touch over the years. She was the closest thing I had to a real friend in the Agency days."

"When was the last time you saw her?" I asked.

"Seven months ago. We had a holiday together."

"A holiday?"

"Yeah, you know, a vacation. They call it a holiday in Europe. We did a cruise of all things. We were scheduled to do an expeditionary trip to Antarctica in two weeks, but . . ." She ducked her head and caught her breath. "But she'd disappeared."

"What do you mean, disappeared?" Skipper asked.

"I mean, I can't find her. She's not answering her phone or email. Naturally, I got worried, so I went to her house and nothing. She's not there. The neighbors said they hadn't seen her in several days."

"Did you call the police?" I asked.

Teresa laughed. "She lived on Isla Mujeres, in Mexico."

"So, did you call the police or not?" Hunter asked.

Teresa looked at me. "Do you want to tell him, or should I?"

I sighed. "The cops on Isla Mujeres are nothing more than glorified golf cart tow truck drivers. There's no real crime on the Island of Women, so anything serious like a missing American would fall under the jurisdiction of the federales, who aren't particularly interested in searching for a missing American woman."

Hunter leaned back in his seat. "I see. Does, or did, Ms. Bingham have any family? A husband? Kids?"

Teresa said, "The lives we led didn't lend themselves to white picket fences and two-point-five children. Clandestine Service officers don't go to PTA meetings, Mr. Hunter."

"It's just Hunter, ma'am. Mister makes me feel old."

She winked at him. "And ma'am does the same to me." The moment passed, and Teresa said, "So, back to what I suspect you did while I was exiled down the hall. You probably ran my passports to see if I happened to be anywhere near the places the dead former operatives were found." She pulled out a stack of passport books and dropped it on the table beside Skipper. "I have five passports with five different names. These are all five. Feel free to run them all you'd like."

Skipper pushed her glasses up the bridge of her nose. "You have six, at least, and I've already run all of them."

Teresa slipped a hand into a pocket and withdrew a sixth passport. "You're at least as good as I expected. So, are you going to help me find the people who are killing off former CS officers or not?"

I made eye contact with every face in the room, and no one flinched. "No, we're not going to help you."

The silence in the room felt like a moment from one of Penny's movies, and I said, "We don't *help*. We complete missions, and that's exactly what we're going to do on this one. We're going to find the people or person responsible for those deaths, and we're going to make them pay."

Chapter 8
The Whole Truth

Having spent a lifetime in a world where emotion often leads to extinction, Teresa Lynn wasn't prone to displays of emotional reactions, but the retired spook allowed herself the luxury of putting on a sincere smile. Her shoulders relaxed, and her breathing slowed. "Thank you, Chase. You don't know how much this means to me. I told you those people weren't my friends, but that wasn't completely true. Friendship in the Agency is practically forbidden, but we're all human behind the credentials, so their lives were important to me, even if we didn't call ourselves friends."

"You don't have to thank us," I said. "I'd like to believe you'd do the same for us if the roles were reversed. We do have some in-depth questions for you, though. Are you ready to dig into this thing?"

She nodded. "I've been ready for weeks."

Skipper took the floor. "Let's start with something simple. How did you find out about the deaths of McAllister, Emerson, and Phillips?"

Teresa licked her lips and swallowed the lump in her throat. "I guess we should talk about them one at a time."

Skipper pulled her laptop closer, and I picked up my legal pad.

"Who do you want to start with?" Teresa asked.

Skipper said, "Let's talk about Alexander McAllister. You said earlier that Clandestine Service officers don't often have families. I think you said something like, there's no time for white picket fences and PTA meetings."

Teresa said, "That's right, but Zander—Alexander was his full first name—he was the exception. In fact, he was the exception to a lot of things. He managed to maintain a marriage for almost thirty-five years, and by all indications, it was a happy one. I only met his wife once, so I really don't know her except for the things Zander said."

"If theirs was a happy marriage, why did it end?" Skipper asked.

"Pancreatic cancer. Maria died about five years ago. They had two daughters and three grandchildren—two girls and a boy. The hunting trip was a birthday present for the oldest grandson, Alex. He was named after his grandfather."

I scribbled furiously on my pad while Skipper typed a few notes as Teresa spoke.

Teresa glanced toward the kitchen. "Would you excuse me while I get a glass of water?"

Singer hopped to his feet. "Keep your seat. I'll get it for you."

A minute later, she took the glass from his hand and looked up at the deadliest man I've ever known. "Thank you, Jimmy."

"Call me Singer, ma'am. Jimmy left the scene a long time ago."

She sighed. "Isn't it interesting how we become who our environment dictates that we be?"

"It certainly is," he said.

Teresa took a long drink and dabbed at the corners of her mouth with the napkin Singer delivered with the glass. "You asked how I found out about Zander's murder."

We waited in silent anticipation, but when her answer came, I wasn't convinced she was telling the whole truth.

"He didn't answer an email."

"An email?" I asked.

She looked away. "Yes, an email. He always answered my email within twenty-four hours, and usually within minutes."

"But he was on a hunting trip with his grandson in the wilds of Wyoming and Montana. Even if he were alive, he probably couldn't send or receive email from there."

She smiled. "You didn't know Zander. He loved the outdoors, but only in short bursts. He was a bit of what we'd call a diva today. He didn't mind *getting* dirty, but he wouldn't *stay* dirty. He slept in good beds in good hotels with central heat and air, and he loved technology. He and Alex may have been in the woods by day, but you can bet your bottom dollar they weren't sleeping in tents. They were staying at the Bighorn Lodge near Sheridan, Wyoming."

Skipper's fingers flew across the keyboard, and she spun the laptop so I could see the home page for the lodge.

I scanned the screen and stopped after the line that boasted fast, dependable Wi-Fi. "So, if he didn't answer your email, how did you know he was in Montana?"

She pressed her lips into a thin horizontal line. "He wasn't in Montana when he was murdered. He was in Wyoming."

Skipper pulled off her glasses. "According to the news story, his body was found on the Crow Reservation in Montana."

Teresa said, "The story is correct. His body *was* found on the reservation, but that's not where he was killed."

"How could you possibly know that?" she asked.

"Because I went to the site with Alex, Zander's grandson."

"Wait a minute," I said. "You went there? When?"

"A few days after he was murdered. I contacted Zander's daughter, Caroline. I told her who I was and that I was concerned, and I asked if she'd heard from him. That's when she told me about the shooting."

"So, you went to Wyoming?" Skipper asked.

Teresa narrowed her gaze. "This is beginning to feel like an interrogation."

"It's not an interrogation," I said. "We just want to understand the details so we can determine exactly what happened. The more we know about the killer or killers, the better chance we have of identifying them."

Teresa raised her eyebrows. "I told you what happened. Three former Intelligence officers were assassinated. We're wasting precious time talking about what's already happened while the killers are still out there, likely hunting their next victim, who very well could be me."

I slid forward on my seat. "I understand your frustration, and we're going to find the people responsible, but if you want our help, you have to let us do our job the way we do it. We aren't vigilantes. We want to know the truth and as many facts as possible before we embark on a manhunt."

She closed her eyes, took a long breath, and slowly let it out. "Okay, what else do you want to know?"

"The nagging question is, how do you know he was killed in Wyoming and not Montana?"

"That's what I was trying to explain to you. When I went there with Alex, he showed me their hunting spots."

"He's a kid, though. How do you know he—"

"He just turned seventeen. He's an Eagle Scout and works as a fishing and hunting guide. He's young, but he's no kid. He showed me precisely where he was hunting, and then he took me to the spot where Zander was supposed to be."

"Was there any evidence of foul play at Zander's spot?"

"Not one single drop of evidence of any kind."

"Then how could you know that's where he was killed?"

She leaned back and took another drink. "Because the spot where Alex said Zander should've been was burned to a crisp."

I slumped back into my seat. "So, somebody shot Zander, moved his body, and burned the spot where they killed him to cover up any evidence of the crime."

"That's my theory."

"Did the local authorities do any forensics at the scene where they found the body?"

Teresa said, "Wyoming authorities aren't interested in investigating a murder site where there was no evidence of anything except a small fire. And the local authorities where Zander was actually found were the tribal police. Unless you're Native American, you're not getting past the front door."

I glanced at Clark, and he stood. "I'll get her."

He returned a few seconds later with Celeste and her long, black ponytail braided down her back.

I said, "Teresa Lynn, meet Dr. Celeste Mankiller, our technical services officer."

"You've got to be kidding me," she said.

"Nope, not kidding."

I spent the next two minutes detailing the situation to Celeste, and when I finished, she said, "I'm Cherokee, not Crow, but nobody in Montana knows that. Let's go."

Packing for a mission is a vastly different thing than packing for vacation, so a stop in Georgia was a necessity en route to Montana. We landed at the airport in St. Marys and convoyed to the house.

I stepped from the Suburban and offered our retired spook my hand. "Welcome to Bonaventure. We'll change clothes, pack some gear, and head for Little Bighorn."

She took in the house and property. "Nice place. Contract work must be good. Maybe I *do* need a job after all."

I checked my watch and asked, "Would you like the nickel tour? It's probably too late to fly to Montana this evening anyway."

"In that case," she said, "I'd love the tour."

We started on the third floor of the house. "This is the operation center when we're running missions from here. Skipper and Tony take shifts, but Skipper is always on duty when it hits the fan."

Teresa let out a low whistle. "This is nice. I've been inside a lot of embassies, and I've never seen any of their op centers that could outdo what you've got here."

"Thanks. Skipper designed and specified everything in this room and behind the walls. We've even got a supercomputer— whatever that is—in a hardened underground bunker. I like to call this place Skipper's lair. She lets us use it for staff meetings, but we all know better than coming in here without her permission. Come on. I'll show you the range."

I took her through the firearms training facility, including the shoot house. "This is where we work up for close quarters battle. As you can see, we can configure doors and windows any way we want. It's built of double-stacked railroad crossties so we can live fire in here without worrying about stray bullets."

"This is amazing," she said. "It's better than what we've got at the Farm."

"Training is crucial. We have to stay at the top of our game. Otherwise, we come home in body bags."

"I like it," she said. "I knew you guys were good, but I had no idea you had your own compound. Who pays for it?"

"We do. It's part of the cost of doing business and staying alive. It's just home, though. We're not big fans of the word *compound*."

"I get it," she said. "Thanks for the show-and-tell."

"We're not finished yet. I still have to show you my favorite spot on Earth."

I led her along the bank of the North River until she saw the boat. "Is that yours, too?"

"Spoils of war," I said. "She's called *Aegis*, but she's not a tactical asset. She's just for fun. The gunboat is inside the boathouse. It's a highly modified Mark Five patrol boat."

"A Mark Five? Seriously?"

"Yes, ma'am. We do our best work on the water."

"Former SEALs?"

"Not hardly," I said. "Most of us are former SF except for Hunter and Disco. They're retired Air Force. Hunter was a combat controller, and Disco was an A-Ten driver, among other things."

She said, "Yeah, I got that from his history with Zander in Budapest. What about you? Were you SF as well?"

"No. Gator and I are civilians. He played football at K-State, and I played a little baseball. We were just athletes who needed a little excitement in our lives."

She laced her hand around my arm. "I'd like to hear that story someday."

I glanced down at her hand resting casually inside my elbow, and she said, "I really want to thank you for doing this, Chase, but I need you to understand that I can't afford to pay you. I probably can't even cover expenses."

"We asked a lot of questions in New York. Do you remember any of them being about money?" She shook her head, and I said, "That's how it'll stay. When this is over, you'll owe us one. It's never a bad thing to have an ex-spook on speed dial."

She squeezed my arm. "Sincerely, thank you."

"You're welcome. Please keep one thing in mind, though. If you lie to us or hide information—what Penny calls 'a lie of omission'—we're done."

"I understand," she said. "Now, show me this favorite spot of yours."

We stepped into the gazebo overlooking the river, and she ran her hand along the worn, weathered cannon barrel serving as the centerpiece.

"Something tells me there's a story here."

"You might say that. Clark and I pulled that old girl out of the mud a couple miles from here. We believe she came off either a French or British man-o'-war during a little skirmish in eighteen twelve."

She smiled up at me. "Really?"

"Yes, ma'am."

We slid into a pair of Adirondack chairs, and Penny stepped into the gazebo a few minutes later.

"This looks cozy."

"Just wrapping up the nickel tour," I said.

She leaned against the cannon. "That's what I thought. And I knew you'd forget about clothes for Teresa, so I'm here to remind you."

Teresa said, "I've got a couple of changes, but if this thing turns into a fight, I don't have any gear."

I palmed my forehead. "What would I do without you, my dear?"

Penny rolled her eyes. "We've been through this before. You'd chase blonde Russian girls all over the world until you caught them all or died of exhaustion."

Teresa perked up. "Oh, so Russian blondes are your kryptonite."

Before I could defend myself, Penny said, "You have no idea."

The former spook appraised my wife as if she were for sale. "I've known a lot of Russians in my life, and I've never seen one who could compete with you, so I suspect Chase feels the same."

"Wholeheartedly," I said. "Now, let's get you some gear before whatever this is turns into something worse . . if that's possible."

Penny stepped from the gazebo. "Dinner will be here by the time you're finished downstairs."

"We'll hurry," I said.

I cleared the three levels of security to grant myself access to the basement armory and gear locker. It obviously wasn't Teresa's first time in an equipment issue. She chose weapons, spare mags, holsters, boots, pants, shirts, and body armor in minutes, and we beat dinner to the dining room, but only by a few seconds.

Travis, a local aspiring chef, rolled in his cart with two assistants at his side, and the table was a masterpiece in no time. Like most dinners at Bonaventure, that one became a family affair, and everything felt right with the world. Well, almost everything.

With dessert plates and coffee cups empty, the family dispersed, and Penny planted Teresa in a second-floor bedroom.

I opened the humidor and produced a fistful of Cubans. "Anybody up for a drink and a smoke?"

Clark, Hunter, and I settled in the gazebo with Cohibas ablaze, and Singer took his seat without a Cuban.

I stared through the honey-colored nectar in my tumbler. "All right, guys. Let's have it. What's on your mind?"

Clark took a sip and pretended he hadn't heard me. Hunter stared into the rafters above our heads.

But Singer, the moral compass of the family, didn't look away. He seemed to focus directly into my soul. "How far are we willing to take this thing?"

I was on the verge of experiencing another of Singer's life lessons that have come to mean more to me than any other wisdom I'd ever possess.

"What do you mean?" I asked.

He didn't hesitate. "We're going on a manhunt, Chase. Those only end in one of three ways. We kill him, he kills us, or we give up. I don't ever remember giving up."

I let his words wander through my mind. "It's not too late to back out."

Singer lifted his glass of tea that wore the same look as our bourbon. "That sounds a lot like giving up to me."

"So, what do you think we should do?"

He said, "There's only one thing we can do, and that's come to terms with the fact that we're probably going to stop some beating hearts without any sanction besides our own morality. I say we spend some time on our knees listening to God before we start playing God."

Singer's infallible wisdom didn't fall on deaf ears. I spent more than a few minutes in communion with God before falling asleep, and when I awoke in Penny's arms, my conscience was clear. I was ready to follow the road beneath my feet to its ultimate end and pray the end of that road wasn't also the end of me.

Chapter 9
What About the Russian?

The GPS approach into Sheridan County Airport in northern Wyoming began on the eastern edge of the snow-covered mountains of Bighorn National Forest, at ninety-one hundred feet, and traced a line to the north-northwest, descending into the airport nestled some forty-two hundred feet above the North River I called home, nearly fifteen hundred miles behind us. The foreign landscape wasn't the only thing that was vastly different on the edge of the Rockies. The air was crisp and cold as winter's imminent breath whispered ominous promises of blizzards to come. I would spend no more time in that environment than was absolutely required to begin our journey down the curving, forbidding road.

The rented four-wheel-drive SUVs Skipper arranged waited like chariots beside the FBO, and we wasted no time offloading bags and equipment sufficient to sustain us at stop number one.

I slid my credit card across the counter. "We should have a hangar arranged, and please top off all tanks with Prist. The brakes are off."

The young lady entered the details of my card into her computer and slid the plastic key to everything back across the counter. "We'll pull your Gulfstream into hangar two and top it off. Our twenty-four-hour number is on the back of this card, and if you'll give us an hour's notice when you're ready to go, we'll have the plane ready when you arrive."

"Thank you, ma'am. We'll probably be less than two days, but I'll let you know."

On the way to the rented Suburbans, Gator asked, "What's Prist?"

I said, "I forgot. You're not a plane guy. Prist is an additive to keep the jet fuel from turning into gelatin in freezing temperatures."

He nodded. "I'm not saying I'm not an airplane guy. I just didn't take to it at the Farm. Maybe it was the instructor. He wasn't very patient."

"I remember," I said. "He wants his students to memorize the Airplane Flying Handbook, whether they understand it or not."

"Exactly, and academics weren't really my thing. I like the physical stuff. Well, not the physical stuff you and Clark taught, but you know what I mean."

"Yeah, I know. I've been there. Do you want to learn to fly?"

"I don't know about the jet, but the other stuff back in St. Marys looks like fun. Especially the Mustang."

I laughed. "The Mustang isn't a company asset. It's Penny's. But she lets me fly it sometimes."

"Seriously?"

I said, "You'll figure it out someday. It's all theirs. We just get to play with it."

"Ah, I get it. I've got to be honest. I'm not sure how you guys make a relationship work in this job. Most women—"

I laid a hand on his shoulder. "We didn't marry most women. We married exceptional women who don't need a man to form their identity. They're strong, capable individuals on their own. They don't need us. They want us, and that's what makes it work."

"If you say so. But I've never met a girl who'd be okay with me running off for weeks at a time without telling her where I was going or when I'd be back."

"She'll show up," I said. "Just give it time."

"What about the Russian? The one in New York."

"That one isn't a woman. In fact, I'm not even sure she's human. I've seen her kill half a dozen men without breathing hard. She'll kill you and play in your blood."

"How did she learn to do that?"

"She was a Russian SVR assassin in another life, but old habits die hard."

We pulled into the parking lot of the Bighorn Lodge, a massive log structure sitting in a valley that gave way to frozen rocky peaks stretching into the heavens. It looked like a postcard. The clerk behind the counter slid a collection of keys toward me, and we stowed our gear.

Celeste pulled me aside, wearing a look of concern. "What exactly is it you want me to do up here? I'm not one of your soldiers."

"You're right. I can teach almost anybody to soldier, but you're a key to a lock we can't pick. I want you to get the tribal police to talk about Zander McAllister."

"I don't have to carry a gun, do I?"

"You can if you want."

She shook her head. "No, that's okay. I'll pass. How do you want me to approach the tribal police?"

"I originally thought we should make an appointment to talk with the detective assigned to the case, but I've changed my mind. To them, it's not a case anymore. So, I thought it might be best if we knocked on their door."

"Am I going in alone?" she asked.

"No, I'll be with you."

She seemed to think about my answer for a moment. "Maybe it'd be better if I went alone. I can wire up, and you'll be able to hear everything, but since we're playing a game of look-at-me, I'm-like-you, I don't think it's such a good idea for me to ride in there with a paleface in tow."

I grabbed my chest. "That's insensitive, and I'm offended."

She gave me a shove. "Good. Now you know how it feels."

"I'll give it some thought," I said. "But first, we're going on a little field trip."

I knocked on Teresa's door, and she opened it with her cell phone pressed to her ear.

She waved for me to come inside, then ended the call and tucked away the phone. "That was Alex, Zander's grandson. I told him we wanted to see the spot where his grandfather was killed and the place they found his body."

"What did he say?" I asked.

"He sent me the GPS coordinates and offered to fly up here to lead us in there."

"Can you find the spots without him?"

"I can, but it'd be a lot faster if we had a helicopter."

I patted my pockets. "Darn it, I didn't bring my chopper."

She sighed. "I'm serious. There will be a lot of snow up there, and I don't think the rental company would like us taking their Suburbans off-road."

"How about snowmobiles?"

She said, "Let's plot the coordinates on a map and take a look."

We convened in my room and opened my laptop. I entered the coordinates Alex gave Teresa, and they populated on a topo map on the screen.

"That's rough country," I said. "Your helicopter idea might be the only way. It would take hours to get in there on snowmobiles."

Kodiak leaned in and studied the map. "It would take amateurs a few hours to get in there, but I could do it on a good snow machine in a little over an hour if we could get to the trailhead to the southeast."

I followed his finger on the screen as he traced the best route into the hunting sites.

Teresa leaned around me to get a good look at the map. She said, "Maybe, but where can we get a good snow machine?"

"Surely, somebody rents them around here," I said. "Check with the front desk."

Teresa picked up the phone, had a brief conversation, and hung up. "She gave me a number to a backcountry guide who rents them, but she didn't know if he would let us have them without a guide."

I said, "Kodiak, you speak their language. Call 'em up and see what you can arrange."

Two minutes later, Kodiak covered the receiver with his hand and looked up. "How much cash did you bring?"

"Plenty."

He removed his hand from the mouthpiece. "We'll be there in half an hour."

I said, "That sounded productive . . . and expensive."

Kodiak said, "Exactly. He won't rent them to us, but he'll sell us six high-end machines. If we bring them back in good shape, he'll buy them back for eighty percent of the purchase price."

"What's the purchase price?"

He smiled. "Five grand apiece."

Teresa let out a whistle. "That's thirty thousand bucks."

I raised a finger. "No. It's thirty grand if we don't bring them back. It's only six thousand if we don't destroy any of them."

"That's still a lot of money," she said.

I lowered my chin. "Do you want to find the people who are killing your friends?"

She nodded slowly, and I said, "Let's go get our snowmobiles."

Kodiak said, "You'll sound more in the know if you call them snow machines."

"Whatever," I said. "Let's go for a ride."

We made the deal with the backcountry guide, and he fueled all six machines and strapped spare fuel cans onto each of them. He asked, "How are you going to haul them?"

Kodiak pointed to the Suburbans. "With those."

The guide laughed. "What are you going to do? Put them on top?"

I said, "For thirty grand, I thought you'd at least provide a trailer."

"Trailers are expensive. I've got one I can let go, but it'll cost you the same as another machine."

I stuck out my hand. "Fine. But we get full price for it when we bring it back."

He stared at my outstretched hand. "Eighty percent. Just like the machines."

I glanced at Kodiak, and he shrugged.

I said, "I've got a better idea. We'll pay you five hundred bucks to deliver and pick up the machines at the High Country trailhead."

The guide stared at each of us in turn, then finally said, "You're bringing everything back, aren't you?"

I said, "Yes, sir."

"Take the trailer. But if you wreck it, it's five grand. I've got a business to run here."

Kodiak loaded the six machines as if he'd done it a thousand times, and we made the trailhead in half an hour and set off on our new steeds. Kodiak led the way, taking it easy for the first ten minutes while the rest of us learned the machines.

It took two hours to reach the first site, where Zander McAllister was likely killed. The evidence of the fire was still there, even though a blanket of fresh snow covered the ground.

Kodiak stood beside a burnt tree and scanned the landscape. "If I were hunting from this area, I'd set up right here. He knew what he was doing if this is where he was."

"This is definitely the place," Teresa said.

The look on her face was anger knocking on the door of rage, and instead of taking advantage of the opportunity to get her to blurt out something she hadn't mentioned before, I let the emotions boil.

"Singer, if you were going to assault a target right here, where would you set up?"

Our sniper took in the surroundings with the eye of a seasoned killer. "It depends on the weapon, but if I were planning to move the body, I'd get in nice and close. I don't miss, but just to be safe, I'd move into a range that would guarantee a kill shot. I wouldn't want McAllister to shoot back." He kept scanning the area and finally pointed to an elevated position to the west. "There. See those two boulders?"

I searched the snow-covered hillside until the two lumps came into view. "I see them."

"That's where I'd be. Even an average shooter couldn't miss from there, and it provides both easy access to get to the body and to escape if something went wrong." As if he'd spotted a nugget of gold, Singer stepped forward through the snow, never taking his eyes off the ground. He took a knee beside a small scrub bush and cradled a stem in his palm. "Check this out."

We walked over and stared into his hand.

I said, "What am I supposed to see? It's a stick."

"It's not just a stick," he said. "It's a broken stick. Look, it's snapped off clean, but no other branches of the bush are damaged. If an animal had stepped on it, there would've been several broken branches, but there's only one. That can only mean one thing. A bullet flew through this bush on its way to its intended target."

I drew an imaginary line from the boulders to the burnt spot beneath the tree. The line perfectly pierced the bush in Singer's palm.

I said, "Okay, Teresa, the evidence supports your story so far. Let's head for Indian country."

It took less than fifteen minutes to ride our machines across the Montana state line and onto the Crow Reservation. Kodiak pulled to a stop beside a tree with a small piece of yellow flagging hanging from a branch, and we shut down our engines.

Teresa pointed to the flagging. "Somebody pulled down the crime scene tape already, but they missed a piece." She pointed to a spot beneath the tree. "That's where they found him."

Kodiak stepped to the spot and examined the scene in every direction. "This is sloppy."

"What do you mean?" I asked.

"You can't see more than two hundred yards in any direction from here. Nobody would hunt from this spot. It'd be a waste of time."

I asked, "Is it possible McAllister could've been shot at the first site and somehow made it here on his own before he died?"

Teresa said, "There's nothing this way for miles, so he wouldn't have come this direction. Alex was a half mile back down the trail. If anything, he would've moved toward Alex, not away from him."

Kodiak shook his head. "If he was shot by a pro, there's no way he could've escaped after being shot. The shooter would've kept firing until he went down."

Singer nodded his agreement.

I took a knee and raked away the thin layer of snow beneath the tree. "I don't know anything about forensics, but would it do any good to take a soil sample and look for blood?"

Teresa said, "I already did that. There was human blood in the soil at the first site, but none here. The blood type matched Zander's."

"Who tested the soil?" I asked.

"A friend."

As we headed back to our snow machines, a mechanical growl sounded from the northwest, and we froze. A vehicle that looked like the cab of a truck mounted on the treads of a tank rumbled across the snow.

"Who could that be?" Kodiak asked.

I said, "It doesn't matter. We're trespassing, no matter who it is. Move!"

The six snow machines roared to life, and we raced southward, away from the approaching vehicle. As we ran, just like Lot's wife, I couldn't resist the urge to glance over my shoulder every few seconds. I didn't turn into a pillar of salt, but I didn't like what I saw.

I thumbed the throttle to its stop, willing the machine to accelerate, but no matter how hard I pushed, we couldn't outrun our pursuers. Kodiak was in the lead and afflicted with the same urge as me. He made a visual head count and waved for us to follow. In the next instant, he threw his machine to the left and across an embankment leading into a ravine. Our engines roared as we descended the slope at breakneck speed.

Another glance over my shoulder revealed the vehicle still giving chase. It bounded across the lip of the embankment and slid sideways until the driver finally recovered and continued closing on us. As we approached the bottom of the ravine, a river appeared, and I panicked. We were stuck between an unknown potential enemy chasing us and a thirty-foot-wide river that had yet to freeze over.

I immediately regretted my decision to bring five other people on the excursion. If the people chasing us were the same people who killed Zander McAllister, they wouldn't have any qualms about adding to their body count. We were armed, but not well. Each of us carried a pistol, and Singer had a rifle. I didn't relish the idea of our afternoon turning into a gunfight, but it was certainly shaping up that way.

To my surprise, Kodiak kept his machine at full throttle as we approached the flowing river. He raised his left arm and waved frantically for us to continue following. I trusted him, but I wanted to know his plan.

In that instant, everything changed as geysers of snow from the ground exploded around me with every bullet strike. Whoever they were, our pursuers had just upped the ante, and we had no option other than returning fire. Shooting backward while riding a snow machine downhill at sixty miles per hour may have been the most difficult thing I'd ever done, but in that moment, it was the only action that might save our lives.

A column formation would give the unknown assailants a smaller target, but lining up would make it impossible for anyone except the trailing machine to fire back, so we settled into a wedge formation and kept our throttles buried. We fired without aiming, hoping to disable the vehicle behind us, but he kept coming, and the river's edge grew ever closer. When we reached the waterline, we'd have no choice but to turn and fight. With any luck, we'd disable the vehicle before reaching the bottom, but it wasn't looking good.

My heart pounded so hard I could hear it over the thunder of the engine between my knees and the blasts of our pistols in the air. We were on the verge of a serious gunfight in the Montana backcountry, dozens of miles from civilization.

I prepared myself for the coming fight. I would intentionally lay my snow machine on its side, use it for cover, and empty my pistol through the windshield of the coming vehicle. I believed the rest of my team would do the same, but Teresa was a wildcard. My plan was logical, but I had no idea what was happening inside her head. Keeping her alive was critical, but our situation was quickly becoming an exercise in keeping ourselves alive.

The rushing water of the river was close enough to almost taste, but Kodiak wasn't slowing down. I expected him to make a hard turn to the south and run parallel to the river until we reached a position we could defend. High ground would be our best option, but I was coming to believe we were running out of options to choose our battlefield. We were being driven into unfamiliar territory with rapidly depleting ammo and aggressors obviously intent on driving us into the frozen ground.

At the last instant before reaching the water, I leaned right to brace myself for the ninety-degree turn to the south, but Kodiak didn't turn. The skis of his snow machine hit the water, and the track sent a rooster tail of river water high into the air. We blindly followed him onto the surface of the river, and to my utter disbelief, the snow machines didn't sink. Our momentum, coupled with the thrust of the tracks, sent us shooting across the water as if on Jet Skis.

Kodiak left the river and climbed the bank on the opposite side, with mud and snow flying in every direction behind him. Each of us followed suit and barreled up the embankment. Once back on snow, we turned south and accelerated until our machines were at full speed. With a full head of steam, Kodiak turned left, and we followed him into the tree line.

As the forest around us grew in density, we turned toward the southwest and finally back onto open ground. We pushed the machines to their limits until the trailhead, our Suburbans, and the empty trailer came into view. The loading took only seconds, and we were back inside the trucks without any bullet holes in our bodies.

Chapter 10
It's What We Do

"Well, that was interesting," were the first words out of my mouth when we gathered inside my room back at the Bighorn Lodge.

Teresa said, "I was impressed."

Hunter chuckled. "Me, too. I can't believe that thing—whatever it was—kept up with us."

Kodiak chimed in. "That *thing* is called a snowcat. A bunch of companies make them. They're essentially a high-speed bulldozer with an enclosed cab. They're used for all sorts of stuff in the snow. They can plow roads and haul groups of backcountry skiers and hikers in and out of places a vehicle with tires can't go. Some of the ski patrol guys even use them as ambulances on the slopes."

Teresa said, "I wasn't talking about the snowcat. I meant I was impressed with your team's ability to adapt, fight back, and escape."

Clark huffed. "Yeah, it's impressive what folks can do when they're being shot at. We're not good at getting dead. That's one of our selling points."

"Seriously," she said. "A lot of Clandestine Service guys wouldn't have identified the snowcat as a threat. You didn't hesitate."

Clark said, "We're not Clandestine Service guys. We're operators. When we go to work, it's just us out there. There's no full might and force of the federal government waiting to ride in and pull our butts out of the fire. We get in, do the job, stay alive, and get out. Comparing us to CIA Clandestine Service officers is like comparing apples to dump trucks."

The look on Teresa's face said she hadn't been around Clark long enough to understand, so I stepped in with some logic that actually made sense. "I may have made the decision to run, but it was Kodiak's knowledge and skill that got us out of there. Combining skill sets to survive and fight another day is what we do best."

She cocked her head. "Why did you make the decision to run so quickly?"

I took my first sip of coffee. "We were somewhere we shouldn't have been without permission. That's Crow Reservation land, and we've already learned dead bodies don't get much respect up there. I figured it was a fifty-fifty proposition whether the snowcat was friend or foe. If they were friendly, they wouldn't chase us if we ran. If they were foe, sticking around to have a chat was a potentially deadly option, so I erred on the side of staying alive. It was the right decision this time, but we made one nearly critical mistake . . ."

Singer placed his cup on the end table. "Yeah, we did, and we can't let that happen again."

Celeste stared at us wide-eyed and pointed two thumbs at herself. "Not a soldier here. What am I missing?"

Singer said, "We carried pistols into a rifle fight. Handguns serve only one purpose, and that's to keep you alive while you're fighting your way to a rifle."

Celeste said, "I guess I learned something new today. So, who do you think was inside the snowcat? Could it have been the tribal police?"

I picked up my phone and called the op center back at Bonaventure.

Skipper was on the line in an instant. "Nice of you to check in."

I didn't waste time playing word games with her. "I need to know who operates snowcats inside the Crow Indian Reservation."

"Well, I'm fine. Thanks for asking. And how are you?"

"This is serious, Skipper. We took rifle fire from somebody in a heavy, tracked snow machine inside the southern edge of the reservation. I need to know who operates those things up here."

"Sorry," she said. "I'm on it."

As the clicking of her keyboard echoed through the phone, I punched the speaker button and laid it on the table.

She asked, "Was there an insignia on the vehicle?"

"I don't know," I said. "I was too busy running for my life and shooting back to look for stickers."

Celeste said, "Most importantly, does the tribal police have any of those things?"

"I'm looking. Give me a couple of minutes. Oh, wait. Is everybody okay?"

"We're good," I said. "But it was close."

I grew more impatient with every tick of the second hand until Skipper said, "It wasn't the tribal police. They have snowmobiles, but nothing bigger than a two-man machine. The National Parks Service has several, but they're all painted orange."

"This one wasn't orange," I said. "I think it was blue and white, but I can't be sure."

Singer nodded. "Chase is right. It was blue and white."

"In that case, it wasn't the Parks Service. I'll stay on it, but I don't have many answers right now. Have you talked with the tribal police yet?"

I said, "No, that'll happen tomorrow morning. Get back with us as soon as you have information on who operates a blue and white snow machine in the area."

"You got it," she said. "Anything else?"

"That does it for now. Good job on the SUVs and the lodge. It's nice."

"It's what I do. TTFN."

I pocketed the phone, and Gator said, "TTFN?"

"Come on. Don't tell me you don't know Winnie the Pooh," I said.

He sat, clearly clueless as to what I was talking about.

I said, "Tigger, Piglet, Kanga, Roo, Christopher Robin . . . Nothing?"

He shrugged. "Yeah, I know, but what's that got to do with TTFN, whatever that means?"

"Ta-ta for now," came the chorus from the team.

Gator shook his head. "We just got shot at, ran for our lives, turned snowmobiles into Jet Skis, and now we're quoting cartoon characters?"

I refilled his coffee cup. "Just like Skipper said, it's what we do."

Kodiak and Clark returned the snow machines and came home with twenty-four thousand dollars and change and some solid local intel.

We were gathered around the largest table in the dining room of the lodge when Clark bent down beside me. "We need to talk."

I pushed away from the table and stood. "Excuse me for a minute."

In the massive lobby of the resort, Clark spoke barely above a whisper. "Snowmobile guy said he heard a rumor about a gun-fight on the mountain and wanted to know if we saw anything. I slipped him a nice tip and asked where he heard the rumor." He paused and checked our surroundings for prying ears, but we were still alone. "He wouldn't give me a name. He said something about it being a small community and that word gets around."

I said, "I don't see how any of this is helping us."

"I'm not finished yet. Hear me out. He said he also heard a rumor that some feds were snooping around up there. He heard it had something to do with a missing CIA agent or something."

"Oh, really?" I asked.

"Yeah. I didn't take the time to tell him the CIA doesn't have agents, only case officers. I only listened, and he said it's just local scuttlebutt."

Before he was finished talking, I had Skipper on the line. "Look for feds with snowcats."

She cut me off. "Way ahead of you. I came across an appropriation request and approval to purchase one tracked, all-terrain vehicle capable of operation in arctic and mountainous conditions. Guess who."

"I don't have time for guesses. Tell me who, when, and where."

She said, "The *who* is the U.S. Department of Interior."

"Parks Service?" I asked.

"No, definitely not. They have a separate budget. This is a discretionary purchase out of a special-use budget for CONUS operations."

"Keep talking," I said.

"The when was last week, and the where was Billings, Montana."

"Please tell me there's a description."

"There's not," she said, "but who's your girl?"

"Spit it out!"

"Geez! Give me a minute to gloat, would you? I found the dealer in Billings. They've got a website with pictures. Check your phone."

I pulled the phone away from my face and brought up the text message Skipper sent. When it opened, I couldn't believe my eyes. It was a blue and white snowcat on the showroom floor at the dealer in Billings. "That's it!"

"I thought so," she said. "I called the dealership to inquire about it, and they said they could have another one in less than six weeks, but the one in the pictures just sold last week."

I said, "I wish you were here. I'd kiss your forehead and tell you how great you are."

"Save it, snow bunny. Enjoy the cold, and let me know if you need anything else."

"There is one more thing," I said. "If you can find out which tribal police detective worked the McCallister case, that'd give Celeste a nice starting place in the morning."

"I'll see what I can do. See ya."

Clark and I made our way back to the dining room, where every eye at the table looked up in anticipation.

I gave them a nod and asked, "What's for dessert?"

We finished the meal, enjoyed dessert, and headed upstairs, where I briefed the team on what Skipper had dug up.

Hunter said, "So, those guys were CIA?"

"Not likely," Teresa said. "The CIA isn't officially authorized to conduct operations inside the United States except intelligence gathering operations against suspected foreign operatives. It's more likely it was the FBI or a contractor."

"Why do you think they shot at us?" I asked.

She said, "They're looking for the people, or a person, who killed a retired case officer. We fit the profile, and we ran like guilty people. They may not have had probable cause to employ deadly force, but that's something they could spin, should it ever get out."

I said, "So, regardless of who they were, they're working for the federal government."

"Probably, but not officially," Teresa said. "Those things get a little murky. That's why I always preferred working overseas."

I turned to our gadget guru. "Are you still up for going in there tomorrow morning?"

She said, "If they don't shoot at me, I am. Maybe I should take Singer with me. He seems to be the only one smart enough to bring the right gun to the right fight."

"We won't be far away," I said. "I don't think we have anything to fear from the tribal police except deception and denial, neither of which will kill you."

Celeste smiled. "I may have a trick or two up my sleeve for the meeting if they get too quiet."

* * *

The next morning, Celeste sat at the kitchen counter, nursing her fifth cup of coffee.

I said, "It's your big day."

"Yeah, I know. I've been thinking about it all night, and I'm more than a little nervous."

"There's no reason to be nervous."

"Easy for you to say. You're some kind of James Bond, and I'm a scientist."

I slid onto the seat beside her. "All you're doing is asking questions. Keep it civil and walk away if it gets heated. Nobody is going to shoot at you. The worst thing that can happen is a detective throws you out of his building. I got shot at yesterday. Compared to that, anything that happens to you today is going to be a cakewalk."

"You make it sound so easy," she said. "I'm a lab rat."

"You're a lot more than a lab rat. You're the smartest person I know, and if anybody can pull this off, it's you."

"What if they figure out I'm Cherokee and not Crow?"

"I don't think they're going to start another Indian War because you're not Crow and you asked a few questions."

She chuckled nervously. "Okay. I guess I can do it. Just don't leave me in there if you hear something suspicious."

"Don't worry. I won't."

She took my arm. "Promise?"

"We won't let anything happen to you, I promise. And I almost forgot. Skipper sent me a text. Detective Rivers was the investigator for McAllister's case."

She placed her cup on the table. "Well, at least that's somewhere to start."

She wired herself for sound, and we tested the communications. Everything worked exactly as she designed.

The drive to the tribal police station was quiet, but Celeste seemed to relax a little more with every passing mile.

When we pulled into the parking lot, she said, "I think I should have a gun."

I laughed. "What are you going to do? Start a gunfight in a police station?"

She sighed. "Okay, but next time, I get a gun."

"Deal," I said. "Now, go get 'em, Chief Mankiller."

She rolled her eyes. "My grandmother was the chief. I'm just like a minor princess or something."

"I don't think the Cherokee have princesses, but if they did, you'd certainly have a crown. Now, go in there and do your thing, Princess."

She closed her eyes, took a long breath, and exhaled as if casting out a demon. The door flew open, and her feet hit the ground like thunder. "I've got this."

I pulled away to avoid leaving a black SUV full of commandos sitting in the parking lot of the Crow Tribal Police station, but we didn't go far.

There was no reason to believe anything would go wrong, but I had every reason to believe we could get her out of there if it did.

"Good morning, ma'am. How may I help you?"

That's a good start, I thought.

"Is Detective Rivers available?"

The first voice said, "And your name, ma'am?"

"Mankiller."

"I'm sorry, what?"

Celeste said, "That's my name. Mankiller. Would you like to see my ID?"

I turned to Clark. "I'm loving the confidence."

He said, "Me, too. We'll see how she does when she gets in front of the detective."

"*If* she gets in front of him."

"Oh, she'll get in. I'm sure of it."

The first voice said, "Wait here, Ms. Mankiller. I'll see if Detective Rivers is available."

I pressed the button to transmit to Celeste. "You're doing great. Keep it up."

She whispered, "Cut it out. I'm working here."

Clark put on his crooked grin. "It's a good thing we didn't give her a gun."

Celeste's transmitter was tuned to broadcast any sound in her immediate area above thirty decibels, or the volume of the typical whisper. The mechanical sound of a door unlocking came through the speaker, and someone said, "Ms. Mankiller, I'm Detective Rivers. What can I do for you?"

Celeste said, "I'd like to talk with you about Alexander McAllister, the corpse discovered at the southern extreme of your reservation. I understand you're the senior investigator on the case."

"Who are you with, Ms. Mankiller?"

She raised her voice. "I'm with my people, who aren't fond of having dead white men showing up on the reservation."

Clark raised an eyebrow. "She's getting a little strong. Should we reign her in?"

"Not yet. Let's see how Rivers reacts."

The detective said, "Come to my office. There's no need to discuss this out here."

Clark said, "Okay, it sounds like it's working for her."

We listened to footsteps and another door closing.

"Please have a seat. May I get you anything?"

"Some answers would be good, Detective. Let's start with who he was."

Rivers appeared to rearrange himself in his chair. "If I may ask, Ms. Mankiller, are you an investigator of some sort?"

Celeste cleared her throat. "Have you heard of the Bureau of Indian Affairs, Detective Rivers? We made the formal request last week, but your office hasn't responded."

"And what request was that?"

"We asked for a full report and a copy of the case file. Is it your practice to ignore such requests, Detective?"

Clark said, "Did you tell her to go in there impersonating a BIA investigator?"

"No! I didn't tell her to do anything except get what information she could. She's improvising."

"I don't like it," he said. "It's too easy for her to get busted on a claim like that. Rivers is going to call the Bureau the second she leaves, and the gig will be up. We've got to get her under control."

I held up a finger. "Let's give it another minute."

Rivers said, "Forgive me, but I never received your request. Could I see your credentials?"

Clark palmed his forehead. "I knew it. Get her out of there."

Celeste said, "Of course, Detective. May I see yours?"

"Does she have credentials?" Clark asked.

I shrugged. "I guess we'll find out."

Rivers said, "Thank you, uh, Dr. Mankiller. Wait here, and I'll retrieve the file."

Celeste said, "I'll come with you. The Bureau isn't interested in a partial file. Since your office ignored our request, I'm sure you understand my insistence."

"Yes, of course. Follow me."

We heard more footsteps and doors opening and closing.

Rivers appeared to be talking to someone else. "I need the sealed McAllister file from two weeks ago."

A new voice said, "Sure. Give me a minute."

Rivers said, "We have a procedure for handling all investigations involving a fatality that requires the file be sealed and a log entry made every time it's opened and resealed."

Celeste didn't answer, and I didn't know if we'd had a comms failure or if she was playing the role of the stern investigator.

"Here it is. Sign the board. You know the drill."

Rivers said, "I assume you need a copy."

Celeste said, "You assume correctly, and if you don't mind, I'll watch as you make the copies."

The hum and clicks inherent of a copier filled the coming minutes, and Celeste spoke softly. "Off the record, Rivers. What am I *not* going to find inside that file?"

"Off the record?" he asked.

She said, "We don't want this thing to ever see the light of day, so give it to me straight. And yes, we're off the record."

Rivers said, "It's not ours. It was a drop-and-go. He was clearly killed somewhere else and dropped on the reservation. If you ask me, whoever did it wanted the story to die right here on the rez. He was an old guy . . . obviously a hunter."

Celeste said, "Obviously? Did you recover his rifle?"

"Uh, I don't think . . . I'll have to . . ."

"If he was obviously a hunter, Detective, where was his rifle?"

Rivers said, "We assume—"

"Assume? Is that how investigations are conducted out here? On assumptions? Look, Rivers. This thing has the weight to raise a lot of questions. We're still off the record, okay?"

The detective said, "Yeah, okay."

"Let's take a walk back to the file room. I'd like to have a copy of the log."

"Are you doing what I think you're doing, Dr. Mankiller?"

Celeste said, "I wouldn't know, Detective. I'm not a mind reader, and unlike you, I don't make assumptions."

The sounds appeared to be those of the two returning to the file room.

Rivers said, "We need to make a copy of the file log."

A clipboard snapped, and Celeste said, "I'll make the copy when I get back to my office. You don't object to that, do you, Detective Rivers? Your career has been far too clean to sully it with something like this. I think we understand each other, right?"

I could almost hear the smile on the detective's face. "Yes, ma'am, we certainly do. And it was a pleasure never meeting you."

"Likewise, whatever your name is. Good day."

Clark waved toward the windshield. "Go, go, go."

I threw gravel and snow from beneath the tires and arrived at the front door of the station at the same time Celeste emerged from the building.

She slipped onto the seat and slapped the file and the copy onto the center console. "That's how it's done, boys."

Clark grabbed the file. "Bureau of Indian Affairs? Really? How did you get BIA creds?"

Celeste smiled. "I got them from a brilliant tech services officer I know, who works for the coolest team of bad-ass operators the world has ever seen."

Chapter 11
Just Cause

We pored over the file Celeste masterfully acquired from the Crow Reservation Tribal Police, and we learned nothing.

I said, "This barely qualifies as a case file. What would these guys do if they caught a real case?"

Celeste tossed her copy onto the coffee table. "If it's anything like the Cherokee Reservation, they don't get much real crime to speak of. It's mostly petty stuff—car wrecks and domestics."

I waved the file in my hand. "Maybe they didn't know what to do with this one."

Celeste grimaced. "I don't think that's it. They knew what to do, but they wanted it to go away, and I gave them the escape route they were looking for."

"Do you think this will ever make its way to the Bureau of Indian Affairs? I don't want to get busted on that one."

Celeste slid her phone onto the table. "Check this out."

A ringtone sounded through the speaker before an electronic voice came on the line. Eventually, we found ourselves listening to an employee directory, and Dr. Mankiller's name was fourth on the list. Celeste pressed the numbers for her make-believe extension, and three seconds later, her phone rang.

"How did you pull that off?" I asked.

THE SILENT CHASE · 95

She gave me a wink. "Don't mess with the tech services chick. We can do magic, and if we happen to be full-blooded Native American, it just might be black magic."

"I'm glad you're on our team."

She grinned. "I'm in love with being on your team. I never got to do cool stuff like this at the DOJ. So, when do I get a gun?"

I said, "It's on my list. Don't let me forget."

She rolled her eyes. "Yeah, right."

"Where's Teresa?"

Clark said, "She wasn't feeling well, so she's taking a nap. I think she's exhausted. It's been quite a month for her. I'd be ready for a nap, too."

"You're always ready for a nap. Let's talk about what we learned."

"From the file? Nothing," Clark said. "It might as well be a jay-walking case."

"I don't mean just the file. I mean the whole thing. We learned that somebody working unofficially with the federal government is willing to kill anybody who comes nosing around the dump site."

Clark said, "I've been thinking about that, and I'm not so sure they were shooting to kill. Looking back on it, now that our heart rates are under a hundred, I think they may have been missing on purpose to scare us off. Think about it. How does somebody fire that many rounds and hit none of us? It doesn't make sense."

"I disagree," I said. "A snowcat at the speed we were moving isn't exactly a stable platform. I think there were two people on board—a driver and a shooter. They might've had a third guy, but he would've been stuck in the middle with no way to fire at us. If I'm right, they had one guy hanging out a window, bouncing all over the place, and snapping off rounds in our general direction. When I first spotted the fire, it was because of the bullet strikes in the snow a foot away from me. If he was missing on purpose, he was a heck of a shot to get that close under those conditions."

"Maybe you're right," he said. "The whole thing just feels strange to me."

"Yeah, getting shot at during a high-speed chase through the snow definitely qualifies as strange. Let's back up and look at the big picture."

"Lay it out for me," he said.

"Somebody was willing to shoot at us on American soil, and they were very likely working for the government, either officially or not. That's thing number one. Number two is the ease with which the tribal police were willing to dump the case file. They're not idiots. They've got a reason why they don't want that file hanging around. If this thing is a coverup, they don't want blood on their hands."

Clark said, "I'm with you so far."

"Third, Zander McAllister's rifle is missing. Where is it? Who took it? And most of all, why did they take it?"

"There are only three reasons somebody steals a gun," he said. "They need money, they're afraid the rightful owner might use it on them, or they're planning something sinister with the weapon and don't want it tied to them."

I said, "You could be right, or it could be an oversight on the part of whoever moved the body. They may have thrown the rifle into their vehicle and forgot about it. Not everything is sinister. Sometimes, it's just sloppy."

He said, "Do you see anything sloppy about that operation? I don't. Whoever shot him and moved the body was good enough to do it all without being seen. I think it had to be at least two people. Moving a body is tough without some help."

"I agree. Now, when we look at the whole thing, it boils down to one simple conclusion. Teresa was telling the truth about what happened up here. Everything she told us checks out, and the kicker for me is the fact that somebody was willing to shoot at us. That makes her story even more credible."

Clark played with his graying beard. "Be careful, College Boy. It's starting to sound like you may be looking for reasons to believe her instead of looking for the truth."

Through the years with Clark Johnson, I never knew him to avoid making eye contact when he scolded me, and there had been more scoldings than I care to remember, but that time, he didn't look up. He stared into space as if lost in thought.

"I can assure you that I'm approaching this mission with the utmost caution. I question everything until I know, and yes, I want to believe her, but my first loyalty is to this team, and I will never decide to put us in harm's way when I think we're being lied to."

He said, "I wasn't questioning your loyalty to the team. I just want to make sure you're being objective. Teresa saved your life overseas, and that's impossible to forget. Loyalty is earned over time and strengthened by repetition of action."

I said, "I believe her. What does she have to gain by lying to us? She knows we're smart enough to bust her if she tries to scam us, and she's experienced enough to know we'll walk away the second we catch her in a lie. She's asking us to put our lives at risk for people we don't know. An ask like that isn't something a career Clandestine Service officer would make lightly."

"I agree with you," he said. "I just need to know that your head's in the right place."

"My head is good, and it's right where it needs to be for this mission. Unless Teresa shot McAllister, moved his body by herself, convinced the tribal police to throw away the case, and sicked that snowcat on us, she's clean in this thing, and I believe her."

Clark finally looked up. "I'd follow you into a burning building wearing gasoline underpants, College Boy, and so would everybody on the team. You're one of the best natural leaders I've ever known. Just remember the number-one rule of leadership . . . Question everything except yourself."

A female voice from the other side of the room said, "Is that what all of this was about?"

Clark and I looked up to see Teresa Lynn standing in the doorway with fury in her eyes.

She said, "Did you come all the way up here and spend all this money just to test my honesty?"

My first instinct was to deflect the accusation, but instead, I said, "Come join us, and I'll tell you what this is about."

She stood frozen for a moment before moving into the room and claiming a seat. Before I had a chance to begin, she said, "If you don't trust me, look me in the eye and say that. I'll find a way to pay you back what you've spent on this little truth-detecting field trip of yours, and I'll go after this guy, or guys, by myself."

The little psychologist inside my head wanted to let her vent as long as she needed, but it was time for leadership, not psychotherapy.

I said, "Everybody who looks at a situation sees it differently. You described what happened up here, and I thought I had the picture, but I was wrong. I didn't have the full picture until I saw it for myself. Now I see it, and now I have a sense of the type of adversary we're up against. I'm asking a team of men and women I love to walk into Hell with me because you asked me for my help."

I paused and studied her softening posture.

"When I ask this team to do something, they do it, trusting that I wouldn't ask anything of them that I wasn't one hundred percent willing to do myself. I needed to know who and what we're facing, and now I do. This wasn't about a check on your honesty. It was about assuring myself that whatever this is, it's worth getting myself or my men hurt or killed over."

She took a long breath and relaxed, so I continued. "This thing is clearly a thorn in the Agency's side. Otherwise, they wouldn't go to so much trouble to cover it up and try to kill us in the meantime. We're going to see this thing through to its end, and we're going to find the answers you need."

She closed her eyes. "Forgive me for being defensive. I'm tired. I don't feel good. And even though it kills me to admit this, I'm scared. Whoever's doing this has a kill list, and I have every reason to believe I'm on it."

"I understand," I said. "It's perfectly natural to be afraid. I would be, too, but more than that, I'd be furious, and that's just as dangerous. We'll go about this methodically, but quickly and without emotion. That's how we stay alive . . . all of us, including you."

She nodded. "I understand, and again, I'm sorry for overreacting."

Clark beat me to the punch. "Don't be sorry. Be better."

That brought a little smile to Teresa's face. "I like that. Mind if I steal it?"

"It's all yours," he said.

Teresa bit her lip for a moment. "Thank you—both of you—for what you're doing. Do you plan to go to Glenn Phillips's place in Virginia and Ty Emerson's house in the Philippines?"

I asked, "If we do, will we find anything you haven't told us?"

"I don't think so," she said. "Getting any kind of real answers in the Philippines is out of the question, and aside from an autopsy report for Glenn, I can't imagine there's anything to see in Newport News."

"Then where are we going next?" I asked.

She said, "We need to know what happened to Pam Bingham."

"In that case," I said, "it looks like we're headed to Mexico. How do you feel about ships?"

Teresa recoiled. "Ships? What kind of ships?"

Clark chuckled. "It sure ain't Royal Caribbean, but the food's just as good. Maybe better."

Chapter 12
The Brave Lion

I made the call to Bonaventure. "Good evening, Skipper. We'd like to schedule a Western Caribbean cruise, please."

"Cute," she said. "Let me guess. You'd like luxury accommodations aboard the *Lori Danielle.*"

"You're really good at this travel agent gig. Maybe you should consider a career change."

"Done. I quit."

I panicked just a little. "On second thought, let's renegotiate your contract."

She chuckled. "I thought you might be willing to negotiate. I'll get Captain Sprayberry on the horn. Where would you like to rendezvous?"

"That depends on where they are. We'll need to make a stop at home to gear up, but we can meet them at their nearest port, as long as there's an adequate runway somewhere close."

"I'll get back with you. How did Celeste do with the tribal police?"

"She wants a gun," I said.

"So, give her one. Everybody else is armed. Why not her?"

I groaned. "Because I'm afraid she'll take over the world. I think she might be some sort of evil genius. She had way too much fun impersonating an investigator from the Bureau of Indian Affairs."

"Look at her go," Skipper said. "I take it that means she talked them out of every morsel of information they have."

"She did better than that. She came out with the original case file in her hands."

Skipper chuckled. "Teach her to speak Russian and fight with a knife, and you'll never have to call Anya back in."

"I don't know about that."

"That would make Penny happy."

I shivered a little. "Let's talk about something else."

"Chicken. I'll talk to Captain Sprayberry and call you back."

"We'll be on the plane in an hour," I said. "We're headed home for a quick turn."

I gave the airport a call, and they promised to have the *Grey Ghost* fueled and waiting when we arrived.

"Unless you guys want to stay up here for the Wyoming winter, let's break camp and head for warmer climes."

Kodiak stared out the window. "Can't we vote on it?"

I said, "Sure. All those in favor of Marley, mangos, and margaritas say aye."

A rambunctious chorus of ayes filled the room, and Kodiak stuck his hands in his pockets.

I threw an arm around his shoulders. "I'll make a deal with you. If we survive this mission, you can teach the rest of the team to snow ski when it's over. How's that?"

He put on his best Forrest Gump face. "But you ain't got but one leg, Lieutenant Chase."

"In that case, I guess that means I've only got one to break."

"That's one way to look at it," he said. "So, are you serious? Do you really want to learn to ski?"

"No, I don't want to, but I want you to enjoy the winter, so I'm willing to make the rest of us suffer through it."

He stuck out his hand. "It's a deal. After seeing how you guys took to the snow machines, you may be better skiers than you think."

The lady at the airport kept her word, and the *Grey Ghost* was perched on the ramp just outside the FBO when we pulled up. It took the team only minutes to stow their gear aboard the plane and find their seats.

Just inside the cockpit door, I took a knee and watched Disco flip through the preflight checklist. I said, "Would you mind if I put Gator up here with you for a few minutes?"

He glanced over his shoulder. "Sure, that's fine with me. Are you trying to set the hook?"

"He and I had a little talk about flying, and he thinks he wants to do it. He clashed with the instructor at the Farm, so he got a bad start."

"Sure, send him up here. We'll have some fun."

I made my way through the cabin of the Gulfstream, where my team was settling into the softest seats on any airplane in the world. Gator was already situated and had his book open on his lap.

I knelt beside him. "What are you reading?"

He flipped over the novel. "It's a Clive Cussler story. I guess I should be reading something nonfiction, but fiction gives my brain something to do instead of thinking about, well, you know."

"Yeah, I know. We all need something to flush out the demons. I've got a better idea than the novel if you're interested."

He brightened. "Sure. What is it?"

I took the book from his hand. "Hop in the right seat up front, and Disco will take you through the departure and initial cruise phase of the flight. If you like it, stay up there. If not, come on back and pick up your library book."

"Seriously?"

"Absolutely," I said.

He unbuckled his seat belt. "I've never been in the cockpit of a jet, so I won't be any help, but I'm in."

"I think Disco can handle it without your input, but he'll teach you a few things. If you decide you like the front seat, we'll start your training when this mission is over."

"Thanks, Chase. This is really cool of you."

I took his seat and flipped back to the front of his book. I wasn't a stranger to Cussler's writing, but I hadn't read that particular novel. By the time we were cruising at forty-three thousand feet, I was completely engrossed in the story.

My sat-phone chirped right in the middle of a scene I didn't want to stop, but when I saw Skipper's face on the screen, I thumbed the answer button. "Go for Chase."

Skipper said, "Good news. The *Lori Danielle* was on her way to Bermuda to pick up scientists for some counting whales project or something. I wasn't interested, and Captain Sprayberry clearly wasn't, either. I think he's an action guy like us. Anyway, he's flipping a U and heading for Bonaventure. They'll be here tomorrow afternoon."

"Nice work," I said. "That'll give us just enough time to pack up and get our shots. If you don't mind, call that Flower Girl and have her bring her bag of needles over. We're headed to Mexico, so our immune systems might discover a germ they're not familiar with."

Skipper moaned. "Her name is Cindy Flowers, not Flower, and she's not a girl. She's a woman who just happens to be a registered nurse. I'll make sure she brings an extra big needle just for you."

"We'll be home in a couple of hours."

We clicked off, and I dived back into Gator's book, secretly hoping he liked being in the cockpit. Fifteen chapters and two hours later, we touched down at our private airport with Gator still up front.

By the time my boots hit the tarmac, Don already had the fuel nozzle connected to the plane and fuel flowing.

I stepped close enough for him to hear me over the engine and pump of the fuel truck. "How's it going, Don? Do you need anything?"

"No, I'm good. Thanks. Everything is running as it should. I ordered a few replacement runway lights a couple of days ago. I should've asked you before I spent the money, but you weren't around."

"Nobody knows this airport better than you. Order whatever you need, whenever you need it. If I didn't trust you, you wouldn't be here."

He gave me a nod. "Thanks. You know I'll take care of the place."

I walked away to find Disco and Gator inspecting the exterior of the Gulfstream. "What did you think of the front seat?"

Gator said, "I'm hooked. Disco says you've got a One-Eighty-Two."

"We do," I said. "It doesn't get much love, but it's in the back of hangar two."

He glanced at the hangar. "I think I'd like to get started when we get home. I can pay for the—"

I cut him off. "No, you can't pay for anything. Flying is a big part of what we do. You don't pay for shooting on the range. Training and staying current on every skill we can develop makes us more capable. Disco is a great instructor, and he'll have you well-qualified before you know it."

Gator said, "That's exactly what Disco said about you."

"There's no shortage of instructors around here. Clark's a CFI, too. Between the three of us, we'll turn you into a pilot in no time."

We convoyed back to Bonaventure, and I pulled Teresa aside. "Tell me about Pamela Bingham."

"What do you want to know?"

"Everything you know."

She said, "This could take a while. We may need to have a seat."

"Follow me."

I led her through the kitchen and down the back stairs to the gazebo, where I took a seat in my favorite Adirondack. "Let's start with what we're going to find on Isla Mujeres."

"Have you been there?" she asked.

"A couple of times, but I never stayed long enough to get a real feel for the place."

She crossed her legs. "It's a quiet little island. I've never known there to be any real crime. Pam has—or maybe had—a small house at the south end of the island. Like I told you before, I went there to check on her, but she wasn't there. I didn't go inside, but I checked all the doors and windows. There was no one inside and no sign of damage. Everything seemed to be in its place, and the house was locked up tight."

"So, there were no signs of a struggle?"

"Not that I saw," she said.

"How about a car?"

"As far as I know, she didn't have a car. Most people on the island use golf carts to get around. The weather is always nice, and it's a small place. There's no real need for a car."

I asked, "Was her golf cart there?"

Teresa shook her head.

"Why didn't you go inside?"

She said, "I flew commercial, so I didn't have my picks, and I didn't want to break any glass to get in. The last thing I needed was to get arrested in Mexico."

I drummed my fingers on the arm of my chair. "No, Teresa, the last thing you need is for your name to come up on the kill list we're chasing."

"Touché."

"Tell me about Pamela."

She twisted in her seat. "As I told you, we went through the Farm together, but we never shared a posting. Our professional paths crossed a few times throughout the years, but our friendship was mostly cards, letters, and the occasional phone call before email became a thing. After technology took over, we talked more often through email, and we grew closer."

I didn't like having to ask the next question, but the answer could potentially reshape our investigation. "Was it a romantic relationship?"

She smiled. "No, but I understand why you have to ask. She and I are only interested in men, but the lives we led weren't conducive to long-term romantic relationships. We're colleagues who share a friendship."

"You said you took a cruise together?"

"Yes, we did eleven nights through the Mediterranean. It was really nice. She spent most of her career in Central and South America, so the Med was a treat for her. I had mostly European and Near East assignments."

I made a mental note of the fact that Teresa spoke of Pam in present tense. Maybe it was wishful thinking on her part, but subconsciously, she didn't perceive Pam as being dead, only missing.

"I need to ask a question that'll involve some classified information. Everyone on my team has a TS clearance, a signed NDA, and

I believe we have the required need to know. You said your professional lives crossed a few times. I need to know about the assignments the two of you worked on together."

Something over the river caught her attention, and she stared into the marshland for a long time. When she finally turned to face me, the concern on her face spoke volumes. "She and I ran an operation in South Africa. There was an American diplomat who'd been compromised, and we were assigned to get as close to him as possible and feed him misinformation. The plan was for him to pass the information along to the agent who was working him."

"Did it work?" I asked.

"It actually worked a little too well. The agent who was running the diplomat recruited Pam and me. It was an espionage grand slam."

She just used a baseball term. Am I being played, or was it coincidental?

"A grand slam," I said. "How so?"

"We busted the diplomat, stopped the flow of real information into the hands of the . . . adversary . . . and we convinced the foreign agent we were more valuable sources than the original target."

"Wait a minute," I said. "The two of you let a foreign operative run the two of you as sources and kept feeding him bad intel?"

She nodded. "Yeah, exactly."

"For how long?"

"Eighteen months."

"Has that ever been done before?"

She said, "Sure. It's not all that rare, really, but it's hard to keep up the ruse. Case officers and marks behave very differently, and it's tough for one to pretend she's the other."

"What was your cover story?"

"Pam and I didn't operate together per se. We were working the same agent, but from different angles. Her legend was as a senior executive in a South American oil exploration company with extremely close ties to several government officials in Central and South America."

"Okay, slow down," I said. "I'm a paramilitary operator, not a spy, so that's not my world. Break it down for me. First, what government was the foreign agent working for?"

She chewed on her lip for several seconds. Her hesitance concerned me, but refusing to break eye contact can be a far more powerful motivator than pushing, so that's the game I played.

Finally, she said, "China."

"China? A Chinese agent ran you and Pamela as spies for eighteen months?"

"Almost eighteen," she said.

"How did it end? Why and how are you still alive?"

"Nothing ends well. Otherwise, it wouldn't end. It was getting hot, and keeping up a cover for that length of time isn't easy. The whole thing was falling apart, so the Agency decided to fake Pam's death before the Chinese put all the pieces together and ended her life for real."

My head was swirling. "So, the obvious answer is the Chinese are the ones gunning their way up the kill list."

"Hang on a minute," she said. "You're jumping to conclusions without knowing all the information. My cover wasn't a complete lie. We let the Chinese intel officer *learn* that I was an attaché in the predecessor of the Bureau of Near Eastern Affairs, Arms Control and International Security branch, Bureau of Political-Military Affairs."

"That's a mouthful," I said.

Teresa chuckled. "You should try fitting all of that on a business card."

"Okay, so you let your position leak to the Chinese agent, and he started licking his chops, right?"

"Not exactly. It's more complicated than that. We let him see Pam and me together on several occasions and let him listen in on a few scripted conversations she and I had about classified material. Letting him believe we were a couple of cackling hens who weren't smart enough to keep our mouths shut is what opened the door, but when I got sloppy with some supposedly classified State Department documents, that's what really got his attention. I intentionally left a file marked 'classified' with Pam when she was scheduled to meet with the Chinese agent."

"You can tell me his name," I said. "You don't have to keep referring to him as the Chinese agent."

Ignorance must have flashed all over my face when she said the Chinese agent's name was Bahadir Kaplan.

"Were you expecting something like Chaoxiang Chen?"

I said, "I guess I didn't realize the Chinese ran agents who weren't actually Chinese."

She said, "You're great at killing people and breaking things, aren't you?"

"It's what we do," I admitted.

She said, "The espionage side is a little different. Section two of the Social Affairs Department in the Chinese Ministry of State Security is responsible for intelligence collection. You can think of them like the Clandestine Service branch of the American CIA. How many white guys named Billy Bob Smith from Alabama do you think we run in Bangladesh? Just like us, the Chinese put case officers all over the world who fit in wherever they're assigned. Bahadir Kaplan was Turkish, and I don't know if that was his real name. Translated into English, it means something like 'brave lion.' That's a little hokey, even for the Chinese."

I was suddenly a baseball player on a soccer field, but I was running as fast as I could and trying to keep up. "Do you know if the three dead former case officers are connected to Kaplan in any way?"

"I don't know about Ty Emerson and Glenn Phillips, but Zander was in on the same operation as Pam and me."

"What was his role?"

She said, "He was the senior case manager."

Chapter 13
Sea Monsters with Knives

My pea-sized brain was turning to mush as I tried to create an organizational chart to represent an American CIA senior case manager, a pair of case officers—one pretending to be an attaché, and the other, a South American oil exploration executive—and Turkish agents working for the Chinese Ministry of State Security. I couldn't imagine how anyone could keep such a convoluted mess organized in their heads. On that day, I was grateful to be a knuckle-dragging trigger-puller.

Thankfully, I was saved by the bell, or more correctly, saved by the buzz of the rotors of the MH-6 Little Bird racing through the sky just above treetop level. Teresa and I pushed ourselves from our seats and stepped from beneath the cover of the gazebo to see the chopper turn into the wind and nestle gently onto the lawn a hundred feet away.

Teresa asked, "Is it safe to assume that's a friend of yours?"

"It is," I said. "Come on. I'll introduce you to the best chopper pilot in the business."

The pilot and her sidekick stepped from the machine, and I said, "Teresa Lynn, meet Barbie 'Gun Bunny' Brewer, former U.S. Army Apache pilot with a couple combat tours under her belt and a chest full of medals that'll never tell the whole story.

And this is Ronda No-H, CPA and the baddest door gunner you'll ever meet."

The women shook hands and exchanged pleasantries.

Teresa said, "Well, Chase, it would appear you've surrounded yourself with strong, beautiful, capable women."

"It's good work if you can get it," I said. "I suppose you two are the advance party. This must mean the *Lori Danielle* isn't far behind."

Barbie pointed toward the ocean. "She's that way about two hundred miles. She'll be in on the morning tide when the sun comes up tomorrow, but No-H couldn't wait to see her man, so the captain ordered me to get her off his boat to shut her up."

I nodded toward the house. "Disco's inside. Make yourself at home."

Teresa, Barbie, and I made no effort to keep up with Ronda, but we followed her up the steps, across the gallery, and into the house, where we found Clark leading Gator through the refrigerator.

"What are you two doing?" I asked.

"Trying to find something to eat. We're starving," Clark mumbled through a mouthful of something.

Barbie said, "Hey, guys. Nice to see you again."

Gator grinned. "Nice landing."

I could've sworn she almost blushed.

She said, "I left the keys in the ignition if you want to take her for a spin."

Gator laughed. "I'd spin that thing right into the house. I'm a long way from any front-seat time in a chopper, unless you're up for a new student."

"Maybe we could work something out," Barbie said.

Gator tipped his imaginary hat. "Looking forward to it."

Clark gave him an elbow. "Quit flirting, and grab that pie."

"Some things never change," I said as we headed for the room Penny called *the parlor*.

I never knew what that word meant, but I liked the room, regardless of its name.

Twenty minutes into conversation and relaxation, the sound of the Little Bird's T63 turboshaft engine whistled through the house, and Barbie's ears perked up. "I guess Gator's taking her for a spin after all."

"Don't worry," I said. "I'm sure Clark and his full belly are with him. They probably won't break anything."

Barbie stood. "There was a nasty little wind shear just above the treetops. I should let them know before they take off."

Everyone in the room followed Barbie back onto the lawn, but we were too late. Clark pulled the Little Bird off the ground and climbed into the wind from the south. We watched as he took Gator through his first few seconds of rotor-wing training. Just as they climbed above the trees and the peak of the roof, the wind shear Barbie encountered hit the Little Bird like a hammer and spun the tail to the east in an instant.

It was impossible for us to know what was happening inside the cockpit, but whatever it was resulted in the Little Bird spinning through a hundred eighty degrees and settling until the tail rotor struck an upper branch of a two-hundred-year-old oak tree. The flight was over, and all that remained was the crash.

We stared in disbelief as the chopper spun and drifted away from the house with the painful sound of mechanical destruction cracking through the air. Hunter and I yanked our phones from our pockets, dropped them to the ground, and sprinted side by side toward the dock.

Neither of us watched as the Little Bird and our teammates plunged toward the darkened waters of the North River. We dived in unison from the end of the dock at the same instant the chopper hit the water. I raised my head, desperately praying to see it floating on the surface, but my prayer was denied.

The emergency flotation system only partially inflated on the left skid, sending the doomed machine onto its right side with the rotor blades coming apart in flying shards as they struck the water.

Hunter and I powered through the outgoing current as hard and as fast as our arms and legs could carry us. We reached the wreckage at the same time and raised our heads from the water as we labored to fill our lungs with the air our bodies would demand in the coming minutes.

Hunter said, "I'm going deep for Clark. You get Gator."

We submerged together as if attached by an unseen force, and the world around us turned black in utter darkness. Feeling my way into the cockpit, I discovered Gator still strapped into his seat with his body leaning toward the other side. He was jerking violently and twisting his torso. No matter how hard I pulled against his five-point harness, I couldn't release the catch. With his body position and constant motion, there was too much force holding the release in place.

I tried to calm him down by patting his shoulders and upper arms, but he shoved me away. Wrestling with an athlete fifteen years younger than me, underwater, was the last option I wanted to explore, so I drew my knife, determined to slice him free of his restraints. The nylon webbing succumbed to my blade, but it took both of my hands to accomplish the task. I had to protect Gator's body with my left while cutting the webbing with my right. The battle consumed oxygen at an incredible rate, and my lungs screamed for fresh air.

I only needed to cut four of the five straps to free him from his confinement, but every move I made was countered by a defensive blow from Gator. He was fighting me and something else at the same time, and both of us were losing. If I didn't cut him free, he'd drown. If he knocked me out, I'd drown. If whatever he was fighting overcame him, we might both drown. Nothing was going right, and I was growing more confused and desperate for air by the second.

My chest convulsed, and my brain ordered my body to find fresh air, but I was determined not to surface without Gator in my arms. The battle continued for what felt like hours, and the tell-tale signs of an impending blackout from oxygen depletion poured through me. There was no choice left. I had to breathe, and I had to do it in the next few seconds if I was going to survive somebody else's helicopter crash.

I planted my feet against the frame of the chopper and kicked for what I hoped was the surface. A light above beckoned to me like a beacon, and I prayed it was the sun and not the ethereal light of death's undeniable call. I broke the surface an instant later and drew in a fresh gulp of air. Forcing myself to hyperventilate, I emptied and refilled my lungs several times.

The dive back into the obsidian pit found Gator limp in his seat, and I thumbed the harness release. It fell open in my palm. I wrapped my arms around my teammate and kicked away from the chopper for the second time in as many minutes. Carrying his two hundred pounds to the surface made the ascent slower than before, but we still reached the light in seconds, and I rolled him onto his back.

Assessing my situation took only an instant. Dragging Gator back to the dock wasn't an option. His body had been without air too long already, so I shoved his limp form onto the partially inflated pontoon still attached to the skid and then climbed on top of him. I shoved the heel of my hand against his diaphragm, hoping to force at least some of the water from his lungs. I couldn't tell if the water running from his face had come from his lungs or his beard, but I wasn't going to let him die in my arms.

Hunter broke the surface with Clark held against his chest, but I didn't have time to check on either of them. I kept my attention focused on my patient. I pinched Gator's nose and pressed my mouth over his, forcing the air from my lungs into his. I repeated the breath twice more and shoved a pair of fingers against the skin of his neck where his carotid artery should've been. The steady beat of his heart thumped against my fingertips, and I forced another breath into his lungs.

It sounded like I was deep inside a well, where every sound echoed endlessly. There was no time for me to be concerned about my condition. All that mattered in the moment was keeping Gator alive.

Finally, after several more breaths, he coughed, rolled onto his side, and vomited water, bile, and death from his body. I leaned over him as he opened his eyes, and although I couldn't decipher his garbled words, his lips beckoned, "Is Clark free?"

I raised my head and torso to see Hunter cradling our old guy against his chest. He was gagging, spitting, and probably cursing, but he was alive. I threw a finger into the air, and Gator followed it to see what I saw. Satisfied, he closed his eyes and lay back against the pontoon.

Penny motored toward us in *Aegis*'s RHIB. Barbie knelt in the bow and pulled Gator across the tube and into the boat. He landed with a thud between her legs and drenched her with filthy river water. Penny pulled Clark aboard from the stern, and Hunter and I climbed across the tubes.

We motored back to the dock, and Penny tied us alongside. Clark and Gator sat up, each catching their breath, and I climbed from the RHIB and took two steps on the dock before falling on my face. I peered down to see my electronic prosthetic frozen in position at the end of my stump. In the same moment, I reached for my ears and found nothing where a pair of hearing aids should've been. I was still a warrior inside my chest, but I was quickly running out of body parts to throw back into the fight.

I sat up, and Skipper stepped beside me with a towel in one hand and a fresh pair of hearing aids in the other. I took her offered gifts and put them both to excellent use.

As everyone's heart rate returned to normal, I grabbed Gator's shoulder. "What were you doing down there? I was trying to cut you free, and you were kicking my butt."

He wiped water from his eyes. "I was trying to get Clark out of his harness. I couldn't leave him down there, and I didn't realize you were trying to rescue me."

"What did you think I was? A mermaid?"

He shrugged and turned to Barbie. "No. She's the only mermaid around here. You were just some sea monster with a knife."

Chapter 14
Anchors Aweigh

"We can't leave what's left of the Little Bird in the river," I said. "It's a hazard to navigation, and it might still be salvageable."

Clark dried his hair and stared into the water. "How are we going to move it? It weighs almost two thousand pounds when it's not full of water. We don't have anything that can pluck it out of the river."

I turned to Mongo. "How much can the crane aboard the Mark Five lift?"

"Around two tons," he said. "But there's a lot more than a ton of water inside that thing."

"Let's try it," I said. "What's the worst that can happen?"

Mongo crossed his arms. "The cable could snap and kill everybody within twenty feet."

"There is that," I said. "How about the crane on the *Lori Danielle*?"

Mongo said, "Probably ten times as much as our crane on the Mark Five."

"In that case," I said, "let's strap some lifting bags to it and drag it into the boathouse until the ship arrives in the morning."

Mongo nodded. "I like that idea a lot better. There's very little chance of getting anyone cut in half by a snapped cable with that plan."

Hunter and I rigged a dozen lift bags to the foundering chopper that had been a spectacular flying machine less than an hour earlier but now more closely resembled a stepped-on black widow spider. We attached a towline and bridle, and Penny pushed the throttle full forward in the RHIB. The bow rose higher and higher, but the Little Bird didn't budge.

She pulled off the power. "The RHIB doesn't have the muscle. We need something bigger."

Every eye turned toward the boathouse, and my boat-handling wife grinned from ear to ear. "I'll be right back."

Minutes later, she backed the massive Mark V to within ten feet of the wreck, and Hunter attached the line. With the engines barely above idle, the hundred-thousand-pound boat dragged the carcass across the river as if it were nothing more than a fly. It took a little maneuvering to get the chopper into the boathouse, but we pulled it off.

With the wreck secure for the night, Clark said, "You know, we're required to notify the FAA about this."

"About what?" I asked.

He shook his head. "You're a lot of trouble, College Boy."

* * *

Just as predicted, the Research Vessel *Lori Danielle* arrived on the morning tide and hoisted the demolished chopper with little effort.

"What do you want us to do with it?" the crewman on the crane asked.

His question rattled me. "I haven't thought that far ahead yet. Give me a minute." I pulled out my phone and dialed the only number that came to mind.

"Dis here be Kenny LePine, me. Who dat be, you?"

Cajun Kenny LePine was the most eccentric person I'd ever known. Aside from being pure Southern Louisiana, he owned more heavy equipment than anybody in Camden County.

"Good morning, Kenny. It's Chase."

"Dat be who you be, you. How you is, you?"

"I'm doing all right, Kenny. Thanks. I'm sorry to call you so early . . ."

"Early? What you talkin' 'bout, you? Dis ain' early for Kenny, no. Half da day be done over. What you need from ol' Kenny, me?"

I'd never come to understand the language Kenny spoke, but I tried to answer the question I thought he asked. "We crashed a helicopter in the river, and—"

"Whoa, right der, you. Erebody, dem, day be a'right? Ain' nobody hurt nor graveyard dead, no?"

"We're all fine, Kenny. But we need a flatbed to haul the wreckage to our hangar. Do you have a truck and trailer we could use for a couple of hours?"

"Where you be at, you?"

"We're at home, and we've got the wreck on the deck of the ship."

Silence filled the line for a long moment, and I thought I could hear Kenny scratching his head. "So, you don' wan' nobody knowing you done crasheded dis helicopter, no?"

I let my brain play with the word *crasheded* for a while. "That's right. We'd rather not draw any attention."

"Den you done called da righ' man, you. Ol' Kenny be der in no time, me. Now, tell me true. Ain' nobody hurt nor ready to be put in da groun' dead?"

"I thought we lost Gator for a few minutes, but everybody's okay. Thanks for the concern."

"Gator?" he asked. "Dat soun' like somebody I done be knowin' for all my life, and his'n, too. Do dat be Gator LeBlanc or Gator Boudreaux? No, dat ain' make no sense, no. Gator LeBlanc won' be gettin' in no helicopter after dat airboat done took off mos' o' his arm."

I laughed, but deep down, I wanted to hear the story of Gator LeBlanc losing his arm in an airboat accident. "I guess you haven't met the new guy. We named him Gator after he jumped on the first alligator he'd ever seen. It hauled him into the river, but he came out alive with all of his fingers and toes, so naturally, he got a new name."

"Das right zackly how Gator Boudreaux would do. He ain' 'fraid o' nothin', him. I be der in dus a minute, me. Bye now."

I was terrified that I might one day begin to understand Kenny, and that was the last thing my brain needed to deal with.

Kenny showed up exactly as promised and talked to Gator for ten minutes. I was amazed that the new guy could understand the Cajun until Kenny climbed back into his truck and Gator turned to me with bewilderment all over his face. "What was *that*?"

I couldn't resist. I said, "Dat be Cajun Kenny LePine, him."

Gator waved me off. "No, don't ever do that again. That was terrible."

The crane operator aboard the *Lori Danielle* lifted the mangled chopper from the deck and placed it on Kenny's trailer. We strapped it down and covered it with a tarp for the short drive to the airport.

I climbed into the cab with Kenny. "Where's Earl this morning?"

He blushed. "She be restin' up, her. Ol' Kenny done come home las' night feelin' frisky, me. 'Cause when da weather backs off da way it do down in da fall like dis here, whoo-wee, I gar-ohn-tee ol' Kenny be needin' him some lovin' from dat fine woman, her. I tells you dis wiff my hand done raised to da heavens, me. Dat woman be da wild-cattingest woman dat ever been on dis here ol' Earth, she be."

I threw up both hands. "Kenny, if you don't stop talking, I'm going to throw my hearing aids out the window."

He roared with laughter and slapped the steering wheel. "You sho' nuff be some mo' kinda mess, you. Point da way you wan' me to go wiff dis here all-to-pieces, tore-up airplane."

"Let's go to the airport," I said. "We'll put it in hangar three."

After a call to Cotton Jackson, Earl's brother and top-notch aircraft mechanic, I was convinced we had two thousand pounds of scrap aluminum and what may be a salvageable turbine. I put Mongo to work restoring the General Electric Minigun. It was almost as expensive as the rest of the helicopter in its entirety.

Kenny dropped me off back at Bonaventure, and I pulled Barbie aside. "Do you have any time in a Bell Four-Twelve?"

She said, "A couple hundred hours in the civilian model, and a thousand or so in the Huey, the military version."

"You get better every day," I said. "Will it fit in the hangar bay on the ship?"

"Not without the blade folding kit."

I said, "I didn't like spending the money for the kit when I had the new rotor blades installed, but I'm sure glad I did it now."

She said, "You have a Four-Twelve?"

"We do."

She shook her head. "I really want to be you when I grow up."

"You wouldn't like it," I said. "Between my prosthetic leg, rebuilt hand, and hearing aids, I'm practically a cyborg."

"Yeah, but you're a cyborg with extremely cool toys. Point the way to the chopper, and I'll get reacquainted."

Instead of pointing, I drove Barbie to the airport and opened the electric door on the largest of our hangars. "There she is."

Barbie climbed out of the Microbus and stuck her head inside the 412, then she let out a low whistle. "Nice." She stuck her head beneath the fuselage and pointed toward the cargo hook. "This thing's got plenty of muscle. We could've used it to pull the Little Bird out of the river."

"I didn't think of that," I said. "Let's pull her out."

She climbed onto the tug and pulled the chopper out of the hangar on its cart. I sat in the left seat while Barbie familiarized herself with the radios, instrumentation, and checklists.

When she was satisfied with the groundwork, she said, "Let's take it for a spin to make sure I'm still safe."

Thirty seconds into the flight, I relaxed as the flying machine became an extension of Barbie's hands and feet. We spent half an hour putting her and the chopper through their paces before she said, "I think I remember how to do this."

I was confident she could safely handle the chopper without my involvement. "Yeah, put me back on the ground and test your theory about folding blades and the hangar deck."

As the afternoon shadows stretched their way across the river at Bonaventure, we kissed the ones we loved and set sail for the Yucatan Peninsula.

After leading Teresa Lynn around the ship and describing the vessel's capabilities, she said, "What's next? Are you going to tell me you've got a couple dozen satellites orbiting overhead for your exclusive use?"

I chuckled. "A couple dozen satellites aren't enough to cover a college campus. We've got thousands at our disposal, but the people who own them don't always know we're borrowing them."

She ignored the quip. "So, the ocean is your primary area of responsibility, but you don't have any former SEALs on your team."

THE SILENT CHASE · 125

"I don't think we have a primary area of responsibility. The ship gives us capabilities most teams don't have, but we're far more than a maritime force. You've seen us in action on the ground."

She put her hands on her hips. "Chase, you've got more capabilities than most small countries, but you still didn't answer my question. Why don't you have any SEALs on the team?"

"I have the utmost respect for SEALs. We've worked with them on several operations, and there's no question that they're some of the finest operators on the planet. Our team came together organically. We didn't actively recruit anyone. It just happened that we ended up with Green Berets instead of SEALs, so far. Who knows what the future holds? We may end up with a couple squids before this mission is over."

"I see."

"Do you have some special affection for the SEALs?"

She giggled like a schoolgirl. "Every woman on Earth has a special affection for SEALs."

"That's not what I meant."

"I know," she said. "I asked the question because it seems like the agency who provided this ship for you would insist on you having a SEAL or two around."

"There is no agency that provides things for us. We work for . . ." I took a long pause. "Let's just say it's not an agency."

"Then what is it? The CIA hires a lot of contractors, but not ones with a warship and small air force."

"No, we don't work for the Agency. We report to a board of directors who offer assignments."

"Offer?"

"Yes. We're not ordered to do anything. We're offered assignments, and I decide if we'll accept them after discussion with the team."

"*You* decide?"

"That's right."

She stared at me as if trying to decide if she should let me live. "I'm intrigued. Have you ever considered bringing a retired Foreign Service officer on board?"

"I'd have to see her résumé," I said. "Come on. Let's get some dinner. We eat as a family whenever we can. We'll be in Isla Mujeres this time tomorrow evening, and we'll likely be too busy to enjoy a nice meal together."

She checked her watch. "It has to be a thousand miles to Isla Mujeres. There's no ship on the water that can cover that distance in twenty-four hours."

"There's at least one, and you're on it. It won't take twenty-four hours, though. We'll do it in less than twenty. You'll see."

"That's not possible. There are limits to how fast a displacement hull can go, no matter how hard you push it."

As if on cue, the engineers deployed the hydrofoils, and the *Lori Danielle* rose out of the water like a phoenix from the ashes and accelerated to what felt like sixty knots.

"You're exactly right about a displacement hull, Ms. Lynn, but things are rarely as they appear, and if they are, well then, we perceived them incorrectly in the first place."

She said, "You're far too young to dispense wisdom like that, Mr. Fulton."

"I'm afraid I can't take credit for that one. I borrowed it from Professor Robert 'Rocket' Richter, the wisest man I've ever known. I'd like to believe he's looking down on us tonight and laughing his butt off at the idea of my team working with a former spook to hunt down a killer we know nothing about on a playing field made up of the entire planet."

Chapter 15
El Gato

I was wrong about our ETA to Isla Mujeres off the coast of the Yucatan Peninsula. We ran all night on the foils, making just over sixty knots, but high winds and rough seas put us back in the water in the Straits of Florida, where we made only forty knots in the heavy conditions and arrived off the coast of the island just after dark.

Laying offshore, Teresa Lynn watched the island as if her old friend might stand up and wave from the beach. "Do you have a plan?"

I stood beside her on deck and wondered what was happening inside the head of the spy. "I do. We'll take the RHIB ashore tomorrow morning and knock on Pamela Bingham's door."

"She won't answer."

"Maybe not, but it's always polite to knock before galivanting into somebody else's house."

Captain Sprayberry dropped the anchor in the lee of the island, giving everyone aboard a gentle night on the hook. We took full advantage of the opportunity to give our bodies and minds the rest they'd earned.

As the sun peeked over the quiet chunk of dry land just five miles east of Cancun, we put six men and one former lady-spook ashore in our tactical RHIB and rented the two largest golf carts we could find.

We carried stamped passports bearing names that somewhat resembled our own, courtesy of Dr. Mankiller and her remarkable counterfeiting capabilities. I didn't anticipate anyone asking to see them, but having the documents granted us an additional layer of cover, and in our business, every layer counts.

Hunter drove our cart, and I sat beside Teresa on the back seat as she directed us toward Pamela's house near the southern tip of the island. The neighborhood was a collection of multistory homes with well-manicured gardens, and smaller houses with a few fruit trees congesting the narrow lots. Most of the homes had walls or fences, but they looked as if they'd been built for aesthetics and not security.

Teresa pointed ahead and left. "Pam's house is coming up. It's the blue one with the white awning."

I laid a hand on Hunter's shoulder. "Let's do a drive-by and circle the block."

He nodded, and I turned to point out the house for the second cart of commandos trailing us.

"It certainly looks vacant," I said.

Teresa stared at her friend's property. "She was a stickler for keeping everything neat. I've never seen her lawn in that condition."

The back side of the block gave us a nice little gift I hadn't expected. The lot directly behind Pam's house was vacant, with only the foundation of a former house nestled in the center. We pulled onto the lot and positioned the golf carts behind a pair of bushes, providing at least some degree of concealment.

Clark stepped from his cart and grabbed his lower back, so I stepped beside him. "Are you all right?"

He twisted and stretched. "Yeah. We hit the water pretty hard, and the mattress on the ship isn't exactly a Tempur-Pedic."

"Let's have the doc take a look when we get back on board."

"Don't worry about me. I'm as tough as a long-tailed cat on a hot tin kitchen."

"Well done," I said. "You managed to screw up three clichés with one blow. Stay here with the golf carts, Brokeback. We've got more than enough manpower to search the house."

To my surprise, he didn't protest. Instead, he slipped back behind the wheel and rested a foot on the dash.

The rest of us walked the perimeter of Pam's house, peering into every window as we passed. At the front door, I gave the knock I promised, but as Teresa predicted, no one answered. With my lockpick in hand, I took a knee and worked the deadbolt. It gave way in seconds, and I stuck the tools inside the keyhole of the knob. It was even more willing to surrender to my touch, and we were inside in seconds.

"Hello? Anybody here?" I called out, just in case someone was standing behind a doorway ready to pull a trigger.

My voice echoed through the emptiness of the small home, and I gave the order to clear the house. We broke off into two-man teams and searched every room. Even though my nose didn't pick up anything, part of me feared we'd find Pam's body in the bathtub. However, the search yielded nothing but an abandoned house. I wasn't questioning my team's ability to clear a house, but I walked through every room myself, cataloging its condition and contents.

Back in the front room, I leaned against the sofa. "Did anybody else notice what isn't here?"

Mongo and Singer smiled and gave Gator a look, offering the new kid a chance to shine.

He didn't waste it. "If this woman was anything like the rest of us, she would've had a go bag, and I didn't see one."

"Excellent catch," I said. "The rest of us are thinking the same thing."

Teresa said, "Pam would've definitely had a go bag, and I'm pretty sure I know every item she would've had inside."

"How much cash?" I asked.

"At least the equivalent of a hundred grand American in various foreign currency."

"Passports?"

"Probably only one. Getting caught with multiples when you're not on the job can get tricky."

"Cell phone or other comms?"

Teresa dropped her head. "She would've had a satellite phone, but I've called the number seven times, and there's no answer."

"Why seven times?" I asked.

"Like everything else in my life, it's a code. In this case, seven calls meant I won't call again, and I'll monitor one particular sat-phone number and await a call from her."

I glanced at Gator, and his expression told me he was locking that tidbit away for later use.

While I had his attention, I asked, "What should we do next?"

He answered immediately. "Get out of this house and make it look like we were never here."

That garnered a hardy chuckle from the team, and I said, "That's excellent short-term tactical thinking, but I was looking for our next *big* move."

He said, "I'd want a list of probable locations Ms. Bingham would likely go if she had to bug out, and I'd start that list with the places Ms. Lynn can name."

I turned to Singer. "Give your protégé a cookie. He's learning."

Gator grinned. "Everybody loves a cookie."

I ignored him. "Let's check the exterior for cameras on our way out."

Teresa said, "I've already done that, and there are none. I also checked for cameras at the airport and the ferry terminal. The airport officials acted as if they'd never heard of a camera, and the so-called security at the ferry terminal recycles their tapes every two days. And, of course, they'd already overwritten the video from the time period when Pam would've left."

I said, "I'll take Gator, Hunter, and Teresa to canvas the neighbors to the south, and the rest of you can knock on a few doors to the north. We'll meet back at the boat in thirty minutes."

Door-knocking yielded the same result over and over again. They last saw Pam two weeks ago, and her cat makes the rounds through the neighborhood, gobbling up the charity cat food. No one knew anything more than that.

Frustrated, I said, "Let's go. We could knock on every door on the island, and we'd get the same story."

Teresa agreed, and we headed for the golf cart. As we pulled from the vacant lot, an old man with a well-worn machete stepped from the side of the road and stood directly in front of us with his blade held high.

The three commandos in the cart reached for our pistols, but Teresa said, "Take it easy, guys. I don't think he's a threat."

Gator scoffed. "He's standing in the middle of the road with a machete raised over his head like a sword. What part of that doesn't look threatening?"

"Just take it easy," she said.

We stopped far enough away to maintain a nice, comfortable buffer between us and the knife.

The weathered man said, "*Estás buscando a la señorita Pamela?*"

Teresa still showed no sign of concern, so I put my Spanish to use. "Yes. Do you know where she is?"

The man lowered his machete and took a step toward us. "My name is Hector, and I live on top of the hill up there." He pointed with his knife. "I am worried for her. She left quickly, and her cat is sleeping on my doorstep. I am coming down to clean her yard for her. She would be embarrassed to see it now."

Teresa took over the conversation. "Did you see her leave?"

"Yes. I was walking to mass with my family, and she came riding by on her bicycle very fast."

"When was this? Do you remember the date?"

He cocked his head as if he didn't understand. "It was Sunday morning, three weeks ago, but I don't know the date. I don't know the date today. When is she coming home?"

While Teresa continued questioning Hector in flawless Spanish, I studied the hillside where the old man claimed to live.

When a break in their conversation came, I asked, "Before she left, did you see anyone around here who shouldn't have been here?"

Hector shrugged. "I don't want to get into anyone's trouble."

"You're not in any trouble, Hector, but if you saw someone, we need to know. We're Pam's friends, and we're worried about her, too."

He rubbed the tip of his machete with a calloused hand. "There were two men near my home on Friday, and maybe Saturday, before she left. They were watching her house from the trees beside my house. I had three small dogs, and they don't like strange men. They barked, and now I have only one small dog, and he doesn't make noise."

"Can you describe the two men?" Teresa asked.

Hector leaned in and stared at Hunter. "One of them looked like him."

Hunter said, "What's he saying? Why's he looking at me like that?"

"Relax," I said. "He's telling us how one of the men who was watching Pamela's house looked like you."

"It wasn't me," he said.

I laughed. "He knows it wasn't you. The guy just looked like you. Stand up so he can get a better look at you."

Hunter stepped from the golf cart, and Teresa said, "Take a close look. Was the man the same size and everything?"

Hector studied Hunter. "He was taller, but same size." He motioned with his hands to indicate the breadth of Hunter's shoulders.

"And his face looked similar?" Teresa asked.

The old man smiled, exposing very few teeth, and tried to speak in English. "All gringos look the same." He laughed at his own joke and slapped his leg.

Hunter rolled his eyes and climbed back into the cart. "We don't all look the same."

Gator nudged him. "We kinda do."

"I'll kill you in your sleep, rookie."

In spite of my desire to laugh, I asked Hector, "What about the other guy?"

"He wasn't a gringo. He was black and bigger than the first man. Not as big as you, but also strong. He had a beard like the first man, though."

I glanced back at Pamela's property. "Do you take care of her yard for her?"

He shook his head. "No, she takes very good care of it and always keeps it looking nice. I don't want her to come home and see it like this."

I pulled a few bills from my pocket and stepped from the cart. Shaking his hand, I pressed the bills into his palm. "Thank you for taking care of her place while she's gone. We're going to find her and make sure she's okay. I'm sure she would appreciate you looking after her yard."

He eyed the bills, and out came the random-toothed grin again. "*Gracias, señor. Gracias.* I will make sure her garden is very nice for her when she comes home. You will tell her I am caring for it, yes?"

"It'll be the second thing I tell her when we find her."

He thanked me again and turned away, but before he pulled off, he turned back and asked, "What will be the first thing you tell her, señor?"

I gave him a wink. "That her cat is just fine."

Chapter 16
The Mind of a Spy

I met Captain Sprayberry in the ship's mess for noon chow, and obviously to his surprise, I held a blueprint of his ship. Brushing his plate aside, I unrolled the drawings on the stainless-steel table and stuck a finger in the center of the page. "What's this?"

He recoiled. "Well, it appears to be a deck plan of my ship."

"You'd be correct, but specifically, what are these two compartments right here?"

He pulled his glasses from his shirt pocket and slipped them on. After studying the page for a moment, he removed the glasses and looked up. "They're laboratories."

"What's inside of them?"

He palmed the drawings and slid them away, returning his plate to its previously held position of honor before the captain. "Nothing right now. They're configurable spaces for the scientists who use this ship as a research vessel. Why are you bothering me while I'm trying to eat?"

"I need to configure these two spaces for my research project, and technically, I qualify as a scientist."

"Technically?" he said as he forked a bite of pork roast into his mouth.

"That roast looks delicious, and yes, technically, I'm a scientist, so can I have these two compartments or not?"

He wiped his mouth. "It is good. You should stop playing architect and join me. Oh, and sure, you can have the labs. It's pretty much your ship, anyway. What can I do to help?"

I rolled up the drawings and tucked them beneath my arm. "Send up two welders with torches, an electrician, and somebody with a broom and dustpan."

He lifted a slice of cornbread from his plate. "Oh, is that all?"

"For now, but we'll need more electricians and probably a carpenter by the end of the day."

"Then, for Heaven's sake, let me abandon my lunch so I can gather your support staff."

"Don't abandon it," I said. "Feel free to take it with you. After all, you *are* the captain. You're allowed to do stuff like that."

"Nice of you to notice." He pulled a radio from his belt. "Engineering, Captain."

"Go for engineering," came a crackling response.

"Send somebody with a torch up to Lima Seven, and if you can spare an electrician, send one of them up, too."

"Wilco, Captain. Anything else?"

Barry looked up at me with contempt in his eyes. "Yeah, have the welder bring up a broom and pan for Chase. He needs something to do."

I snatched the remaining cornbread from the captain's plate and shoved it into my mouth. "Thanks, Cappy. You're the best."

Just like the gazebo back home at Bonaventure, I had a favorite spot on the ship. The officers and crew of the *Lori Danielle* called the area the fantail, but since I'd never worn a Navy uniform, it was just the stern deck to me. I spent hours back there with my eyes cast into the heavens, naming every star I could remember and making up names for the ones I didn't know. I loved imagin-

THE SILENT CHASE · 137

ing the lives of ancient explorers who stood on creaking, swaying decks, watching those same stars hundreds of years before I was born. I wondered if they shared the same fears and delights as I bore on my shoulders and in my heart. Did dreams of the unknown fill their minds with anticipation and excitement, or were their nights fraught with terror of what they might find on the next shore, on the next island, or in the jaws of the coming storm? Most nights, I carried all of those emotions. I longed for the adventure of what lay around the next corner. Who would stand and fight, and who would lie down and surrender? Would I find a thousand answers to a thousand questions, or would I find only my demise on the tip of the next spear I would face?

Time has no meaning on the sea. The ocean remains as she was the day after Creation, unmolested by the hand of man and unaltered by the relentless echoes of time. Perhaps men like me bore more in common with the ocean than with the ever-changing dusty surface that was untouched by the salty sea. Perhaps I would continue the fight until there was no fight left burning in my chest, and I would fall at the hands of a timeless enemy, only to be reborn—my ambition, my drive, and my devotion raging inside the soul of another man in the endless line of fighters who soldiered beneath the banner of freedom and refused to allow death's cold hand to quench the valorous flames within.

That day, beneath the early afternoon Caribbean sun, I wasn't musing over ancient mariners. I was holding a mission briefing. My ever-expanding team gathered with grumbles of complaint for having been called outside without plush chairs and Skipper's digital monitors hanging overhead.

"All right, that's enough," I said. "We've outgrown the combat information center for these briefings. There simply isn't enough space in Skipper's lair for us to hold these sessions anymore. I'm working on that, and we'll soon have a nice conference room that used to be a pair of side-by-side laboratories. The oceanographers might cry a little, but that's somebody else's problem. For now, we need to talk about our next port of call."

Clark arched his back, stretching the bruised muscles that had to be stabbing him with every breath. "Is Curaçao an option? It's always nice this time of year."

I said, "I like the suggestion, but this one isn't up to me. Teresa, let's hear the short list of spots where Ms. Bingham is likely to run."

She pulled a small pad from her pocket and stepped beside me. "Believe it or not, Clark, Curaçao is one of the possibilities, but it's not near the top of the list. Former Intelligence officers spend their retirement looking over their shoulders. You guys know that feeling as well as we do, but most of the time, retired intel folks like me don't have the lethal skill you have, so we run instead of fighting. I'd fight because running isn't in my blood, but Pam was an intellectual like Skipper. She wasn't a hitter. When we pick a bug-out location, we spend a lot of time thinking about where an enemy would expect us to go, and we generally avoid those spots. However, there is a school of thought that says we can use those spots because the bad guys would never expect us to do the expected. I know that's convoluted, but that's how the mind of a spy tends to work."

Each of us was tuned in and hanging on her every word as she continued her master class in post-career espionage.

Teresa cocked her head as if carefully considering her next words. "I believe she's in Tierra del Fuego, and if you want my reasons, I'll lay them out for you, but it won't change my mind."

Clark and I locked eyes immediately, but neither said a word. Teresa was obviously finished with her portion of the briefing and willing to turn the floor—or the deck—back over to me.

I said, "Okay, let's hear the other three."

"The other three what?" Teresa asked.

"If she's not in the Land of Fire, what are the other three possibilities in the top four?"

Teresa bit her lip. "Curaçao, as Clark mentioned, for obvious reasons. Oslo, Norway, because she has an affinity for Viking men and reindeer steaks. And my house."

"That's an interesting list," I said. "And if both you and she are on the hit list, that rules out your house."

Clark said, "I'd like to know why you're excluding Curaçao."

She smiled. "You really want to go to the South Caribbean, don't you?"

"Not in August. But now? Yeah."

Teresa took a moment to stare at the steel deck beneath our feet. "She's not in the islands because she developed skin cancer and had several places removed from her ears and neck in the last year. She wouldn't run to the sun."

"Wait a minute," I said. "She lived in Mexico. It's just as hot here as it is in Curaçao."

"You're right," she said. "But Curaçao is a tourist destination where people worship the sun. She would stand out if she spent her time inside wearing long sleeves and an enormous hat every time she walked outside. Here in Mexico, she lives in a house with a yard full of shade trees and very few tourists. Nobody gives her a second look if she covers up here on this island. Curaçao is another story entirely."

Clark threw up his hands. "That's the story of my life. Instead of an island paradise, I have to go to the bottom of the world."

I checked the time. "Let's break for lunch. They're serving pork roast and some amazing cornbread in the mess. Get down there before it's gone. I need Clark and Skipper with me for ten minutes, and the rest of us will meet back here in ninety minutes. Enjoy your lunch."

Clark rolled his eyes. "Get it right, College Boy. It's noon chow, not lunch."

I led him and Skipper to what had been a pair of empty laboratory spaces. The torchman was finished, and my broom and dustpan lay waiting for my hands.

Skipper's eyes turned to saucers. "Wow. What's going on here?"

I extended both arms. "This is our new conference room. Somebody will clean up this mess, and the ship's carpenter will build it out per your specifications."

Skipper said, "My specs? Why?"

"Because I want you to have the capability to give detailed briefings up here, exactly like you can down in the CIC, so the electricians are standing by to run the cabling you need. Ronda No-H has the checkbook open and waiting. I want you to turn this into a conference room that would make any CEO proud."

Clark appraised the space. "Will there be a snack bar?"

I planted my hands on my hips. "Get it right, landlubber. It's called a gedunk, not a snack bar."

Chapter 17
The Mirror

Construction continued on the new conference room, and Skipper morphed into the closest thing we had to an interior decorator.

Captain Sprayberry met us in the middle of the debris. "Yep, my suspicions are confirmed. You're clearly destroying my ship from the inside out."

"Think of it as capital improvement," I said. "We're making your ship more user-friendly."

"For you," he said. "The science geeks aren't going to share that opinion."

"I've got an idea about that. We'll have a chat later, but right now, we need to talk about the bottom of the world."

He lowered his gaze. "Antarctica?"

"Almost. Tierra del Fuego. How long?"

The captain closed one eye and seemed to draw a mental nautical chart in the air above his head. "Six to seven days, depending on traffic. We've got the fuel to run on the foils the whole way as long as we don't attract any unwanted attention."

I sighed. "Six days is an eternity when you're running for your life."

"Are we running for our lives?"

"No, we're running for someone else's life. Is Gun Bunny available?"

He handed me his radio. "She's always available for you."

I held the mic to my mouth and pushed the button. "Gun Bunny, Alpha One."

A second later, she answered. "Go ahead, Chase."

"I need you to run your boyfriend and mine over to Cancun."

"Give me twenty minutes to get the chopper out and rigged, and I'll meet them on the helipad."

"Roger. Thanks."

I stuck the radio back in the captain's hand and pulled Skipper from a task that seemed to be all-consuming. "What are you doing?"

She growled. "I'm playing architect, and I suck at it. What do you want?"

I glanced at the sketch beneath her fingertips. "Yeah, I think you should stick with being the world's best analyst and leave the drawing to somebody else."

"I know, right? I'm trying to make Mike understand what I want, and I can't seem to put it into words."

I pointed at the paper. "I'm not sure you can put it into pictures, either."

She planted her hands on her hips. "Did you interrupt me for some meaningful purpose or just for your personal amusement?"

"I had a purpose, but I'm having a pretty good time with that personal amusement thing."

"What do you need, Chase?"

"I'm actually here to ask what you need. We're headed to the tip of South America, and it'll take the ship at least six days to make it. That's too long to wait. I'm sending Clark and Disco for the Gulfstream, and I need to know if you want to stay aboard the ship or come with us."

She eyed the construction project under her direction. "I can do pretty much anything here that I can do at home, so if it doesn't screw up your plan, I'd rather stay on the ship."

"Fine with me. Just make sure your first priority is the mission."

She said, "Don't worry. Once I get the carpenters to understand my vision, I'll be chained to the CIC."

I left the demolition zone and found Disco in Ronda's office. "Imagine finding you down here."

He flinched. "I was just . . ."

I said, "I hate to break up the party, but we need the *Grey Ghost*. The ship's too slow to get us to Tierra del Fuego when we need to be there, so I want you and Clark to go get the plane and pick us up from Cancun."

"What about the gear?"

I leaned against the hatch. "Ah, good point. Ronda, are you busy?"

She shot a thumb toward Disco. "I was trying to get some work done, but he won't leave me alone."

"He's a lot of trouble," I said, "but he's pretty, so I guess we'll have to live with him."

"I guess," she said. "I'm never too busy for you. What do you need?"

"I need as many tickets as you can get on the next thing smoking to Miami or preferably Jacksonville."

"I'm on it, but don't get used to it. This is Skipper's job."

"I know, I know. But she's neck deep in the remodeling project upstairs."

Ronda said, "I heard about that. The captain's a little grumpy about it."

"He's grumpy about everything."

Her fingers didn't move as quickly as Skipper's across the keyboard, but it was close. She studied the screen, frowned, and leaned back. "I can get eight to Atlanta or four to Jacksonville today. Miami is booked up, and Charlotte is . . . ."

"We'll take the four to JAX. What time does it leave, and is it coach or first class?"

"I was only searching coach, but it looks like there are three in first class, so that makes seven total. And it leaves in two and a half hours."

I chuckled. "They'd kill each other fighting over first class if we stuck four people in the back, so grab the three in first class for Clark, Disco, and Gator."

She cocked her head. "That's an interesting trio."

"I'm sending Gator so the two old guys don't have to break their backs packing gear."

A few keystrokes later, she said, "Done."

Disco left to retrieve Clark, and I found Gator lying on the stern deck behind a .338 Lapua Magnum, with Singer sitting beside him and conducting a master class. "What's going on here?"

Singer looked up. "We're having a little clinic on engaging moving targets from a moving platform."

"Sounds like fun," I said.

Gator twisted to look up at me. "It's not. I'm starting to doubt that I'm sniper material."

Singer slapped him on top of his head. "Don't say that. If you couldn't learn to do this, I wouldn't waste my time teaching you."

"Yes, sir."

I winked at Singer and gave Gator a nudge with my boot. "Pack up. You're done. We're flying you back to the States."

The terror on his face *almost* made me wish I hadn't pulled the cruel joke.

He looked at Singer as if his mentor could do something to override my declaration, but Singer played along. "On your feet, kid. You heard the boss. You're done."

The newest member of the family drew his knees beneath himself and lifted the rifle from the deck, but Singer threw an arm across the weapon. "What makes you think Chase would send you packing and let you handle our weapons on your way out the door?"

Gator returned the rifle to the deck and slowly stood. I'd never seen a more defeated soul.

"Did I do something wrong? I thought I was . . . I mean . . ."

I couldn't keep a straight face any longer. "Relax, kid. We're just messing with you. You're flying back to Bonaventure with Clark and Disco to play human pack mule. We need you to hump every piece of gear they point to and grunt. We're heading for Tierra del Fuego, and we need the Gulfstream and a second set of gear. We don't have what we need to operate in that environment."

Relief washed over him, and he gave Singer a shove. "I'll get you for that."

Singer threw up his hands. "What? I was just following orders. Chase is the one you've got a beef with."

"Yeah, but he's the boss. I can't—"

Singer cut him off. "Everybody's the boss until you're not the new guy anymore. Just ask Kodiak."

"That's enough," I said. "I want you to think about what gear we'll need down there. Do you know anything about the environment in Tierra del Fuego?" He shook his head, and I said, "Good. That means you don't have any preconceived notions to overcome. Do some research, and come up with a team packing list on the flight back home. Compare your list to what Disco and Clark have you pack, and if you have something listed that they don't pack, bring it up. It'll be a good learning opportunity for you, and it'll keep them on their toes."

Gator's concerned look crept back in. "I don't know how I feel about telling Mr. Clark he forgot something."

I shrugged. "Don't be afraid of him. He's just a big teddy bear masquerading as a commando."

Gator scoffed. "I know you're the boss, but there's nothing teddy about that bear. I'll make sure he knows I'm following *your* orders if I bring up anything that's not on his list."

Gun Bunny pulled the Bell 412 off the helideck with three passengers on board, two of whom crashed on their last helicopter flight. I watched Gator sitting beside Barbie with his hands on the controls as the hardened combat pilot flew with the precision of a surgeon.

Singer said, "I like seeing that."

"What?" I asked.

"Gator in the front seat. That wreck in the river didn't scare him away. He's a keeper, you know."

I watched the chopper climb to the west. "I'm glad you brought that up. How's he doing on the rifle?"

He tapped the Lapua with the toe of his boot. "We couldn't shoot here, so we were just doing theoreticals, but he's got the mindset and the patience. I'm not always going to be around, so it'll be good for my heart knowing I'm leaving you with a competent overwatch."

"Whoa! Where are you going?" I demanded.

"Nowhere anytime soon, but there will come a day when I'm too old to climb into a nest and stay awake for two days."

I relaxed. "I don't like the thought of losing you. You're a lot more than just a sniper on this team."

"Thanks for that, but I'm working on the new kid in that realm as well."

"How's that coming along?"

Singer stared at his boots for a moment. "He's got a lot of demons chasing him around. Watching your parents die isn't something that goes away."

I swallowed the lump in my throat. "Trust me. I know."

He threw an arm around my shoulders. "That's why you took him on, isn't it? You think if you can get him through it and turn him into a warrior, you'll be able to believe you can get over it, too."

I've never been good at looking into the mirror, but the one Singer held in front of me cut me to the bone. "I don't know. Maybe. What happened to my parents was over two decades ago."

Singer smiled. "Contrary to popular belief, time doesn't heal all wounds. Some of those scars can only be erased by a divine hand. It doesn't matter how long ago it happened. They were still your parents, and that's a tough pill to swallow."

I nodded, but I didn't have the wherewithal to speak without having my voice crack.

My friend and spiritual mentor pulled me tight against his side. "I know, brother. I've been there, too. The difference is that I'm the one who pulled the trigger and sent my father to the grave."

I blew out the breath I'd been holding. "I'm sorry. I was being selfish. I didn't think about what you went through."

"Never be sorry. I'm in good hands. I've made peace with my past, and I'm living for an eternal future. Just because I quit running from them doesn't mean those demons aren't still chasing me, too. The important thing is to know we've got a shield to keep them at bay. That spiritual shield is true power, but God gave us more than just that shield we can't see. He gave us each other because He knew we needed brothers to hold us up when we got too weak to stand on our own."

He stopped talking and let the Caribbean wind whisper across our skin as his wisdom soaked in. Then he said, "You, me, and Gator . . . we've got a common bond the others don't have. But we've also got each other to remind us what we're capable of, and we've got each other to take care of."

I longed to have the insight and brilliance of our sniper, our moral compass. He always seemed to know exactly what should be said, and more importantly, what shouldn't be said.

He let his arm fall from my shoulders, and he picked up the rifle, but he wasn't finished holding up that proverbial mirror of his. "I know you're the psychologist, but even an old, dumb sniper like me can see the truth."

I cocked my head. "What do you mean?"

He smiled. "It's obvious, Chase. You love and protect Skipper because she's the spirit of the baby sister you lost. You let Dr. Richter become the father you lost. You adopted Gator because you see yourself when you look at him. And this is the one you'll deny the most . . ."

He had my attention, but I had no idea where he was about to lead me.

He motioned toward Teresa Lynn, who was stepping through the hatch and onto the stern deck. "You're protecting her because to you, she's the mother who died at your father's side in the jungle down in Panama twenty years ago."

Chapter 18
Giddyup

I spent the next thirty seconds of my life reevaluating every decision I'd ever made.

How could I not see what Singer identified at first glance? What keeps me from understanding why I never think of my team as anything other than my family? The University of Georgia piled a stack of useless letters at the end of my name, and all those years of learning to understand the human mind left me blind and ignorant of my own condition. Is my yearning for a family stronger than my ability to cope with the loss? What else am I embracing that's meant to fill the chasm left in my heart when my family was torn from my life? Am I wrong in treating those around me as family? Does that window on the world put the people I love in peril? Does it weaken me as a leader, as a friend, as a brother?

Teresa Lynn laid a hand on my arm and drew me back from my cosmic introspection. "Chase, are you okay?"

"I'm good. Sorry. I was just thinking."

She laughed. "I'd say. You were a million miles away. Is everything all right?"

"It is. I was planning to come find you, so I'm glad you're here. Listen, I'm committed to finding the person or people killing your colleagues, and the next step in doing that is finding Pamela Bingham."

She leaned against the rail. "Thank you again for all of that."

"Save the thanks until we're successful. For now, we have to focus on getting to Tierra del Fuego. I dispatched a team back to Georgia to pack gear and retrieve the jet. They'll be back in Cancun, most likely tonight, but no later than tomorrow morning. The ship, even though she's one of the fastest ships on Earth, isn't fast enough to get us there when we need to be there. We'll catch the jet in Cancun, and the ship will rendezvous with us in a week or so."

She said, "If we're still in South America in a week."

"Exactly. Regardless of where we are, if there's water, the ship will be there. If I'm going to start a fight—or finish one—I like having the fastest battleship on the planet in my back pocket."

She said, "If I had that option during my career, I would've done the same."

"I do have a few questions about Ms. Bingham."

Teresa said, "Shoot."

"First, do you know where she'll be once we get to Tierra del Fuego, or is this another hunting expedition?"

"I know where she *should* be. Of course, she doesn't own the property. That would be ludicrous, and she'd be too easy to track down. There's a cabin at the end of a long inlet. The only ways in are through the mountain pass or across the water. Both are easy to monitor."

I said, "That makes it sound like she's security-minded, but that didn't seem to be the case on the island."

"She was. You just didn't see it."

I scowled. "I don't think we would've missed cameras or sensors. She was pretty open from all angles up there."

Teresa glanced toward Isla Mujeres. "You didn't see them because they weren't there."

"That's exactly my point."

"What you don't know is *why* they weren't there. Either she or her killer removed them."

I said, "Both sound unlikely. Why would she or her killer take the time to dismantle cameras and remove all evidence that they were there? That takes time, and from what I saw, she left in a hurry . . . and still alive."

"I agree, but I know Pam. She would've had a solid security system, and it would've been highly mobile—something she could take down in minutes."

"But why would she take it down? If she's running, every second counts."

"She would've taken it down because there would be evidence on it that she wouldn't want anyone to see . . . not even me."

"You may have to explain that one to me later, but for now, let's assume she took it with her."

Teresa shook her head. "More likely, she destroyed it. Carrying extra gear that doesn't have much practical value while on the run isn't something she would've done."

"All right, I'll buy that. But in the big scheme, it doesn't matter. We have to work on the belief that she's still alive until we know differently, and that presumption leads us to South America."

"Agreed," she said. "What else do you want to know?"

"Since she hasn't contacted you, should we assume she can't or just hasn't?"

"The only reasons she wouldn't contact me—especially since we had plans together—is if it's impossible for her to do so or if she feels like contacting me would put me in grave danger."

"Which of those two things do you think it is?"

"I hope it's the latter because I'm in pretty good hands when it comes to being attacked. I don't exactly feel vulnerable with you."

"That's high praise," I said. "We'll do our best to keep you—and her—alive, but there are a lot of variables in this thing, and we're accustomed to stacking bodies after somebody else solves the mystery."

She almost laughed. "The body-stacking is the easy part. Identifying the correct bad guys is the tricky job."

"Speaking of the correct bad guys, do you have any suspects yet?"

She stared into the distance to the south. "It has to be tied to the South African op. There's no other reasonable connection between all of us."

I rapped on the railing with my knuckles. "I think you might be making one assumption too many."

She turned to face me with inquisition in her eyes, and I said, "You're assuming whoever is killing your colleagues is part of an operation that tied all of you together."

"Yes, that's the logical assumption."

"It would be if there was some solid evidence that you're on the kill list, but so far, no one has taken any shots at you. What if your colleagues are being picked off one by one because of a connection they had that didn't involve you?"

She furrowed her brow. "Are you suggesting that I'm paranoid?"

I softened my tone. "We're all paranoid. That's one of the things that keeps us alive. I'm saying you might be making connections where there are none. Is it possible that Ty Emerson, Glenn Phillips, Zander McAllister, and Pamela Bingham had a connection that doesn't involve you?"

My question seemed to hit her like a freight train—as if she couldn't comprehend a scenario in which she wasn't tied to the action.

She stammered. "I . . . I mean . . . I don't . . ."

The hardened exterior of the career case officer cracked in that moment, and I said, "It's just a possibility. I'm not saying I'm right.

I'm just saying we have to play all the possibilities. That's the only way to keep ourselves from getting tunnel vision on this thing. If all of our barrels are trained on twelve o'clock, our flanks and rear might as well be welcome mats."

She gave me the beginnings of a smile. "Spoken like a true warrior."

She and I made our way to the CIC and pulled up a collection of high-definition aerial photos of the Land of Fire. Teresa took the mouse and zoomed into a small town at the eastern extreme of Lago Fagnano. "That's the town of Tolhuin. That means 'like a heart' in the Selk'nam language."

"I'll take your word for it. Is this where your friend's cabin is?"

She panned to the east. "No, but this is the closest airport."

I pulled up the airport data and groaned. "We could get the Gulfstream down and stopped if there was no ice on the runway, but it's too short for us to take off again. What other options are there?"

She panned south. "The big airport, if you can call it big, is in Ushuaia. It's geographically closer to the cabin than Tolhuin, but the mountains make the cabin almost inaccessible from the south, unless you're a mountain goat."

I studied the pictures. "Ushuaia is our only option with the Gulfstream."

The mountains sucked me in, and I couldn't look away. "Do you know how to find a topo map of that region?"

She looked up. "I can barely run my iPhone."

I called Skipper away from her hardhat area on the upper deck, and it took her less than thirty seconds to bring up a topo overlay.

Teresa zoomed in until a small dark area nestled into the foot of a mountain slope appeared. "That's the cabin."

The terrain was steeper than anything I'd seen in the Afghan mountains, and far more ragged.

"If God were making the perfectly defendable spot, that would be it," I said. "The water is the only good way in, and it's wide open in every . . ." I yanked my phone from my pocket and thumbed a contact. "I need you in the CIC as fast as you can get here."

Less than two minutes later, Singer pushed through the hatch. "What is it?"

I pointed toward the dark spot on the aerial photo. "Where do you set up to put a bullet on that target?"

"What target?"

Teresa moved the cursor over the shadow. "Believe it or not, that's a cabin."

Singer squinted and moved close to the screen. "I see it now, but that's one tight target. The elevation to the south is too steep to get a usable line of sight, so that forces a sniper onto or across the water. How wide is that inlet?"

"That's not an inlet," Teresa said. "It's a lago."

"What's a lago?"

I said, "Apparently it's a lake in that part of the world."

Singer pulled a chair beside mine and slid onto it. "Three miles is artillery range. Nobody's ever made a shot that far with a rifle. That may be the only sniper-proof piece of ground on the planet."

"How about from the water?" I said.

"Sure, but you're in the open for miles in every direction. It might as well be a stage with spotlights and a sign that says, 'Look! I'm shooting from here!'"

He leaned back in his chair, and I said, "Give me a down-and-dirty assault plan on that cabin."

"With us, or a conventional force?"

"Us."

He reached for the mouse, and Teresa surrendered it.

He panned, zoomed, squinted, and sighed. "Covert or overt?"

I said, "Covert."

He didn't hesitate. "I'd hike in through the mountains on the north side of the lake—*lago*—with two young, strong guys humping an M-one-twenty mortar tube and ten M-fifty-seven high-explosive mortars. I'd do the math twice and pray I got lucky enough to hit the target with one of the first three rounds. Once that tube gets hot, the math changes, and the chances of hitting a target that small from seven thousand meters start to look like lotto odds."

"That's your covert plan?"

He shrugged. "It's covert because I'd sink the tube and mortars in the lake and disappear into the mountains for weeks if necessary. Nobody's going to find me in that environment if I don't want to be found."

"I can't wait to hear your overt plan," I said.

His one-word response said it all. "Gunboat."

We sat in silence and contemplated the mortar idea until Teresa said, "They won't hit like that. It'll be silent and look a lot like the shooting in Montana."

Singer said, "Not in that terrain, it won't. A pack of Boy Scouts with slingshots could defend that place. It's almost perfect."

"Almost?" I asked.

His wheels were obviously churning inside his tactical cranium. "Yeah, almost. If one guy, or maybe two at the most, had the spine to pull it off, they could brave those slopes and get behind the cabin. They could put a suppressed round through the kitchen window and hike back out, but that's billy goat country. I could've done it when I was twenty-five, but these days, I sound like a Rice Krispies commercial when I stand up."

I let his idea circle the drain in my skull for a few seconds. "I call dibs on Snap, so do you want to be Crackle or Pop?"

He scowled. "Why are we assaulting the cabin? I thought we were here to get Ms. Bingham out, not pin her down."

156 · CAP DANIELS

"We're not assaulting. We're counter-assaulting. The people who want her dead probably have plenty of twenty-five-year-olds they can turn loose in those mountains. It's our job to find them before they find her."

Most shot-up, beat-up, broke-up old gunners would walk away, but Singer, my brother, put on a Clark Johnson crooked smile and said, "Giddyup!"

Chapter 19
Professor Mongo

We called the remainder of the team into the CIC and briefed the plan. Clark, Disco, and Gator were still airborne somewhere between Mexico and Jacksonville, but at least two of them were going to hate my plan.

When the briefing was complete, I said, "That's it. Any questions?"

Mongo raised an enormous finger. "Is it too early to apply for retirement?"

I tossed a pencil at him. "There's no retirement plan in this game. You know that. Old warriors never die. We just smell that way."

Singer said, "Seriously, Clark can't pull this off, and we can't carry him out if he goes down in those mountains."

As the reality of our way of life washed over me, I felt my heart sink into my gut. "You're right. He's not going to take that little morsel very well, but I'll talk with him about it."

He stared down at my prosthetic leg. "It's time for a little tough love for you, too. I'm not sure you've got the—"

I silenced him with a raised hand. "I made a commitment. When was the last time you watched me walk away from a commitment?"

"I get it," Singer said. "I do. But your commitment extends to the whole team. I'm sure we all feel the same about that. We're an extension of you, so the team will fulfill that commitment. Take a look at that topo map and tell me you can manage that terrain as well as you could before you lost that leg."

"You're right about the terrain. It's nasty, and it won't be easy for any of us, but I'm going. If I bite it up there in those mountains, just roll me into the lake and get yourselves out of there."

"You know that's not how this works."

Mongo waded into the conversation. "For the record, I agree with Singer, but I've known you long enough to know you're not going to stay behind. If you bite it up there, *I'll* carry you out, but I'm throwing that robot leg of yours into the lago."

"I can always count on you, big man."

Singer looked away and then turned back to face me. "I didn't mean any disrespect, Chase. I'm just thinking about the best way to make sure we can move fast and silent *and* make it out alive."

"Relax. I always want your opinion, and your perspective never fails to be unique and valuable. Don't ever hold back whatever you're thinking. I may not like it, but I'll always listen."

"Thank you for that," he said.

I checked the time. "Ring Clark's phone. Give him the good news about our plan, and make sure he packs accordingly."

The sniper nodded. "You've got it, boss."

While Singer was talking with Clark, I pulled Teresa aside. "I need to know what kind of countermeasures Ms. Bingham is likely to have in place."

"Countermeasures?"

"You said she was extremely security-minded. Will she have her mobile camera system set up down there? Will she shoot at us when she detects us approaching? If she does, what kind of fire can we expect?"

Teresa thought for a moment and said, "Yes, she will have some sort of perimeter security. It may not be cameras, but she'll know somebody or something is coming before we get there."

I jotted down a few notes on my pad. "Keep talking."

"Shooting won't be Pam's first decision. She has two mottos about the use of firearms. The first is, you can't lose a gunfight if you're not there. Her first instinct and action will be to run."

I said, "There's nowhere to run except to the water. Will she have a boat?"

Teresa shrugged. "Maybe. Probably. I don't know."

"That's a lot of help."

"It's all I've got. I think it's wise to assume she has a boat. It'll probably be something small, fast, and agile. Like Singer said, anybody on that lake is exposed and vulnerable. If she runs in a boat, it'll be a good one that she believes will give her the best chance of escaping."

A few more notes hit my page, and I asked, "What's her second motto?"

She locked eyes with me. "Never shoot a large-caliber man with a small-caliber round. If she feels cornered, her bite will be a lot worse than her bark. She'll shoot long and hard with everything she's got."

"That means we have to find a way to let her know we're coming."

She said, "That's not entirely accurate. We have to find a way to let her know that *I'm* coming. She doesn't know you exist."

"The word *we* includes *you*. *We* are a team."

She put on a somber expression. "There's a problem I hadn't considered until this moment."

I leaned toward her. "That's what we need . . another problem."

She seemed to ignore my comment. "There's a chance Pam might not identify me as a friendly."

"What are you talking about? You said the two of you have been friends since you met at the Farm."

"In the world of espionage—the world she and I have lived in for over half of our lives—friends turn into enemies in the blink of an eye. I could stand up, show my face, and walk straight toward that cabin yelling, 'It's me. Don't shoot,' and she might believe I'm one of the people who's trying to kill her. It's a toss-up."

I lay back in my chair and stared at the gray ceiling. "That *is* a problem. Would you be willing to try the satellite phone one more time? We might get lucky and get her to pick up."

"No, she wouldn't, and there are three reasons for that. I explained our code of sevens, so there's no way she'd believe an eighth call would come from me. Second, have you ever been that far south?"

"No."

"I'll put it this way. You can't look straight up and see any communication satellites. It's too close to the south pole. It's likely a sat-phone won't work down there, especially with mountains blocking the horizon to the north."

"Okay, what's the third reason?" I asked.

"Think op-sec. Operational security. Almost every electronic communication device can be tracked. If she's running for her life like I believe she is, the closest thing she'll have to a piece of technology will be a cigarette lighter."

I closed my eyes and let the pieces of our coming operation fall together inside my head, but no matter how hard I tried to fit the pieces in their places, I was always left with a few chunks that refused to find a home.

"So, let me say this out loud, and maybe it won't taste quite so sour. We're embarking on a mission across some of the most forbidding terrain in the world, hoping to encounter a professional assassin or a pair of them. We're then going to eliminate those assassins and press on so we can sneak up on a secluded cabin in which a career Intelligence officer with large-caliber weapons nervously awaits the arrival of anybody coming out of those mountains."

"That about sums it up."

I shook her off. "Oh, I'm not finished. The Intelligence officer in question is running for her life. That means she'll be uber-diligent, and her senses will be at their peak. We won't have any way to convince her we're the good guys, even if her best friend waves and says, 'Hey, girl. It's me. Let's go have a spa day.'"

Teresa started to speak, but I cut her off. "Still not finished. If we do, somehow, manage to get close enough to her to prove we're not a threat, we will have gained very little ground other than finally putting your friend at ease. We still won't know who's behind the killings. Unless Ms. Bingham has some solid intel we're missing, she'll become another liability and responsibility for us."

"Are you finished now?" she asked.

"I've run out of things to say, so, yeah, I guess I'm finished."

Teresa bit her lip and looked up. "First, Pam won't be a liability. She's an asset of the highest order. It's even likely she'll know exactly who's chasing her. Second, if you want out, now's your chance. It's not too late to walk away. This thing has turned into an operation I have no right asking you or anyone else to undertake."

I waited until she finally made eye contact and said, "It was too late for us to back out when you told me you needed my help in Manhattan. We're in the fight until there's nobody left to punch in the face. Like Clark always says, don't count your chickens 'til the cows come home."

I'll never know if it was confusion or appreciation on her face, but I'll always believe it was a scramble of both.

* * *

"It's officially called a yellow dwarf."

I turned to see Mongo standing behind me as I leaned against the stern rail, watching the sun melt behind mainland Mexico. "What?" I said.

He lifted his chin toward the western sky. "The sun. It's classified as a yellow dwarf star."

I couldn't resist, so I asked, "How old is it?"

He stepped beside me and laid a hand on the rail. "The scientific community says it's four and a half billion years old and formed out of a giant, spinning cloud of gas and dust called the solar nebula. Apparently, it was a floating trash pile galivanting around in space about ten billion years after the big bang."

"But that's not what you believe, is it?"

He grinned. "The truth isn't about belief. The truth is the truth, even if a billion scientists disagree. I think it takes an awful lot of faith to believe everything that exists came to be as the result of some random cosmic explosion involving a ball of mass with an unknown origin."

"You're starting to sound like Singer," I said.

He continued grinning. "It's a lot easier for me to believe God created all of this than it is to believe utter chaos morphed into order as beautiful as that sunset."

"I tend to agree, my friend."

We watched the sky turn orange, then purple, and finally, black.

"It's just you and me," I began, "so tell me what you really think about this op."

"We're just two buddies, and you're not the boss right now, right?"

I nodded, and he said, "We're not chasing the killers. We're rescuing Ms. Lynn's friend. If we survive those mountains and whatever she's packing in that cabin, that's when the real work begins."

"Am I too close?" I asked.

"What do you mean?"

I scraped a piece of paint from the rail with my fingernail. "Am I trying too hard to convince myself we're climbing through those mountains to find the killers and not to rescue Pamela Bingham?"

"Probably, but that doesn't really matter. If we find somebody in those mountains and drive a chunk of lead through his skull, it'll just be one of us killing a soldier. The real culprit is probably smoking a big cigar and drinking five-thousand-dollar brandy somewhere."

"Are you saying we shouldn't do it?"

"Nope. We have to do it. But we shouldn't pretend this is the heart of the mission. This is just the good guys' response to the bad guys' opening volley."

Stars—maybe yellow dwarfs or green clovers, for all I knew—began their nightly ritual of claiming the darkened sky as they had for all time, regardless of how long that had been.

"How'd you get so smart?"

He tapped out a drumbeat on the rail. "I'm not any smarter than the rest of you guys. I just pay attention, and I have a pretty good memory."

"That's called humility, if I'm not mistaken. You're the smartest person I've ever met, and as far as I know, you've never been to college."

He waved his massive arms at the sky. "What do you call this? Everything that exists has something to teach us if we'll just shut up and listen. You don't learn that kind of stuff in a classroom. No offense, *Doctor* Fulton."

"None taken, *Professor* Mongo."

Chapter 20
Edge of the World

"Was that a landing, or did somebody shoot you down?" I asked Clark when he stumbled down the stairs of the *Grey Ghost* at the Cancun Airport a few minutes past ten o'clock.

He pointed back into the airplane. "That was all Disco. I wasn't touching a thing."

I laughed. "I'll bet he says the same thing about you."

He shouldered his bag, and I pointed toward the chopper. "We'll get a good night's sleep and leave when the sun comes up tomorrow."

He yawned and stretched. "I like that plan. We're pretty tired."

Gator was next off the plane, and he looked like he'd just been awakened from death.

"Are you okay?"

He pawed at his eyes. "I'm good. It's been a long day. I was just getting some sleep."

By the time Disco finally emerged, I arranged with the FBO to keep the *Grey Ghost* handy and ready for an early morning departure with fuel, snacks, drinks, and ice. My Spanish was better than the clerk's English, so it appeared we reached an agreement.

"Did you see that so-called landing I made?"

Disco didn't look as tired as his traveling companions, but his landing skills told a different story.

I said, "I did, and I hope none of the big pieces fell off."

He ran a hand through his hair. "We didn't have any business flying tonight. We're all exhausted, and there was a nasty storm over northern Florida, but we got above it pretty quickly. We should've taken more help. We've got that old girl loaded down with every imaginable piece of gear, and we're ready to operate anywhere on the planet."

"I'm sorry I asked you to do that. We'll get some sleep, and I'll do the flying tomorrow."

"That'd be great, thanks. Oh, and by the way, Gator was a godsend. He's a human pack mule. That guy never slowed down. I think he touched every piece of gear we packed at least twice. You made a good call bringing him on board."

"That seems to be the consensus," I said. "Singer thinks I picked him up because he reminds me of myself."

Disco shrugged off his jacket and laced it through the straps of his bag. "I can see that. Is that our chariot?"

I spun on a heel, and we walked side by side to the helo.

He climbed in first and collapsed onto a rear seat. "This is so much nicer than the Little Bird. Oh, I almost forgot. Cotton is working on what's left of that thing. He seems to think he can put it back in flying condition for two hundred grand."

"We can't replace it for that," I said. "But I'm not sure we need it."

"Need it or not, it's a million-dollar aircraft. It makes sense to put it back together, if for no other reason than to sell it. If you're going to throw it away, I'll pay the two hundred grand and keep it for myself."

"You're right. It makes sense to fix it. I've got a lot on my mind tonight. I haven't had the day you and Clark pushed through, but I'm tired, too."

We buckled up and closed the door as the rotors began their slow crawl to life above our heads.

He laid his head back against the headrest. "Clark and I were talking about the thing in the mountains in Tierra del Fuego, and we don't want to let you down, but I'm old, and he's still in a lot of pain from dumping the chopper in the river."

I tried not to smile, but I was secretly thankful for not having to initiate that conversation with Clark. "I'm glad you brought that up. I think we need to keep the mountain team as light and quick as possible, so my initial thoughts are to take Singer, Mongo, Kodiak, and Gator."

He opened one eye. "Did you just use the words *light* and *Mongo* in the same sentence?"

"Touché."

* * *

Dawn broke as we were heading to the helipad the next morning. The Bell 412 had no problem carrying the entire team—a feat that would've taken at least two trips in the Little Bird.

Gun Bunny dropped us off, and as promised, the *Grey Ghost* was waiting on the ramp with a red carpet resting at the foot of the stairs.

"Who do you want up front with you?" Disco asked as we climbed aboard.

Gator's eyes lit up, so I said, "I'll take the new guy—whatever his name is—but I'd like to have you up there for the approach and landing in Ushuaia."

"Great plan. I could use a couple more hours of shut-eye."

The line crew pulled the chocks and rolled up the carpet as Gator opened the checklist book. We stepped through the pre-start and engine start checklists slowly enough for him to see and understand every step. With the fires burning and checklists complete, I released the parking brake and said, "She's all yours. Take us to the runway."

He didn't let me get away with the cowboy phraseology in the cockpit. Instead, he said, "Roger. I have the controls."

I smiled at the guy who'd likely become our next pilot. "You have the controls."

Reaching the end of the taxiway, Gator eased his toes onto the brakes and brought the *Ghost* to a stop well before the hold short bar.

I said, "I have the controls, but keep your hands and feet lightly on the yoke and pedals so you can feel what I'm doing."

He nodded. "You have the controls."

"I have the controls."

We ran through the takeoff checklist, I called the tower for our clearance, and we were soon accelerating down the runway with the fully loaded Gulfstream showing off a little. At rotation speed, I released the throttles and placed both hands on the yoke, pulling the ship from the concrete.

I called, "Gear up," and Gator raised the landing gear lever. The lights indicated the landing gear was stowed correctly, and I called, "Flaps up."

Gator raised the flaps, and the airplane was clean for our climb into the flight levels.

English is the universal language of air traffic control, but the radar controller on the Yucatan Peninsula didn't have the diction most international controllers possess. He gave us instructions to climb to flight level three-eight-oh, but Gator turned to me with disbelief in his eyes. "Was that English?"

"It was close enough," I said. "He wants us to climb to three-eight-oh."

"You got *that* from whatever he said on the radio?"

"I did. Set the altitude preselect for three-eight-oh."

"Three-eight-oh," he repeated as he programmed the computer that now had full control of the Gulfstream—under my watchful eye, of course.

I double-checked his work and settled in for the climb. He kept his eyes trained on the panel, and no doubt, tried to fight off the feeling of information overload.

He said, "This is going to suck, isn't it?"

I stuck one finger into the air and another on the altimeter. His look of confusion continued until we passed ten thousand feet.

I said, "Okay, now we can chat. I like to keep the cockpit sterile until we're above ten thousand. The workload is pretty heavy until then. So, what do you think is going to suck?"

"The mountains in Tierra del Fuego."

"You've been doing your homework, haven't you?"

"Yes, sir. This is an opportunity almost nobody gets, so I'm not wasting it. I'm learning everything I can, and nothing about those mountains sounds like a good time."

"I've been doing a little reading of my own," I said. "I've never been to those mountains, but you're right. It's not going to be a walk in the park. Are you up for it?"

"Absolutely," he said without hesitation. "But that doesn't mean I'm going to like it."

I chuckled. "Clark has a saying he likes to throw around."

It was Gator's turn to laugh. "Yeah, he's got a bunch of those, and he gets 'em a little mixed up sometimes."

"You're right about that, but this one's pretty simple and an excellent philosophy in our line of work. Embrace the suck."

"I'll tuck that one away," he said. "Something tells me it'll come in handy for a few decades to come."

"Some things never change."

We leveled off in cruise flight, and Central America gave way to South America. Gator raised himself from his seat and scanned the scenery through the windshield. "I've never seen the Atlantic and Pacific at the same time before."

"You're going to see a lot of things you never thought you'd see if you stick around long enough."

He nestled back into his seat. "I've been meaning to talk to you about that. I know this isn't like a normal job where we have performance appraisals and quarterly goals or whatever—"

"You're right about that, and let me stop you right there. If you were screwing up, you'd know it. We don't need quarterly performance appraisals to let us know how we're doing in this world. If you're staying alive and the bad guys aren't, you're doing just fine."

"There's more to it than that," he said. "I mean, I see how this is more of a lifestyle than a job. You guys are always together. We don't clock out and go home."

I gave him a look. "Stop using terms like *you guys*. You're one of us now. We're going to beat you up and kick you around for a while, but it all happens for a reason. Don't let any of that make you feel less than one hundred percent part of the team . . . part of the family."

"I get it. I've still got a lot to learn. I just want to make sure you guys are happy with what I'm doing."

"If we weren't happy, you'd be looking for another team. Clark and Hunter are going to push you verbally and physically. I'm going to push you psychologically. Singer is going to silently appraise everything you do behind a gun, and Disco will pat you on the butt when you need somebody to cheer you up. It's the way of things."

"I've got a lot of things to say to all of you guys, but mostly, it's just thank you. It means a lot to me that you'd take a guy like me under your wing, so to speak."

"That's a solid attitude, and it's exactly the one we expect from you. Gratitude is one of the most powerful things that happens inside the human mind. When you start taking people and things for granted, you're headed down the wrong path. Keep that attitude, and keep learning. If that ever stops, we'll notice, and we'll straighten you out."

"It's like an accountability partnership, isn't it?"

"That's exactly what it is, but it's not like what your football coach taught you. This team is a little different. Here, we hold each other accountable because it's life and death. If you get lazy or complacent, you'll get yourself, or one of us, killed. You are your own accountability partner first. Push yourself harder than any of us push you, and you'll never feel Clark's boot in your butt."

We flew for a while in silence as the continent below us tapered to a pinpoint at Cape Horn.

Gator motioned out the windshield. "That's it, isn't it?"

"That's what?" I asked.

He never took his eyes off the point where terra became aqua. "The edge of the world."

Chapter 21
Different Enemies

Gator climbed from the right seat, stepped through the cockpit door into the main cabin, and passed Disco coming the other way to replace him.

I briefed our position and planned arrival, and Disco said, "You're the pilot flying. I'm the pilot monitoring."

Keeping things regimented in the cockpit gave us not only a clearer sense of situational awareness, but also left no room for confusion over who was responsible for what.

We flew the approach to Ushuaia, but I couldn't stop looking out the window at the rugged, foreboding mountains that would be our home until we liberated Pamela Bingham from her lakeside safehouse. Nothing about the mountains looked welcoming. In fact, they appeared far more menacing than they had on the aerial photos and topo maps we studied back aboard the *Lori Danielle*.

Disco patted the panel and snapped his fingers. "Fly the airplane. You'll have plenty of time to look at the mountains after we land."

"Sorry. I was just—"

"You were just not flying the airplane is what you were doing. Do you want me to fly the approach?"

"No. I'm good." With my priorities back in order, I called for the approach flaps, and Disco obliged. Just short of the final approach fix, I said, "Gear down."

"Gear coming down," came his response.

A few seconds later, he called out, "Three green. No red. Clear to land."

"Clear to land," I echoed.

It was one of those landings like the perfect drive on a man's favorite par five. Everything felt right, and it was impossible to know for sure the exact instant when the airplane stopped flying and began rolling. I wish I could say that was my typical landing, but nothing was typical about greasing the perfect touchdown in an airplane like the *Grey Ghost*. There were too many variables and too many chances to get one of the thousand little things wrong. Flown well, with the attention she deserved, the *Ghost* would dependably reward her pilot with the praise he'd earned, but fly her incorrectly or ignore her when she wanted attention, she was quick to slap her driver on the back of the hand for minor infractions and across the face for more egregious offenses.

We taxied to the line and ran the shutdown checklist.

I leaned toward the aisle and peered into the cabin. "Sit tight for a minute. I want to check with Skipper before we go be-bopping down the stairs and into the outstretched arms of some overzealous customs official."

Clark held up his phone and waggled it in the air above his head. "I'm way ahead of you, College Boy. I called her before we started our descent and lost satellite service."

"What did she have to say?"

He said, "She's done it again. We're all set up. She's got us a decent-sized rental house and three four-wheel drives. The customs guy decided he didn't have any real interest in a plane full of tourists who'd only be on the ground a few days."

Disco and I unbuckled and climbed from the cockpit. I popped the hatch and lowered the stairs into a world like nothing I'd ever experienced. The feel of the place was more than the crisp, clean air. It was a sensation I couldn't put into words. My first thought was of Penny and how much she'd love the smell and feel of everything at the end of the world.

The airport had its typical fixtures, like most airports all over the world. Massive hangars, planes of every shape and size, and the ubiquitous glass-front terminal welcomed us. I welcomed the familiarity like an old, trusted friend and strolled inside to arrange a nice warm bed for the *Ghost*.

In relatively good English, the lady at the counter put my fear of a language barrier to rest. "You must be Mr. Fulton. I am Emma. Welcome to Patagonia. First time?"

"Thank you. Yes, it's my first time here, but I'm already in love, so it won't be my last."

I expected the next question to be something like, "What brings you to the Land of Fire?" But it didn't happen.

Instead, Emma said, "Your agent made all arrangements, and everything is taken care of. Your airplane will have a nice hangar only for her, and your trucks are waiting inside."

"Inside?" I asked.

"Yes, inside the hangar. Mateo will show you. He is the beautiful boy on the tug outside."

I turned to see a dark-haired man, barely Hunter's size, connecting the tow bar to the nose gear of the *Ghost*.

"Your husband?" I asked.

She covered her mouth and giggled. "Silly. He is my son, and he will take very good care of you."

I drew my wallet from my pocket, but Emma waved me off. "No. I told you that your agent handled everything."

"My agent, huh? Would that be Elizabeth?"

Her broad smile returned. "Your wife?"

"No, ma'am. My sister . . . sort of."

"Family is what matters most."

I repocketed my wallet. "I couldn't agree more."

We followed Mateo to the hangar, where three trucks with canvas covers over the backs waited. I couldn't identify them, but they were, most certainly, not General Motors products.

After Mateo disconnected the tug, I introduced myself and asked, "Are American dollars okay?"

He was missing a tooth, but that didn't stop him from grinning when I shook his hand with a few bills folded in my palm. Without glancing at the tip, he said, "If you need anything, I will be here."

His Argentinian Spanish sounded nothing like the Spanish I learned in the Caribbean as a boy, but I pieced together enough to communicate. I spoke slowly in the Spanish I knew. "Thank you, my friend. We'll only be three or four days at the most."

His goofy grin returned. "No one ever leaves on time from the end of the world. You are here for exploring?"

"*Sí*, exploring in the mountains."

"You have guide? Mountains are dangerous."

"No, we're experienced climbers. We don't need a guide."

His eyes fell immediately to my ankle as if he could see my prosthetic beneath my pants and boot. "No guide?"

"No."

He furrowed his brow. "At least you will talk with guide before you go, yes? Many people do not come back from mountains. It is warm now, so snow is thin, but you still need guide. It is very dangerous."

"Maybe you're right," I said. "Can you recommend a guide who speaks English?"

He pulled a pencil and a torn piece of paper from his pocket and wrote down a name. "Benicio is very good and has many languages."

I tucked the scrap of paper into my shirt pocket. "Benicio it is. I'll give him a call."

Mateo stared at my pocket. "He does not have a telephone. Just ask for him in town. You will meet him before going into the mountains if you are wise. Otherwise, you will meet him when he brings your bodies out of mountains when you and your friends die up there."

Perhaps it was the language barrier, but had Mateo's words been in English, they would've come off as a threat instead of a concerned warning.

"*Gracias, mi amigo. Gracias.*"

As if he knew we weren't who and what we claimed to be, Mateo motored from the hangar and closed the doors, separating us from any prying eyes on the airport.

Clark asked, "What was that all about?"

I pulled the worn slip of paper from my pocket. "He said we need a guide for the mountains, and if we don't have one, this guy will recover our bodies when we die up there."

"Charming, but we can't take a guide with us. A local witness is the last thing we need on this op."

I said, "No, the last thing we need on this op is to get dead because we're stupid. I'm going to talk with this Benicio fellow and at least get a briefing from him before we start our trek. If nothing else, I want to know about the passes and potential for avalanches."

"That's smart, but please tell me you're not thinking about hiring him to take us across the mountains."

"You guys offload the gear and see if you can figure out how to drive those trucks. I've never seen anything like those things. Have you?"

"It's just a truck. How hard can it be?"

I left the hangar and jogged to the terminal, where I found Mateo talking with his mother in a language that was neither Spanish nor English.

He looked up. "Is everything all right, sir?"

I patted my shirt pocket. "This Benicio fellow. Where can I find him?"

"If he is not on the mountain, he will have breakfast and lunch at Cantina Cecilia."

"And where can I find Cantina Cecilia?"

The gap where his missing tooth should've been reappeared. "It is on Avenue San Martin, near Cecilia's Outfitters."

"Thank you. Cecilia must do well for herself."

He continued grinning. "She is Benicio's wife, and you are making a very good decision."

I gave him a nod and rejoined my team in the hangar.

Clark was right, as usual. The trucks were nothing special, and they drove just like anything GM bolted together.

We happened across Avenue San Martin on our way out of town, and I said, "Make the block and drive down San Martin. I want to see if I can find the cantina Mateo told me about."

Clark checked his watch. "My stomach thinks that's an excellent idea."

The cantina turned out to be almost impossible to spot, but the outfitters was not. We parked on the street, and I asked a gentleman coming out of the store if he knew where I could find the cantina. He cocked his head as if I'd asked where the sidewalk was, then pointed directly across the street and didn't say a word.

I followed his finger toward a glass storefront with a small "open" sign hanging crookedly in the window. "That's the cantina?"

"*Sí.*"

"*Gracias.*"

Our first meal in Argentina was unbelievable. We were served mushrooms, wild fruits I wouldn't try to pronounce, and all the salmon we could force into our stomachs.

When we'd eaten until we couldn't move, I touched the wait-ress's arm and put my Caribbean Spanish to use. "Where can I find Benicio? I don't know his last name."

She smiled and pointed toward the end of the bar, where a man who appeared to be nearly a century old sat with his hands wrapped around a steaming cup of something.

I asked, "That's Benicio?"

She nodded with enthusiasm. "Yes."

"Are you sure?"

She nodded with even more energy. "I think I know my grand-father."

"Your grandfather is Benicio, the mountain guide?"

"*Sí.*"

"Okay," I said. "*Gracias.*"

I excused myself from our table and approached the weathered old man at the end of the counter. "Señor Benicio?"

I noticed the cup he was cradling in his twisted, calloused hands didn't hold steaming black coffee as I expected. It appeared to be a hearty stew with far more solid vegetables and cubed meat than broth.

The man didn't look up. He pulled a brown cloth from his back pocket and wiped the surface of the stool beside him. "You are the American explorer."

It wasn't a question. He clearly knew far more about me than I'd ever know about him. I slid onto the newly cleaned seat and ex-tended a hand.

He seemed to study my outstretched hand before his eyes fol-lowed my arm all the way to my face. "Forgive me, but I have been in the water, and my body is very cold. I will shake your hand next time we meet."

I withdrew my hand. "Your English is flawless, sir."

As if he hadn't heard anything I said, he asked, "What is your name?"

Instinct urged me to extend my hand again, but instead, I laced my fingers together on the counter. "I'm Chase, and we're here to . . ."

He stared into his cup. "Do not begin with a lie, Chase. It does not become you."

"I wasn't—"

He interrupted me again. "Why you are here is none of my concern, Chase. What you do in those mountains, or on their other side, is between you and your God. Between me and mine is my responsibility to warn you of the death that awaits you up there."

"That's a little dramatic, don't you think?"

He placed the cup on the counter and pulled his hands from around it. His fingers trembled, and he drew them into fists. "Do you see that?"

I nodded without speaking, and he continued. "This is what happens to a man in those mountains. I was in the water for twelve minutes, recovering the bodies of two Canadian explorers who, like you, did not need a guide. It will be two days before my body warms itself back to the temperature of life."

I watched his knees shake beneath the counter and wondered if the bow in his back was permanent or a temporary condition from the exposure. "Don't you have warming blankets?"

He reclaimed the cup and brought it to his lips. After plucking a vegetable from the mug with his lips, he seemed to savor the taste and probably the warmth. "Some people have warming blankets, but I do not. If the mountain robs me of the heat that I need to stay alive, I will always respect its power. If I begin to believe I can undo anything the mountain does to me with an electric blanket, I will forget how dangerous she can be. Because I am afraid of her, the mountain and I are cautious friends."

I tried to understand his old-world ideology, but it evaded me. I wore a prosthetic because the life I've led took my natural leg. I wear state-of-the-art hearing devices because that same life took my ability to hear from within my head. Perhaps my ideology was exactly the opposite of Benicio's. Perhaps I believed anything the battlefield did to me, short of tearing my soul from my chest, could be resolved by modern medicine. Perhaps Benicio and I had very different enemies.

Chapter 22
Two Days

As Benicio continued his meditation over his cup of stew, I said, "I can't take you with me into the mountains, but I would like for you to talk to my team and me and tell us how to survive up there. I'll gladly pay you well if you'll give us that briefing."

The next time he touched the mug to his lips, he came away with a piece of meat that looked delicious. He closed his eyes and let the protein melt in his mouth. "Tell me about your men . . . and about your foot."

I immediately glanced down at my prosthetic. "How did you know?"

"I'm an old man, and I have spent a lifetime watching men walk on the most dangerous ground there is. I notice everything."

I said, "My team is strong, capable, fit, and well-trained."

"Well-trained, you say? Where were these men trained to survive and operate in the mountains of Tierra del Fuego?"

"Most are former U.S. Army Rangers and Special Forces."

"Most, but not you?"

"No, sir. I'm a civilian."

He ate another piece of meat from his stew. "I know why you are here, Chase, the self-proclaimed American explorer. Those mountains are part of me, and I am part of them. You are not the first."

I scowled. "I'm not the first what?"

He smiled. "Attempting deception is just as bad as lying with your tongue. I will take you across the mountains. I have men to carry your weapons, ammunition, and provisions. To reach the lago is two days for me, but four days for you."

"Why do you think it'll take us four days?"

He shook his head. "I do not think this, Chase. I know this. Remember, I am part of the mountain. I will be warm again in two days, and we will go."

"Two days? That won't work for us. We have to go now."

He shrugged his small shoulders. "If you go now, I will come for your bodies in three days. Your GPS does not function here. Your radios are useless weight. Your confidence is deadly, and your single-minded focus on your target is a loaded gun pressed to your forehead. I know every tree, every stone, every frozen crystal in the glaciers, and every place that has claimed the life of a man in the past fifty years." He paused, studied my eyes, then said, "Two hundred twelve."

Two twelve? The boiling point of water? What's this guy talking about?

As if he'd heard my thoughts, Benicio said, "That is the number of experienced climbers—and others who also believed they didn't need a guide—who died in those mountains and were returned to their loved ones by my hands. These very hands that are crying out to the guisado inside this cup for the warmth to survive another day, so they can do it again and again, as long as this ragged old body can take just one more step."

The old man was a psychologist's dream. Everything about him fascinated me, from his physical endurance to his mental acuity and everything in between.

Of the thousands of questions I wanted to ask, the last one that should've come out of my mouth was the first. "How do you know we have weapons and ammunition?"

His weathered smile looked suspiciously like Mateo's from the airport, so it was my turn to play the mentalist. "You must be very proud of your grandson Mateo."

His smile continued. "Noble attempt, Chase, but spend one year in Patagonia and try to find a man of my age without a grandson named Mateo. I knew you were soldiers from the moment you stepped inside. From the table you chose, you can see all exits, and each of your men memorized the faces of every other man in the room within seconds. You are here to stop the four men who left last night."

I leaned close. "Tell me about the four men."

He placed his cup on the counter and slowly pushed it away. The dark-eyed lady from behind the counter slid a second cup into his hands as steam rose from its surface. Once his hands were wrapped around the second cup, he let out a sigh of pleasure as if his entire body had been immersed in a warm pool.

He reveled in the moment, and I almost believed he'd forgotten my question until he said, "The four men murdered my friend, Alto."

He had my undivided attention, and in that moment, he was the only other human on the planet, as far as I was concerned. I didn't have to ask him to continue when a barely visible tear formed at the corner of his eye. "Alto was my brother, just like those men behind us are your brothers. How far would you go to catch the man who murdered one of them?"

I laid a hand on his shoulder. "To the ends of the Earth."

He slid the cup beneath his chin and let the steam rise across his face. "This is why I will take you across the mountains, Chase. I am correct. You are here to kill those men."

It wasn't really a question, so I didn't answer. Instead, I said, "What are we supposed to do for two days, and can we catch the four men once they have a forty-eight-hour head start?"

He glanced across his shoulder at the table where my team sat. "The man with the red beard and blue shirt. He understands heights and the cold."

"That's Kodiak," I said. "He was a Special Forces arctic warfare and survival instructor."

Benicio nodded. "And the black man. He has the eyes of a hawk."

"You're very good at this. That's Singer. He's our sniper."

"And the woman?"

"She's a long story, but I don't plan to take her across the mountain."

He frowned. "She is very determined."

"Yes, she is," I said as I battled with the decision to tell the truth. "Her friend is on the other side of those mountains. The four men are here to kill her."

Before I could finish, he said, "And you are here to stop them."

"That's just one of our objectives. After we stop them, we plan to pull out the lady's friend and get her somewhere safe."

"Safer than where she is now?"

I ignored the question. "Tell me about the four men."

He nibbled on another vegetable from his stew. "They are younger than you and much smaller. Those are advantages in the mountains. They are strong and formidable."

"Can they make it across the mountains?"

He nodded slowly. "Probably."

"All the more reason to leave today."

He repositioned the cup in his hands. "Go if you must, but I cannot. Who is your tracker?"

"Tracker?"

"Yes, your tracker. The man who can follow another man's trail, no matter how faint."

I looked over the team, and Benicio said, "You don't have a tracker?"

"We do. His name is Clark, but he's injured. He's the man with the blond hair, wearing the University of Alabama sweatshirt."

He narrowed his gaze. "So, you planned to pursue four men in the deadliest mountains on Earth without a tracker?"

"No. Until this conversation, I didn't know the four men existed. We suspected they would come, but we didn't know how many. Our plan was to get to the cabin before the assassins."

He twisted his neck until the bones of his upper vertebrae cracked. "Alto had a family. He was a poor, simple man who loved the mountains, just as I do. Men like him and me aren't the target of assassins . . . only murderers."

"Where will I find you in two days?" I asked.

"Do you have a good truck?"

"Yes."

"Good. I will be here in two days, and I will track the animals who murdered my friend, and you will kill them."

Again, his words weren't a question, so, again, I didn't answer. I stood, and this time, he extended his gnarled hand. I shook it, and the initial warmth from the cup filled my palm, but in seconds, his flesh seemed to draw the heat from my body, and I withdrew.

I said, "Two days."

I returned to my team's table and tossed down a few bills. "Let's go. We've got a lot to talk about."

We mounted our trucks and found the house Skipper arranged. It was simple and small but warm and dry. Although it was autumn back home in coastal Georgia, it was spring at the bottom of the world. Springtime in those latitudes was far more pleasant than the heart of winter would be, but staying warm was still important. I didn't want to know what Benicio had been through when he pulled those bodies from the water, but his refusal to allow electricity to restore his body temperature spoke volumes about the respect and admiration he held for the mountains. I believed his words when he said he was part of the mountains and they were part of him. I wondered if I would ever possess the wisdom of such a simple yet brilliant old man.

"So, here's the deal," I began as Clark finally got the fire to burn in the rugged stone fireplace behind me. "We're leaving in two days."

"Two days?" Hunter said. "Why on God's Earth would we wait two days? We're here and ready to go. You're not making any sense."

I held up a finger. "We're leaving in two days with Benicio, the old man from the cantina."

I detailed the reasons we needed Benicio and why we had no choice other than waiting until he was ready. Then, I pushed past the vegetables to the meat of the stew into which we'd plunged.

"There are four men headed across the mountains. They left last night, and Benicio said they murdered his friend, Alto. They are our primary objective."

Hunter shook his head. "All the more reason we need to go now."

"Benicio says we can catch them, even with a forty-eight-hour head start, and there's no one on Earth who wants to catch them worse than he does. There's nothing more important to him than avenging Alto's murder." I briefed everything Benicio and I talked about and then built my team. "I'm taking Singer, Mongo, Kodiak, Gator, and Hunter. Clark and Disco are staying here to function as an op center of sorts. We won't have any comms with Skipper from the mountains, but I've got an ace up my sleeve for local comms."

Clark's face said he was at least a little relieved he wasn't going mountain climbing. Disco expected my decision, so he took it in stride. The face that concerned me the most belonged to our resident retired spook.

I said, "Tell me what's on your mind, Teresa. We'll come back to the comms."

She inhaled a long breath and let it escape. "I'm going. If any-body has a chance of getting us inside that cabin without getting shot at, it's me. You're wasting time and risking your lives without me."

It was time to don my psychologist's hat. "Let's think about this. You're in great shape, but you're the oldest person here. That alone is enough to ground you for this op."

She leaned in. "Chase, think about it. How will you get near that cabin? Pam doesn't even know you exist. There's no way she'll let you approach."

I didn't have a solid argument, and she was right, but so was I. Taking her across the mountains would slow us down, although she could probably make it across. However, the likelihood of all of us making it across and back without being seriously injured or even killed was low, and those odds got worse with each body we added to the party. That thought rang a bell in my skull.

I said, "I need to know if Pam can make it back across those mountains. What kind of shape is she in, and how old is she?"

Teresa said, "She's in better shape than me and a year younger. She can make it, but that may not be necessary. If she has a boat, and I'm positive she does, egress will be over water and not back over the mountains."

"But you said her boat would be small and nimble," I said. "If you're right, it can't carry all of us out of there."

"No, not in one trip, but once the threat is neutralized, you can make as many trips as you want. There are a few small towns along the southern shoreline of the lake, to the east of Pam's cabin. The highway runs along the coast, giving us a lot of options to get out of there."

I considered her idea. "That's a solid plan, but it hinges entirely on Pam having a boat."

Teresa cut me off. "No, it doesn't. The shoreline is relatively level. Even if there is no boat, we can hike out of there, along the lake, without dealing with a return trip across the mountains. Boat or no boat, that's still the best egress route."

It was my turn to exhale. "Okay, the primary egress route will be east along the lake, with a rendezvous point to be selected before we're finished here."

No one protested, so I continued. "Now, back to the comms. Dr. Mankiller built a set of line-of-sight, low-power relays. They're small, lightweight, and easy to set up. We'll plant one on every peak we cross. That'll allow us to communicate with Clark and Disco here at the house. There will be times we're out of sight of the relays, but from high ground, we should be able to communicate relatively well. Each relay has a small solar panel to power itself. The batteries are small with short lives, but as long as the sun is shining, they'll work just fine."

Teresa locked eyes with me. "I'm going. If you don't want me in your party, I'll go without you. But either way, I'm going."

Chapter 23
Keeping the Peace

The landline in our rented house worked well enough to get a call through to Skipper aboard the *Lori Danielle*.

"Are you making good time?" I asked.

There was a several-second delay before I heard, "We're on the foils in flat seas, so we're a little ahead of schedule for now, but that'll likely change once we're south of the equator. How are the house and vehicles?"

"Everything is fine, as always. We've pushed back our departure into the mountains until day after tomorrow because our guide . . ."

The delay clipped off my transmission with Skipper's. "Why? What could possibly make you wait two days?"

I waited long enough for the line to clear. "Let's end our transmission with *over*. The delay is making this challenging. Over."

A few seconds later, she said, "Okay, but why would you delay your departure? You took the jet because this thing is time-sensitive. Over."

I slowly briefed her on the four murderers—as Benicio called them—and our need for a guide. After a lengthy struggle to communicate everything we needed to share, we signed off and agreed to talk once more before we departed for the mountains.

We spent the next day exploring the southern shore of the eastern reaches of Lago Fagnano. The main road ran near the water's edge at the Argentinian Naval Prefecture, so we probed the perimeter to observe any reaction to our presence. No matter how much noise we made, no one ever came to investigate.

I surveyed the site and found two antennas, a dilapidated collection of structures, and one building that looked like it could house a few people. With our courage and confidence at their peak, we walked up to the single usable building and knocked on the door. No one moved inside, and the knob didn't budge beneath my grip, so I picked the lock and pulled open the door. With my head and shoulders inside the opening, I said, "It doesn't look like anybody's been here for a while. I think we found our rendezvous point."

Mongo hefted Gator onto the roof of the small building, and he shaded his eyes against the glare.

After carefully examining the landscape to the west, Gator said, "I don't think we'll be anywhere near the peaks I can see. Getting comms with this place is going to be tough."

I studied the landscape and tried to picture the map of the area. "If I'm not mistaken, we're about twenty-five miles from the cabin. That's an eight-hour hike if no one's injured."

Mongo said, "I agree. There's enough curvature in the Earth over that distance to block a line-of-sight transmitter."

I pointed toward the taller of the two antennas. "What about from up there?"

Mongo's eyes rose up the rusting metal framework. "I'm not climbing that thing."

Gator hopped off the building and landed beside me like a cat. "I'll do it. Give me the receiver."

I pulled one of the kits from the truck, and Gator slung it over his shoulder. Minutes later, he was a hundred feet above our heads and installing the unit as the antenna swayed in an ever-increasing arc in the morning breeze.

Clark stepped beside me. "Do you remember ever being that fearless?"

"I have a different word for it."

He cleared his throat. "I miss those days."

"What are you talking about? You're still in your prime."

He raised his arms above his head and stretched. "Those days are long astern, I'm afraid. Kids like him are the future."

Gator descended the tower and dusted off his hands. "That wasn't so bad."

* * *

The two days passed remarkably quickly as we let our bodies rest and we consumed the calories we'd need for the trek. Benicio was exactly where he said he'd be when we pulled up to the cantina. He came through the door with a small pack thrown across his shoulder, well-worn boots on his feet, and a knit cap pulled low over his ears and forehead.

By comparison, my team was overpacked. Each of us had a ruck filled with provisions, water, dry clothes, medical gear, ammunition, electronic relay kits, and sleeping gear. In addition to each set of personal equipment, we had weapons still inside the trucks that would become crucial parts of our gear.

Benicio looked us over. "Show me the bottoms of your boots."

We turned like horses and raised one foot, then the other, for his inspection. Apparently, our boots met his standard because he said, "Okay," but then he stopped in front of Teresa, stared into her face for a moment, and then turned to me. "You did not tell me she would come."

"She's coming," I said.

He turned back to face our retired spook and pressed a thumb into her abdomen, and then he did the same to each thigh. After he'd probed until his heart seemed content, he asked, "How old are you?"

"Younger than you," she said.

"How much do you weigh?"

She raised an eyebrow. "More than you."

His frustration, if it existed, was well hidden behind his eyes. "How far can you run without stopping?"

"At least as far as you can."

He glanced back at me and shrugged. "Okay."

Benicio climbed into the cab of the first truck and pointed northward out of the city. We followed his finger and soon found ourselves where the pavement ends and the earth begins. We pushed northward as the terrain in front of us rose to the near vertical, and Benicio said, "Far enough."

The faces of my team turned from those of off-duty fighters and became the masks of warriors perched on the precipice of the battlefield. The laughing, joking, and playful banter ended, and silence claimed the air.

Benicio said, "It is not too late to bring three or four more men to carry your gear."

I shook him off. "Our party is big enough already. We don't need any extras."

"Okay, but after this moment, the option is gone."

I gave him a wordless nod, and he turned toward the mountain looming before us and closed his eyes. A moment later, he whispered something in a language that could've been Latin and crossed himself. That seemingly simple act granted me another level of confidence in our guide, and I shot a glance at our moral compass. Singer gave me a wink.

Benicio then performed a ritual unlike anything I'd ever seen. He stood in front of each member of my team, looked them in the eye individually, and asked, "Are you capable and prepared for what lies ahead?"

Each of us answered in the affirmative, but every word could've been a lie. None of us had any way to know what lay ahead and if we were truly prepared to encounter and survive it.

He ended the ritual in front of me. "Are you prepared to take responsibility for the lives of these people who are willing to follow you into the unknown?"

"I am."

He tightened the straps on his pack and glanced across his shoulder. "Bring the slowest person to the front, and place the fastest in the back. Try to keep up. We will cover as much ground as possible, as quickly as possible, before we must stop for the night."

Teresa took the lead just behind Benicio, and Gator fell to the rear. We tightened straps, checked boot laces, and followed our own personal Master Yoda into the wilds of the Land of Fire.

He walked with his arms swinging in long arcs beside his body, but none of us could keep pace with him without leaning forward and quickening into a slow jog. Benicio's confident stride looked relaxed and well-practiced, but it took us several minutes to find the rhythm to keep adequate spacing and to match his speed.

An hour into the jog, Teresa held up a fist and spoke through heavy breaths. "Hold, please."

Benicio turned but continued walking backward as Teresa took a knee. The team fanned out and set perimeter defense. We gulped from our CamelBaks and caught our breath.

Benicio knelt beside Teresa. "You told me you could run as long as me. I was only walking, and you are already on your knees only an hour into the day. If you cannot keep up, you must turn back now. The trail is gentle and safe back to the road."

Teresa wiped her brow. "I'm okay. I'm not turning back."

He didn't break eye contact. "Your pace will become the pace of movement, and you are slow."

She glared back at him. "I told you I'm good, so let's go."

"Rest and drink water," he said. "We will go again when everyone is ready."

After a few minutes, he said, "The trail is steep ahead, but it is still only walking. Tomorrow we will climb for the first time, but today is only hiking."

We followed in single file as he led us up the steep, winding path that disappeared from sight at several places. The guide's confident movement gave me the comfort to believe we were in very good hands, even in the areas where no trail was visible.

As the elevation increased, the sweat turned cold against my skin, and my thighs burned. I stepped out of our column and trotted to the front, where Teresa leaned into the slope and drove herself forward with determination and grit. "Are you okay?"

She gave me a thumbs-up and kept walking.

Everyone gave the same answer, and I fell back in line in front of Gator. "Are you okay back there?"

"Yes, sir, I'm good. I can carry some of Ms. Lynn's gear if she wants."

I made my way back to the front of the column and unzipped Teresa's pack as we continued hiking. I withdrew several fully loaded 5.56 magazines and rezipped her pack. I stuffed a few in the cargo pocket of my pants and tossed the others to Gator. He stowed the rounds, and I estimated we'd relieved Teresa of fifteen pounds or more.

Just as I settled back into my stride, Benicio yelled, "Stop, and do not move."

Everyone froze, but each of us leaned to see around the person in front of us. In the center of the ascending trail, thirty yards in front of us, stood a puma with her eyes trained on us as if choosing which of us to kill first. Hunter was first to react. He stepped beside Benicio and raised his rifle, but the guide laid a hand across the top of the barrel and pressed the weapon downward.

Like Hunter, every instinct inside of me screamed for me to put a pair of rounds through the predator's skull, but Benicio obviously had a different plan. He laid a hand against Hunter's chest and pressed him backward as he took a knee. Hunter followed the direction, but he kept his rifle at the low-ready position. Our guide spoke in a soft, confident voice in a language I didn't recognize. Maybe it was a dialect of Patagonian puma.

I expected, even hoped, to encounter predators in those mountains, but I anticipated assassins with rifles—not a creature with razor-sharp teeth and an appetite for American flesh.

Benicio continued speaking, and the puma seemed entranced by his words. The aggression in her eyes melted, and his posture softened. My desire to eliminate the threat dissolved the longer our guide spoke. Perhaps he was working harder to soothe the animals behind him than the one perched in front of him. If that was his goal, as far as I was concerned, it was working.

After what could've been an hour, or thirty seconds, Benicio rose to his full height—which wasn't impressive—and the puma watched without changing posture. The fiercest, deadliest close-quarters fighter on the battlefield remained low and curious.

As the standoff continued, a cascade of small falling rocks came from the slope above, and two puma cubs scampered across the trail behind their mother. She divided her attention between the cubs and Benicio until her offspring were safely below the trail and well into the tree line. As if exchanging some sort of ancient understanding between man and beast, Benicio and the puma both made a small sound and parted ways.

The cat bounded down the slope to collect her young, and our guide turned with an enormous smile on his face. "Thank you for not shooting her. Sometimes peace requires more courage than war."

Chapter 24
The Upper Hand

We continued our trek up the ever-steepening slope until the shadows consumed us, and we set up camp at the foot of a sheer rock wall protruding into the night sky. Singer and Hunter posted themselves on perimeter defense.

"What are they doing?" Benicio asked.

"Standing first watch," I said.

His bewilderment remained as he cocked his head. "First watch? Watching for what?"

"Anything that may threaten to harm the rest of us while we sleep."

"Nothing will harm us. The mother cat now knows we are no threat to her cubs, so she won't be a problem. The men we are pursuing are still a mile or more ahead, and they won't turn back. Besides, they have no way to know we are pursuing them."

Making him understand why we wouldn't sleep without someone pulling security would be equally as impossible as him explaining to us how he communicated with the puma. We were from two different worlds, and each would forever remain mysterious to the other.

When dawn broke, Teresa and I were taking our turn as guardians of the flock, and the night had indeed proven Benicio correct. Nothing threatened us through the hours, but that wouldn't stop us from recreating the ritual every time we stopped for each coming darkness.

After MREs and coffee, Benicio said, "It's now time to see if you are the skilled climbers you think yourselves to be."

Gator pointed up the vertical rock wall. "Are we climbing that?"

Benicio pointed to the west. "You may if you wish, but it is much easier to climb that one."

We followed his line of sight to a craggy rock wall that was only slightly less steep than the one above our heads, and we pulled on our climbing gear.

Gator stepped beside me. "I probably should've mentioned this, but I don't know how to climb that."

"Yeah, it would've been a good idea to bring that up, but you'll be fine. Just remember the rule of three to one."

"I guess I don't even know the rules."

"It's okay," I said. "Move only one foot or one hand while three other points of contact are firmly attached to the wall. That's a pretty easy climb. It's jagged and uneven. That'll give us plenty of hand- and footholds. The lead climber will tie off from above and drive anchors and cams as we go. If you fall, it'll only be a few feet before the lines stop you."

He stared at the wall. "What's a cam?"

I pulled the device from my bag. "It's a set of four rounded lobes set on spring-loaded pins that pivot against each other with an anchor point for a line. You pull this trigger and slide it into cracks or crevasses in the rock. That sets the cam. If you fall, the load applied to the anchor will be absorbed by the cams expanding against the rock. Cleaning the cam means to remove it as you ascend. That way, we'll have the anchors for later in that climb or for the next time we start up a wall."

"If you say so."

I asked, "Didn't they teach you any mountaineering at the Ranch?"

"I learned to rappel but not to climb. We did some steep work, but nothing that required cams."

"All right," I said. "I guess this'll be baptism by fire for you."

"So far, everything with you guys has been baptism by fire. I thought I knew some stuff when I left the Farm, but I was wrong."

"You knew more than you realized. It's like drinking from a firehose when you try to learn all the skills at once. It'll come."

He pivoted the cam against his fingers a few times. "Let's give it a go. If Mr. Hunter can do it, surely I can."

Hunter bounced a rock off Gator's chest. "Just try to keep up, kid."

Benicio led the way and scampered up the rock as if it were nothing more than a set of stairs in his house. Hunter followed him and set anchors for the rest of us. Gator climbed ahead of me, and I brought up the rear, cleaning cams and carabiners as we progressed. Our first climb of the mission took slightly less than an hour, and the view that awaited us at the top was well worth the effort.

Each of us stood in awe of the splendor in every direction. The Pacific to the west arced around the southern tip of the Americas and kissed the Atlantic in what looked like a graceful dance from where we stood, but the mariners who traversed the waters of the cape knew all too well how treacherous that kiss could be.

The rough ridgeline offered little in the way of sure footing, so I cautiously made my way beside Benicio. "How far ahead do you think they are?"

"It depends on their skill and how badly they're injured."

"What makes you think they're injured?"

He glanced over the edge behind us. "That is the easiest passage of our journey. Everyone gets injured."

"I see."

We gathered our gear and repacked our rucks.

Our guide said, "We'll move to the east for two kilometers before descending into the next valley. It will be slow, but it will make the next climb much easier. That's something our prey probably didn't know. This is our first opportunity to begin catching up to them."

We followed him and grew more confident with every stride, but caution still ruled the day. A twisted ankle in an environment like that could be devastating.

When we reached the descent point, Benicio said, "We can hike down the northern face. That will take two hours, or we can rappel in only minutes if you brought enough rope."

I turned to Gator. "Would you look at that? We get to do something you know how to do."

He took the shot without retaliation, but something told me he was saving up to lash out later.

I pointed toward the valley. "Estimate the distance to the bottom."

Gator leaned over the precipice, and the wheels in his head churned. When he turned around, obviously ready to share his guess with the class, Singer said, "Don't you dare."

Realization overtook the new guy, and he pulled his laser rangefinder from his pack. A few seconds later, he said, "Seven hundred and sixty yards."

Singer nodded. "When it comes to life-and-death decisions, we don't estimate when we have time to measure precisely."

"Yes, sir."

We rigged lines and descended the sheer face, stopping to reset our lines when necessary to make the long descent as safe and efficient as possible. Benicio was right. We made up at least two hours of time by rappelling instead of hiking down the face.

The day continued with climbs and descents that not only tested our skills but also left us gasping for breath at several points. We situated and activated the small radio relay stations atop every peak we climbed in hopes of maintaining comms with Clark and the ship.

From the top of one particularly challenging peak, Benicio pulled me aside and pointed toward the west. I looked out over the stunning landscape of endless mountain peaks and valleys that looked as if God had dragged his fingers through the stone of the Earth, carving the majestic mountains few men would ever see from where I stood.

Benicio said, "See those passes between the mountains?"

"Yes, sir."

"That is where you'll find the footprints of your prey."

I imagined the four men—well-armed, well-trained, and determined—weaving their way through the comparatively easy mountain passes while my team and I climbed, descended, and clawed our way through the frozen world touching the sky. "Are you still confident we can catch them?"

"We've already caught them," he said. His quiet, humble voice dripped with the confidence of a man who didn't need the approval or permission of anyone else. He was the master of a world few of us could even comprehend—a world of beauty, danger, and mystique that could not be captured by words but must be experienced to appreciate. Understanding a man like Benicio would take a lifetime, but appreciating and respecting him only required seconds.

"How do you know we've already caught them?" I asked.

He lifted a gloved hand toward our sniper. "Have him take a look."

Singer didn't require prompting. Almost before our guide finished the statement, he had his rifle braced against a stone outcropping and his scope focused miles away. We stood in silent anticipation as he scanned the valley floors. He moved the weapon with the precision of a surgeon's hand until he finally froze.

The thousands of hours he'd spent training himself to become part of his environment consumed him, and his breathing slowed to a practiced rhythm that always preceded the final pounding of the hearts of so many men who'd fallen before his barrel, having never heard the shot that sent their souls across the waiting river.

He wouldn't press the trigger in that moment. He would merely burn the image of the men into the folds of his mind. "There they are."

Instinctually, we all followed the muzzle of his rifle and squinted into the distance far beyond the limits of our eyes. I imagined what must've been treading through the minds of the men we'd soon encounter. Perhaps they took every stride believing no one would dare follow them through the forbidden wilds of those mountains. They likely believed they would complete their mission without resistance and cash the checks that would sustain them until the next assignment, the next opportunity they would earn to deploy their deadly skill on the unsuspecting, the next time they would become the hunter stalking a prey that could never escape.

What those men would never know is how close they were to the final steps of their lives, their closing breaths, and the last conscious thoughts they'd ever experience.

Singer lifted his eye from the rifle and turned his attention to the north.

Benicio stepped beside him. "You want to know how quickly we'll close with them, don't you?"

"I do."

He said, "I will put them in your grasp within twenty-four hours."

I slid a hand beneath Singer's rifle and laid my cheek on the stock. It took several sweeps for me to finally see the antlike figures moving slowly to the north. I was tempted to send a round racing through the cold mountain air, but no rifle existed with the capability of sending a bullet that distance with enough force to stop a man. Pressing the trigger would be nothing more than throwing a rock from that range, but I could taste the victory on the wind, and for the first time in the operation, I felt as if we held the upper hand.

I pulled my radio from my pack and pressed the mic to my mouth.

Clark answered as if we were standing in the same room. "Hey, College Boy. How's the hike?"

"We spotted the four guys we're after."

"Did Singer turn out their lights?"

"Not from this distance. We're probably five miles away, but we're closing fast."

"You saw them from five miles away?"

"We saw four objects moving like humans in the right direction through Singer's scope. Benicio says we'll be on top of them in twenty-four hours."

"Is everybody okay?"

"So far," I said. "It's rough country, but we're making it. Have you heard from Skipper?"

"I talked with her a few minutes ago. They're still making great time, and they should be here inside forty-eight hours if everything keeps going smoothly."

"We'll check in from the next peak."

Clark said, "Don't engage without sending me your coordinates. If it goes south, I don't want to have to bulldoze those mountains to find your bodies."

Chapter 25
Bottleneck

The thought of Clark plowing through those mountains in search of our remains didn't surprise me at all. I believe he would crawl through Hell before he'd leave any of us behind, but no part of my plan included leaving any friendly bodies in those mountains.

Leadership comes with more responsibilities than anyone could list in a lifetime. Teresa Lynn spent more time with her left foot on the ground than with her right. Those are the things a good leader notices before they become an issue.

"What's going on with your foot?" I asked.

She quickly lifted her right boot from the ground. "Oh, it's nothing. Maybe just a blister."

"Let's have a look. We've got a lot of ground to cover and no way to get you out if you go down."

"Really, Chase, it's fine."

I said, "Sit down and take off your boot."

The look on her face said following orders wasn't her strong suit, but I didn't care. Mongo figured out what was happening and pulled his med kit from his pack. She planted herself on a rock, and he pulled off her sock.

His trained eye discovered the issue in seconds. "Your feet are wet, and your boots aren't tight enough. Let's get you squared away."

He cleaned and dried her feet while she pulled out a clean pair of socks. With the fresh blister treated, he tied her boots for her and said, "In the infantry, there's nothing more important than taking care of your dogs. If you'd have gone another hour, yours would've been barking like crazy."

"Thank you, Mongo. I've never been in the infantry."

He grinned. "Look around. You are now. If you feel your feet sliding around in your boots, stop us and take the time to fix it."

She gave him a mock salute. "Yes, sir."

We made another climb and two more descents before the sun made its exit.

After camp was built and security was set, Benicio pulled me away from the team. "Is the woman okay?"

"She's fine," I said. "Her boots were too loose, and she got a blister."

"We can't slow down."

I searched his face. "What's on your mind?"

He dropped his chin. "I was wrong about timing. If we intercept those men tomorrow, it will be just before sundown."

"Why is that a bad thing?" I asked.

"There is no moon, so it will be very dark. A terrible time to start a fight."

It was my turn to give the old man a reason to smile. "If I were orchestrating the intercept, that's exactly when I'd want it to happen. The darker, the better. Whoever those men are, they're not elite soldiers."

"How could you know this?"

"If they were as good as we are, they wouldn't be walking in that pass where they're sitting ducks."

He cocked his head. "Sitting ducks?"

"It's an English idiom meaning they're vulnerable and easy to kill. There's no worse condition for a soldier than fighting an enemy who holds the high ground."

"I understand now. I think I have the perfect place for an ambush. Give me your map."

I produced the folded map and followed his weathered finger across the page.

He said, "Here. This is a draw to the east into rising terrain. We will be here an hour ahead of the other men." He slid his finger to the west. "They will come through this narrow pass."

"We call that a bottleneck," I said.

"Okay, bottleneck it is. They will come through here with plans to stop for the night by this stream."

"How do you know?"

"This is what my friend, Alto, would have told them to do. He was a very good guide, and he knew the mountains almost as well as I do."

I forced the map into my memory and drew a battle plan. "Are you sure you can put us in that draw before they get there tomorrow?"

"I am sure," he said.

* * *

Sleep came, and so did the sun. We awoke to one of the most beautiful mornings I'd ever seen, and for the first time in the mountains, I felt truly comfortable. Benicio led the way, and the mountains were far more forgiving than they had been for the two previous days. The climbs were more gentle, and the descents didn't require ropes.

Just as promised, the old man put us in the mouth of the

draw two hours before sunset, and there couldn't have been a better ambush sight if God himself had designed it. And perhaps He did.

Singer took Gator to the best spot on the high ground and set up his sniper hide while the rest of us found positions high enough to provide cover and concealment, but still close enough to the bottleneck to effectively pour fire onto our enemy. I called Clark and gave him our estimated coordinates according to the map, but the detailed terrain description would be the landmark he needed to find us if everything fell apart in the coming hours.

Our radios worked from our positions in the canyon, but no one beyond the surrounding peaks, except for Clark, would ever know what was about to happen in the darkened mountains at the bottom of the world.

The shadows lengthened until the peaks disappeared above us and the valley below became a sea of endless black. Singer's scope and our night-vision monoculars provided enough light for us to tell the difference between a man and a rock, even without the moon looming overhead.

Singer's voice floated in my head. "One, Six, motion to the west approximately one kilometer."

"Roger, Six. Identify when able."

Silence filled the air as everyone did exactly what we'd trained to do in that scenario. We lay in wait for an unsuspecting enemy from a position of strength with far superior firepower. Every ear was trained on the breeze, hoping to hear the unnatural sounds of men treading where they never should have been. The sounds we make in the wilderness are harsh and crashing compared to those made by the creatures who call the environment home. We'd hear our enemy long before we saw them.

My failed natural hearing gave me a distinct advantage. The electronic devices that replaced my eardrums were far more sensitive than the unaided human ear could ever be. Although I couldn't identify everything, I heard every sound the environment made, and I cataloged each one to compare against every other sound I'd hear in the coming moments.

Singer's whisper returned. "One, Six, visual. One man walking point with nods but no visible weapon."

I wouldn't give the order to shoot an unarmed man, but I wouldn't hesitate to let him know he'd stepped into my trap.

"Let him come," I whispered.

Minutes later, Singer said, "Two bandits in sight, both with nods, but no visible weapons."

I leaned to my right to align my sight with Singer's, and the two men came into view inside the hazy lens of my monocular. "Got 'em."

I watched as the two men fumbled their way across the valley floor until reaching the edge of the stream. They stopped, dropped their packs, and withdrew their CamelBaks and canteens. With their water supply replenished, they unpacked a pair of individual tents and nestled themselves near the running water.

Singer said, "One, Six, are you seeing this?"

"Affirmative," I said. "Where are the other two?"

"Unknown," Singer said. "Do you want me to put them down?"

"Negative. Let them fall asleep. Keep your eyes open for the other two."

Two hours into the agony of watching a pair of tents wave in the wind, I reached the point at which I could no longer wait.

I said, "Four and Seven, this is One. Form up on me on the western wall, just out of sight of the camp."

Hunter and Kodiak each acknowledged and stepped silently from their fighting positions. We met at the point I chose and eased our way toward the tents. We moved in silence until I was positioned between the two tents, and Kodiak and Hunter stood at the head end of each tent. They drew their knives and waited for my signal.

My glance back into the mountains was the only trigger required for Singer to say, "Three . . . two . . . . one . . . hit 'em."

The two commandos only feet away moved in practiced unison, each driving a knee onto the center of the body sleeping beneath the tents. The crushing knee shot marked the end of the silence but not the end of our aggression. Kodiak and Hunter sliced through the tops of each tent, creating a gaping wound in the nylon shelters.

Even the world's most elite soldiers wouldn't react well in that moment, but our prey did far better than expected. Hunter's man raised a flailing arm with a glistening blade slicing through the air. Hunter reacted in time to sidestep the stabbing blow, but in doing so, he lost his position of power on top of the man. The man was on his feet in a perfect fighting stance, but the nods he'd worn to find his campsite were nowhere to be found. He was blind, confused, and probably frightened, but he wasn't backing down.

Hunter lunged forward, thrusting his rifle against the man's right wrist in an attempt to disarm him without pulling the trigger. We had the advantage. Our single-tube nods were still in place, so we could see, but our opponents could not.

Kodiak realized what was happening, so he dropped to his knees, with one landing on the man's right elbow and pinning it to the ground. He drove the butt of his rifle against the opposite bicep, rendering the arm temporarily useless.

Hunter's man stepped into him and struck wildly, knocking his helmet from his head and rendering my partner blind.

I needed both men alive for interrogation, but I committed the unforgivable sin of underestimating my opponents in a foreign environment.

Kodiak was handling his man, but Hunter was blind and fighting backward toward the stream. I let my rifle fall against my chest, pulling the sling tight across my shoulder, and drew my pistol. Hunter's fight was growing more violent by the second, and I couldn't afford to lose him.

I took three galloping strides toward Hunter and his foe, but the instant before I grabbed a handful of his shirt, the fighter forced Hunter onto his back in the stream. I followed them down the bank to the edge of the shallow water. Hunter was still fighting, but the man stood over him, making it impossible to put a round through him without risking the bullet slicing through his body and into my partner.

Re-holstering my pistol, I drew my knife and raised it high above my head. A bullet might pass through his flesh, but my blade would stop at its hilt. The instant before I took the striking stride into the stream with my one human foot, Hunter's would-be killer exploded in front of me as if a stick of dynamite had blown from within his stomach. I recoiled, landing on my butt beside the stream, and Hunter clawed backward to the other side of the water as the echoing report of Singer's rifle resounded through the valley.

Stealth was over, so I drew my pistol and hit the light. What remained of the man's body drifted down the stream, bouncing off rocks and twisting with the current. Hunter drew his pistol and illuminated the world in front of him.

Kodiak was still fighting, and I beat Hunter to his side by two steps. My boot to the man's temple ended both his will and ability to continue the fight. Kodiak shoved the limp body away and added a second kick as a final release of adrenaline. The man's unconscious body lay in a twisted heap on top of what had been his tent.

I said, "Six, hold position. Everyone else, bring it in and set security."

Keeping Singer in the overwatch position added a level of security we could never achieve without him.

My team moved in and established a secure perimeter while I dragged the victim of my boot heel to the water. I dunked his face into the stream, time after time, reviving him from his stupor. When he came back to the land of the living, I put him on his face and flex-cuffed his wrists behind his back. Thirty seconds later, I had his ankles tied and his body pressed against a pile of rocks that had likely been in that same spot for thousands of years.

"What's your name?" I demanded.

He spat at me and growled. "Kill me!"

I planted a knee on his thigh, and he bellowed in pain. "What is your name?"

He grunted through clenched teeth. "I said kill me. You won't get a word from me."

A right cross sent one of his teeth flying from his mouth and blood spraying in every direction. "You will tell me who you're working for or I'll tear you apart one piece at a time."

He laughed with blood pouring from his mouth. "You're nothing, man. Nothing you can do to me will make me give up anything. You got no idea who you're messing with."

I took a knee in front of him and clamped my hand around his lower jaw. "You're just number two. I'll walk through you just like I walked through your little buddy when he didn't have anything useful for me. There are plenty more, and I have no qualms about leaving a trail of dead, uncooperative bodies in my wake. Now, who do you work for?"

His answer came in the form of a spray of bloody spittle, but I didn't flinch.

"Aww, isn't that cute? He thinks he can make me mad. What you don't know is that this is my favorite part." I pointed toward my face and waved a circle with my finger. "See this? Behind this is the sickest, most deranged interrogator you'll ever meet. I will cut you and play in your blood while my medic keeps you alive. You're going to talk."

Spittle seemed to be the only language the man knew, so I kept my heart rate down and the smile on my face.

Everyone has a breaking point, but they come in all shapes. Some men wilt and cry like frightened children at the threat of violence against their person. Others seem to thrive on the pain until their body's inability to retain consciousness defeats the will of their mind to resist. I believed I'd seen resistance in all of its forms, but I was wrong.

The bound, defiant man in front of me was a class of warrior all his own. He didn't seem to care that my sniper had blown his partner's body apart. He seemed to have no fear of physical pain. In fact, he seemed to revel in the misery I distributed with my fists. If anything were going to motivate him, it would be the fear of death, and I was more than willing to lead him to within inches of that threshold. Little did I know he would lead me across it.

I drew my knife and backhanded the man with the blade's pommel. His nose opened, and blood poured like a fountain.

"Tell me who you work for."

He let the blood flow down his face and across his battered lips, but his eyes never changed expression. I turned a corner in the interrogation where most men wilt, but my prisoner wasn't most men.

I spun the blade in my palm until the razor's tip landed just below his bottom lip, then I pressed the steel into his flesh until the crimson outline of the blade formed on his skin.

Instead of pulling away from the knife, he raised his chin, offering me his throat. There would come a time in the interrogation at which the man would become a liability. He would no longer be able to walk, and leaving a wounded man alone to die in the wilderness was a sin I wouldn't commit. I would make him believe I would kill him, but tearing the life from a bound man wasn't within my ability.

To my horrified disbelief, my will and ability played little, if any, role in what happened next. Not only did the man offer me his neck, but he also lunged forward, throwing himself onto my knife before I could withdraw it. By the time I reacted, my hand was dripping with the man's blood, and his body no longer possessed its soul.

Chapter 26
Courage, Boys

I shook off the disbelief of the man's willingness to sacrifice his life before giving up his employer, and I turned immediately to Teresa Lynn.

"Think! How many people are dangerous enough to produce that result?"

She looked away from the carnage. "What would make him do that?"

"Fear," I said. "He was more afraid of his boss than anything I could've done to him . . . or even dying. That's the very definition of power. I need a list of people who are that powerful and who have a reason to kill former U.S. Intelligence officers like you."

She said, "It's not coming, Chase. I don't know anyone outside the former Soviet Union or the Islamic extremists who demand that degree of loyalty and get it. We're not dealing with humans anymore. This thing just turned as dark as anything can."

"Where's Benicio?" I asked.

The man stepped from behind a fallen tree. "You want to know where the other two men are, don't you?"

"That's right. Why didn't they come this way? When and where did they break off?"

He waved me toward him with a crooked hand. "Show me the map."

I spread out the paper on the ground at his feet and shined my pistol light on it. He traced a line to the west from our bottleneck until he reached a break in the mountains where one valley became three. "Here. This is the most reasonable place to break into two teams."

Mongo took a knee beside us. "It was a brilliant tactical move. There aren't enough of us to set up two ambush points, so they were willing to sacrifice one pair to occupy us while the other duo continued toward the objective."

"But they didn't know we were chasing them," I said.

The big man said, "Maybe. Ushuaia is a small town, and we were there a long time."

I turned to Benicio, and he held up both hands. "I didn't tell anyone, but that doesn't mean it didn't get out. Rumors are powerful."

I said, "But those men were already in the mountains before we showed up in Ushuaia. How could anyone have told them?"

Mongo groaned. "Maybe nobody told them. Maybe they're just that good. They're not taking any chances, and they're covering all their bases. These guys may be our equals, or even our betters."

I took Benicio by the arm. "Two questions. First, can we get to that split before sunup?"

He nodded. "Yes, the path is low and clear. We can make good time, even in the dark. What's your second question?"

"If we get there, can you track the other two men?"

"Yes. There are only three routes from there, but all of them lead back into the cut where your house sits. It's a three-way divided canyon all the way."

"A straight shot?" I asked.

"No, not a straight shot. There are several turns, but it's not challenging."

I keyed my mic. "Break security, sniper in, we're moving west."

It took ten minutes for Singer to climb down from his hide and join the team. When he showed up, he took me by the arm. "If you had it under control, I'm sorry I took that shot, but it looked like you were in over your head."

"You did the right thing," I said. "The situation was out of hand and getting worse."

I described the actions of the second man, and Singer said, "He was definitely afraid of somebody."

"And it's up to us to find out who that somebody is and stop him."

We formed a long column and pressed westward through the darkness. Even with our night vision in place, there wasn't enough natural light to give us a clear view of the path ahead. We moved as fast as we could without turning our caravan into a carnival act, and we arrived at the point where the other team likely broke off just before daybreak.

Benicio stood in the darkness and studied the mountains climbing away in every direction. I'd never seen him produce a compass, a map of his own, or any other device to help orient himself. I envied his knowledge and understanding of the mountains, but the look on his face in those waning moments of darkness was unlike any I'd seen from him before that moment.

"What's on your mind, my friend?"

He didn't look away from the mountain pass. "I am sorry."

"Why are you sorry?"

"I should have warned you they might take two different routes."

"You couldn't have known that. In fact, it may be better that we didn't have to deal with all four of them. Now we know the degree of their devotion to the mission. They'll fight to the death before they accept failure."

"Be careful, Chase. You only know this of one of the four men. The first died before you could question him, and you have not encountered the remaining two yet."

"You're right, but I'm putting my money on the same mindset across the board. Let me know when you're ready to pick a door."

He wrinkled his brow. "Pick a door?"

I pointed to the three canyons that lay ahead of us to the north. "Yeah, pick a door. Which way did they go?"

He nodded and continued studying the landscape.

I grabbed Teresa. "Have you come up with any names?"

"Not of individuals."

"Let's have them."

She held up fingers, one at a time. "Al-Aqsa Martyrs Brigade, al-Qa'ida, Mujahedeen—"

I stuck a hand in the air. "Think about the two guys we just encountered. Did either of them look or sound Middle Eastern to you?"

She said, "No, but there are mercenaries who'll work for anybody."

"I agree, but it's tough to buy the kind of loyalty those guys showed. A soldier for hire isn't going to throw himself on a knife to avoid interrogation. I need you to tighten the noose. Think closer to home. Focus on the South African op. That's the one thing that ties all of you together."

She stared at the ground, and I said, "Just keep thinking. Our primary focus is getting Pamela safely out of the country. Once she's in our hands and aboard the ship, we can focus on finding out what all of this is about."

She nodded but didn't speak.

When I turned away, I discovered Benicio standing only a few feet behind me. "We must climb."

"Climb? I thought you said you could track them."

He said, "I made a decision that cost two lives. Maybe those men were dangerous, but theirs were still human lives."

"Look, Benicio, if you're struggling with what I might do to the next two guys we encounter, you should've thought about that four days ago. This isn't a humanitarian mission, and we're not aid workers. We're soldiers protecting an innocent woman, and anything that keeps us from accomplishing that mission is expendable, including the lives of the men trying to kill her."

"Remember the puma?" he asked. "She was dangerous, but only because she was defending her cubs. She didn't want to attack us. She only wanted to cross our path with her cubs."

"I get it," I said. "All life is precious and all that, but this isn't a philosophical experience. We're dealing with real evil here. That's the world I live in. I need you, but if you can't objectively support my mission and put your agenda aside, we have to part ways."

He laid a hand on mine. "You don't understand. I am not what you think. What happened back there is tragic, but I understand. I was once a soldier when I was just a boy, so I know your heart. It was once my heart. If you live as long as I have, your heart will soften. I told you I would deliver you all the way through the mountains, and that's what I'll do."

"That's exactly what I need."

He said, "Wait. I'm not finished. I made a mistake yesterday, and that mistake cost you time and put the blood of two men at your feet. I am sorry for that. Today, I could choose a path and lead you all the way to the lake, but it might be the wrong choice. The people we are following are smarter than I expected . . . and more dangerous."

"We're killing a lot of time," I said. "If we have to climb, lead the way, and we'll follow, but we don't have time to discuss every decision."

Without another word, he turned and led us up a steep, rugged incline, but it was nothing like the climbing we'd already done. We made good time and found ourselves on high ground before the sun was high in the sky. When we reached the peak, Gator set up another repeater, leaving just one set left in the pack.

I briefed Clark as we patrolled the ridgeline, scouring the valleys on either side for signs of life.

"That sounds like quite a night, College Boy. Have you put any ideas together on who's behind all of this?"

"Not yet, but whoever it is, they're hardcore."

He said, "Keep your head down and your powder dry. Let me know if you need anything."

"I need a lot of things. A helicopter would be a good start."

He said, "The *Lori Danielle* will be here in less than twenty-four hours."

"Unfortunately, this thing is going to blow up in less than twelve."

Before Clark could respond, Singer called out, "Got 'em! Two-o'clock low."

Every eye turned to the northeast, where a pair of commandos with weapons at the ready pressed slowly to the north with at least a hundred yards between them.

I slipped in beside our sniper. "Tell me what you see."

Without taking his eyes off the targets, he said, "They obviously know something went down with their buddies. They're moving just like I would if I were in their shoes."

"I disagree," I said. "I wouldn't stick to the valley floor. I'd take the high ground."

"Look at them, Chase. They don't have any gear. They're moving light. High ground isn't an option for them."

"Can you pin them down?"

"You know I can. Where do you want them?"

I motioned for the team to huddle up. "Here's the plan. Benicio, Singer, Mongo, and Teresa are moving up the ridgeline to get ahead of our targets. I'll take Hunter, Kodiak, and Gator down the wall into the valley. Once we're in position, Singer will pin them down, and we'll assault from the rear, taking them alive if possible. Any questions?"

Singer said, "I like it. Let's move."

I stuck a radio in Teresa's hand. "Brief Clark, and stay with Singer. Do not get separated. Got it?"

"Got it."

The sniper element moved out at a trot, and my team headed down the slope. "Stay as quiet as possible. Everything will echo once we get below the ridgeline."

We moved as fast as we could without starting an avalanche, and we lost sight of our prey several times. I tried to keep our momentum moving to the north, but the craggy slope didn't always grant me that privilege. We reached a massive outcropping and mounted it on our bellies. It gave us the perfect position to catch our breath and keep an eye on our targets.

Gator slid a pair of binoculars into my hand, and I pressed them to my eyes. "They're looking up."

"At us?" he asked.

"No, I think they may have heard Singer's team."

Hunter said, "No way. Singer would've been silent."

"Yeah, but Teresa and Benicio aren't snipers, and Mongo is, well, Mongo."

I kept my eyes trained on the two men as they stood dead still and stared up the slope toward the precise location where Singer and his entourage should've been. A sickening feeling hit me in the gut when both men shouldered their rifles and a cry of "Shoot her!" echoed through the valley.

Kodiak slid to the outermost edge of our ledge and shouldered his weapon.

I motioned around the rock and toward the valley. "Go! Go!"

Hunter and Gator slid from the ledge and powered down the slope, trading silence for speed. We were seconds away from a gunfight nobody wanted, in a place nobody wanted to be, and Teresa was in the crosshairs.

I radioed Singer. "Six, One. They've spotted you, and they're engaging Teresa."

A beat later, he said, "They haven't spotted us. Hold your fire."

I echoed his order, hoping Hunter and Gator would hear. "Hold your position, and hold your fire!"

Kodiak said, "They're engaging somebody."

Again, the echo came. "Shoot her!"

Five cracks of rifle fire thundered through the canyon, and I called, "Sitrep, Six."

Singer said, "They're engaging a target a quarter mile behind us. We're in position and well covered. They're not shooting at us."

I keyed up. "Four and Eight, get down there and find out who they're shooting at."

Hunter and Gator continued their descent until they reached the valley floor. Six more rifle rounds exploded ahead, and I strained to see the angle of their attack.

I shook Kodiak's boot. "What do you see?"

"Nothing. They're shooting at nothing."

"No way," I said. "Those guys are too good to shoot at a ghost."

That's when the answer came, and it churned my soul. The unmistakable roar of a puma pierced the air, sending every living creature cowering.

"It's a cat," Hunter said. "And she's moving on us."

I ordered, "Hold your fire if possible. Those guys still don't know we're here."

Rifle fire from my team would only serve to worsen the situation and weaken what little advantage we had, but surviving a fair fight with a puma wasn't something Hunter or Gator could pull off. Putting her down to protect themselves was the logical play, but letting her run away—if she would—was the key to preserving our position.

I keyed my mic. "Six, One, if you hear gunfire from us, pin those boys to the ground, and we'll take the fight to them."

He answered, "Roger, One."

Hunter's voice echoed in my head, "She's still coming, but she's trailing off to the east."

I said, "Move to the western wall and let her go. Courage, boys. Courage. Save your bullets for the two-legged fight."

"Easy for you to say," Hunter groaned. "You're not the one in a narrow valley with a three-hundred-pound predator closing on you."

I closed my eyes for the part of a second it took to send up a silent prayer, and it was answered before I finished.

Gator's breathless voice reported, "The cat is clear to the south and still running."

Chapter 27
The Gator's Fury

With that train wreck behind us, I called for a status report.

Hunter was first to answer. "Eight and Four are secure on the valley floor with negative visual on the targets."

Singer said, "Six, Two, plus two are secure with both targets in sight and ready to engage."

I said, "Roger. Seven and I are secure about fifty yards above the valley floor on the western wall. We have one target in sight. Everybody, catch your breath and report ready."

Singer said, "Six and Two are ready."

Hunter wasn't far behind. "Four and Eight ready."

I called Singer. "Are they split?"

"Affirmative. We're inside eight hundred yards, so Mongo and I can pin them down simultaneously."

I said, "Stand by, Six."

"Roger. Standing by."

I ordered, "Four and Eight, press to contact with concealment."

"Roger. Pressing to contact," Hunter said.

I nudged Kodiak's boot. "Still just one?"

He nodded, and I asked, "Do you see a position for a better angle of fire?"

He scanned the valley. "Not from this side. I can move to the valley and back up Gator and Hunter."

I considered our options. "Hold your position here. I'm going down."

I press-checked my rifle and found a round seated anxiously in the chamber and ready to do its deadly work. Sixty seconds later, I was on low, flat ground with Hunter and Gator inching forward ahead of me. I fell behind Gator and reported my position to the team.

Hunter whispered, "Contact, left front."

I peered around Gator's shoulder and saw our foe the same instant he did, but I waited for him to make the call.

He said, "Contact right front."

"Stand fast," I ordered, and Hunter and Gator froze.

I took a long breath and let the coming gunfight play out in my head. No battle plan ever survives first contact, but I needed a track in my head to gauge just how far off the rails our train was going to fly.

With the perfect execution playing on an endless loop in my mind, I ordered, "Hit 'em, Six!"

The earthshaking report of Singer's .338 Lapua rang over the crack of Mongo's 556. The chorus was followed almost immediately by another crack from Mongo and then one more from Singer's massive cannon.

One of the men yelled, "Contact, high left!"

Both men opened fire on the ridgeline, giving us the window we needed to close from behind. Slowly, their rifle fire diminished, then ceased as we approached.

One of the men yelled, "You up?"

"Up!" came the other fighter's response.

I took a breath to order two more volleys of fire to put their heads back down, but Singer and Mongo read my mind. The thunder came, and the two men cowered deeper into their holes like scared rats scurrying into the ground.

Hunter, Gator, and I made our move and advanced with rifles shouldered and muzzles trained on our prey.

The time for silence was long past, and Gator sounded off as he leapt into the hole with his man. "Down, down, down! Face in the dirt! Do it now!"

I couldn't make out Hunter's matching commands a hundred feet across the valley floor, but I had every confidence they were equally effective.

Most fighters would've at least temporarily obeyed, but those men did not. Instead of dropping their weapons and surrendering, they spun, weapons raised and belching fire and lead.

Gator reacted like a cat, ducking beneath the barrel of his man's rifle and driving his shoulder into the man's throat. To my surprise, Gator ran a thumb on top of the man's trigger finger and pinned the trigger to the rear.

If the weapon were on full auto, it would empty the magazine in seconds, but if it were on semi—still effective—the pressure would prevent the fighter from getting off another round. The downside was that he was essentially fighting one-handed, but he was doing fine. I rose from my position to see Hunter pummeling his opponent across the valley. A second later, the man's rifle flew from Hunter's hand, and the fight was over.

Gator was still in it, and everything inside of me wanted to put a round through the other man's knee to stop the fight. Leadership 101 dictated that I let Gator have his victory without my help, and it played out perfectly. The man delivered a couple of nasty blows, but Gator shook them off. Finally, he twisted the man's arm and pinned his rifle beneath his chin. The harder Gator leaned in, the less the man fought back, until the glistening blade appeared.

I watched it happen, and I aimed across Gator's shoulder to send a round through the man's skull before he could sink his blade into my newest teammate's back, but I should've trusted my man. Gator glimpsed the rising blade and delivered a powerful blow to the back of the man's elbow, rendering his knife arm temporarily worthless.

We'd obviously taught the new guy enough to know the fight was far from over because before the feeling could return to his opponent's arm, Gator drew his own blade and buried it to the hilt in the man's thigh.

Somewhere deep inside the animal pacing around in the man's chest, there may have been an ounce of fight left in him, but the indescribable agony of the eight-inch blade buried in his thigh rendered his mind incapable of issuing further commands to continue the fight. He dropped his knife and relaxed under Gator's weight.

The new guy yanked the rifle from the man's hand and sent a crushing strike to his forehead with the butt, rendering him unconscious and possibly permanently lost in the spirit world.

Gator relaxed against the cold ground behind him and glared up at me. "Really? Is that how it is? You're just going to stand there and watch me get my ass kicked?"

His tone was anything but respectful, and he was well justified in his rage, but I said, "You were doing just fine."

He growled, "I was losing at every round, and you just stood there. How 'bout the next time you think I'm doing just fine, you go ahead and shoot the guy in the face? How about that? That'd be hunky-dory in my book."

I bit my lip and tried not to laugh. "Hunky-dory? Really?"

His anger morphed from raging fire to hilarious laughter in an instant.

Before our laughter ended, Hunter appeared, dragging a flailing, hog-tied man by the foot. "When you two get finished with your giggly little slumber party, or whatever this is, I think this guy's got something he wants to tell us."

My partner dropped the man's foot, and it fell to the ground with a thud. He delivered a sharp heel kick to the guy's knee. "Quit squirming around. I'm trying to introduce myself. My name's Hunter, like what I just did to you. You know, hunted you down and stomped your face into the ground. And this is my boss. You don't need to know his name. You can just call him sir. He's got a few questions for you."

Just like the man the night before, Hunter's prisoner spat blood, sweat, and whatever other vile fluid he had to offer. Hunter sent a heart-stopping kick to the center of the man's chest, and every ounce of air in his lungs evacuated. That feeling had happened to me more times than I could count at home plate. The difference was that I would survive the afternoon. He might not.

I grabbed the man's belt and yanked him off the ground several times, trying to shake the air back into his lungs. He finally caught his breath enough to spit again, and I gave him an open-hand slap across the face.

"Be nice. We're trying to show you some courtesy, and you're acting like an animal. Your mommy would be so disappointed in you."

Singer, Mongo, and the plus two arrived on the scene, and I pointed at Gator's victim. "Wake him up if he's still alive, and we'll see which one of these boys decides to talk first."

Mongo reached down and hoisted the unconscious man by a limp arm. "I'll practice my full-contact CPR until he breathes or I break all of his ribs."

Hunter's guy watched our giant drag his partner into the trees before looking back up at me. I stared back at him without saying a word. In situations like that, the man who opens his mouth first is the loser, and now that we'd stopped the coming assault on Pamela Bingham's cabin, I had all the time in the world.

The standoff continued for several minutes until Mongo yelled across the valley. "This guy's wide awake and singing like a bird, so go ahead and put a bullet in your guy's head. We don't need them both."

That did the trick. The man dug at the earth around him in a frantic but wasted attempt to escape. "Wait! Wait! I'll tell you what you want to know."

I ignored his pleading and looked across the open field, where Mongo stood slashing his finger across his throat.

I shot a disgusted look at the man squirming at our feet. "If he says a word before I get back, shoot him in the foot, then the knee, then the hip. You get the point."

Hunter drew his pistol and racked the slide, ejecting a 9mm cartridge into the air. He caught the bullet between his fingers and took a knee in front of his man. "It sure doesn't look like much, does it?" The prisoner looked away, and Hunter grabbed his chin. "I'm trying to have a conversation with you. Now, behave and look at my bullet. Look how shiny and harmless it looks. It's almost cute, huh? I could throw these at you all day, and you'd hardly notice, but let me pitch one your way at around thirteen hundred feet per second and see how cute it looks."

Psychological warfare has always been far crueler than hand-to-hand combat could ever be. Fear scars deeper than pain, and it lasts forever.

When I reached the tree line, Mongo said, "He was dead when I picked him up on your side. I thought you might want to poke around in your guy's head a little, so I let you guys believe he's alive and well."

"Nice work, and excellent thinking."

I crossed the valley at a snail's pace and took a seat beside our one remaining bad guy. I leaned close and spoke just above a whisper. "I don't make speeches like my friend, so listen up. Your buddy over there gave us everything except a name. The next words out of your mouth had better be that name."

I pressed the muzzle of my pistol to his forehead and stared through his head. Little did I know we'd found the weak link.

He said, "We never heard his name. He's just the South African. That's all we know, I swear!"

He didn't cry, so that modicum of dignity bought a morsel of respect from me. I pulled the pistol from his head. "Hesitate just once, and you'll never take another breath. Did you kill the man in Montana?"

"No! I mean, yes, but . . ."

"Slow down, take a breath, and tell me what happened."

Sweat rolled from his flesh. "We killed him in Wyoming and moved his body to the Indian reservation in Montana."

My tone grew softer. "Why did you set the fire on the reservation?"

He furrowed his brow. "We burned the kill site, but that wasn't on the reservation."

"Very good. We're making progress by slowly establishing trust and communicating like the professionals we are. Tell me about Pamela Bingham."

"What do you want to know?"

"Come on, now. You were doing so well. Your chances of surviving were actually looking pretty good, but now you want to play games with me."

"No, that's not what I want. I'll tell you everything. We hit her place in Mexico."

"Where in Mexico?"

"Island of Women. It's in Spanish, but I can't—"

"Isla Mujeres. Very good. Keep talking."

He didn't hesitate. "She wasn't there. She had already bugged out."

"How did you know about this place?"

He squirmed. "We didn't know. The South African knew. I swear, that's all I know."

"Don't clam up yet," I said. "What were you going to do when you reached her house?"

"We were going to burn her out. We've got incendiary grenades and a two-oh-three launcher. She's on the run and scared, so shooting our way in was no good. We were going to burn her out and nail her when she took off. That's why there's four of us."

Does he know about the other two?

"Four of you? What do you mean four? It's just you and your buddy over there in the trees."

"There were . . . I mean . . . the other two."

I leaned in and locked eyes with him again. "Slow down, and tell me about the other two."

He swallowed hard. "We split up yesterday so all four of us couldn't get pinned down with our backs to the mountains in the same place. We were going to approach from different angles and cover all four corners of the house."

"You said *were*, past tense. What do you mean?"

His voice cracked. "We lost comms with the other two, and now I guess we know why."

"I guess you do. What was the plan after killing Pamela Bingham?"

"Report back to the South African for the next assignment. Look, man. I'm number four. I'm low man, and that's all I know."

I pointed across the valley. "That's exactly what your buddy over there said. Both of you can't be low man. That means one of you is lying."

I intentionally didn't ask a question and simply waited for his response. Silence is agonizing for those being interrogated, which makes it one of my favorite tools.

He finally cracked. "I'm telling you, I'm low man. I don't know anything. I'm just a hired gun."

I showed no reaction other than to glance back to the other side, where Mongo was babysitting a dead body.

Several long minutes passed before I said, "Wait here. I'm going to give your buddy over there one last chance to tell the truth, then you and I will finish our chat. Sound good?"

I didn't wait for a response. Instead, I jogged to the tree line, where Mongo sat against a tree with the warrior's corpse resting beside him.

I said, "It's time for a little social experiment."

Mongo stuck his fingers into his ears. "I thought it might come to that."

I drew my pistol and fired a single round into the ground, well clear of Mongo and the dead man.

The giant rose to his feet. "I'll give you time to get back across before I drag him into the open."

"Great."

Back on my side of the valley, I glanced across my shoulder to see Mongo carrying the corpse from the trees. I gave my prisoner a nudge with my boot and pointed across the opening with my chin. He turned to see Mongo drop the dead body from his shoulder to the cold ground. My trap was laid. All that remained was getting the rat to take the bait.

I drew my pistol and ran a hand across the slide. "I guess that makes you both the low man and the boss since you're the only one left."

His Adam's apple rose and fell several times while his mind had to be spinning out of control.

Not wanting to give him enough time to formulate a plan or a decent lie, I said in my calmest therapy voice. "What happens next is up to you. Here is my list of requests. I want the name and telephone number of your handler. I want the telephone number of the South African. And finally, I want the rest of the names on the kill list. When you give me those three things, we'll feed you, give you water, and send you on your way. If you do anything—absolutely anything—other than provide those three things . . . well, let's just say I hope you enjoyed the last meal you had."

He looked up at me with what could only be described as terror in his eyes. "I don't—"

Before he could say another word, I struck him just below his left eye with the butt of my pistol, sending him tumbling onto his side and groaning in agony. Planting a boot on his shoulder and pressing him into the dirt, I roared, "You've reached the limit of my civility."

At least two of his front teeth shattered when I shoved the muzzle of my Glock into his mouth. "No more games. No more lies. We're keeping this simple. I'm going to pull my gun out of your mouth, and you're going to say a name and a number. Anything else sends you to judgment day with your buddy over there."

I withdrew the weapon, and he whimpered. "McMillan. Jacob McMillan . . . embassy . . . Johannesburg. There's no kill list. We got one target at a time. You killed my handler. That's it. That's all I know. I swear!"

I turned immediately to Teresa, and she raised her eyebrows as if to say Jacob McMillan's name didn't ring any bells.

I rolled our prisoner onto his stomach with an aggressive application of my bootheel. "Cut him loose. Check him for serious injuries. And feed him."

"Are you letting him go?" Teresa asked.

"What choice do I have?"

Benicio said, "I will take him back to Ushuaia and turn him over to the authorities."

Hunter leaned down and sliced through the plastic flex-cuffs binding the man's wrists, then rolled him onto his side to cut his ankles free.

What happened next was the epitome of Clark's credo—surprise, speed of response, and violence of action.

The man waited for Hunter to touch the bindings on his ankles with his knife before he burst into action. In an instant, he yanked a small pistol from inside his pants, with a short piece of string tied to the frame, and raised it toward Hunter's skull. My partner caught the motion and threw up a hand to knock the pistol off-line, but it was too late. Three rounds came from two pistols at almost the same instant. The bullet from our prisoner's weapon caught the knife edge of Hunter's hand, but the other two rounds pierced the same entry hole between the prisoner's eyes.

Unsure what to do, I let my eyes fly over the scene in a desperate attempt to piece together what had happened in the previous instant. The prisoner was dead. Hunter was wounded and bleeding. And Gator stood in the perfect stance, with his Glock extended in front of him and a spiral of white smoke streaming from the muzzle.

Chapter 28
Old-Timer

Mongo stepped across the corpse and grabbed Hunter's wrist. He had the wound rinsed and a pressure bandage in place almost before Hunter could react, but when his reaction came, it was far from calm.

Hunter said, "That son of a bitch shot me in the hand! Whose man was he?"

Realizing what Hunter was asking, I intervened, "He was my responsibility."

"Who took him down?"

Gator holstered his pistol. "I did."

Our wounded man leapt to his feet as if launched from a cannon and grabbed two fists full of Gator's shirt. "You put a man down and hog-tied him, but you didn't search him for weapons? What kind of Cub Scout crap is that? If you screw up something that basic ever again, I'll shoot you myself."

Gator planted his palms on Hunter's shoulders and shoved him away. "Get off me! I put two in his head before he could put one in yours, so you're welcome."

I stepped between the two men. "That's enough. It was my fault. I should've searched him."

Hunter reached around me and gave the new guy another shove. "Don't do it again. You got me?"

Gator lowered his head and put on the humility the moment required. "I got you. It won't happen again. It's on me, and I'm sorry."

Hunter shouldered me out of his way and stepped toward Gator with an outstretched hand. "I'm sorry I blew up, but I got shot."

Gator took his hand, and the fight was over.

Hunter stepped away and turned back to the new kid. "You know this means I get to shoot you in the hand, right?"

Gator put on his best gunfighter face. "Good luck out-drawing me, old-timer."

A glance at my watch and the position of the sun in the northern sky sent me to Benicio's side. "How far are we from the lake?"

"Two hours, but if we follow this canyon, we will be back in what you called a bottleneck when the cabin comes into view."

I considered the news. "That's not happening. We have to look at this as a hostile approach on a well-trained Intelligence officer in a fortified position."

"Then we should go up again," he said. "The ridgeline is easy all the way to the lake, and we can break into teams at the northern peak."

"Then, up we go."

Singer had a moment of prayer over the bodies of the men who died in that valley, and we climbed the incline in silence.

Benicio's timing was spot-on, and the lake came into sight two hours after beginning our ridgeline trek. I stood in silent awe of the perfectly blue water stretching in both directions. The surface looked like mirrored glass, and it lay in serenity, nestled among the snowcapped mountains at every point of the compass. Had we not left four corpses behind us, the beauty before us could've been the majestic culmination and ultimate reward for hiking miles of some of the most rugged terrain I'd ever cross, but the reality of our lives and of our mission clawed at the corners of my mind, forcing me back into the dark reality of what lay both behind and ahead of us in that fleeting moment.

We inched forward until the cabin was in sight, and I said, "That's it. We've come a long way just to ring the doorbell."

Teresa said, "I've been thinking a lot about how to approach, and I have an idea if you want to hear it."

I said, "Of course we want to hear it."

She cleared her throat. "I know Pam well enough to know she's got some kind of intrusion detection system in place. It could be anything from tin cans on a string to some kind of high-tech IR laser setup. Whatever it is, we need to find it before it finds us. No matter how basic or how advanced it is, we can use it to communicate with her. If it's a camera system, which I doubt, I can look in the lens and tell her we're here to get her out."

Mongo spoke up. "Why do you think it won't be a camera system?"

She said, "Cameras are power hogs, and the sun isn't visible long enough to keep the batteries charged for very long, even if she had a good solar panel for each camera. I think it'll be some sort of broken-beam or motion detection system."

"How do you plan to use either of those to communicate anything other than an intrusion?"

"I told you about our number game. We use the number seven for everything. If we can find the sensors, we can trigger one of them once per minute for seven minutes. The pattern will be impossible for Pam to ignore, and she should realize it's me."

I asked, "Are you sure she doesn't use that system of sevens with anyone else?"

Teresa shrugged. "What difference does it make? Even if she

does, it will be a friendly, not an adversary. We can't expect her to roll out the welcome mat, but maybe we can get her to poke her head through the door instead of opening fire."

Hunter squeezed his bandaged hand. "What's wrong with climbing down into that cut and yelling, 'Hey, Pam! We're here to help!'?"

"It may come to that," Teresa said, "but she's nervous, on the run, and hypervigilant. She's as likely to answer with gunfire as with questions if we approach that way."

Singer was mysteriously missing from our powwow, and I found him perched on a rock behind his rifle aimed over the lake.

I asked, "What do you see?"

"Nothing yet, but it looks like God himself created this spot for an overwatch sniper. I've got clear angles in every direction and perfect visibility."

"Do you think we'll need overwatch on this one?"

Without lifting his eye from the scope, he said, "Are you sure we *won't* need overwatch on this one?"

"Good answer. Make yourself comfortable. You may be there a while."

Again, without looking up, he asked, "Can I have Gator?"

I considered his request. "I've got a bad feeling about this thing. I'm afraid we'll need all hands on deck before it's over."

He rolled away from his rifle and sat up. "What kind of bad feeling?"

"I don't know, but it feels like I'm missing something. What's your gut telling you?"

He swept some debris away from the rock beneath him. "It feels too easy, doesn't it?"

"It sure does, my friend."

I took a moment to lean against Singer's perch and ask the questions that never have any answers. "Are we doing the right thing?"

Singer slid to the edge of the rock and let his legs hang off the side. He said, "If Penny were down there in that cabin and afraid for her life, would you let anything stand between you and getting her out of there?"

"Of course not, but it's not Penny. It's a retired spook."

"Yeah, it is," he said. "But she's also Teresa's most trusted friend, and I'll bet you'd use those same words to describe Penny."

His wisdom never failed to fascinate and amaze me, but that time, I had a rebuttal. "Is that why we're doing all of this? Just to save Teresa's friend?"

It was time for another life lesson from the sniper philosopher.

He said, "Think about what we learned in the last twenty-four hours. We watched a man kill himself to avoid letting his superior or superiors know he'd failed. We interrogated a man who believed we'd just killed his partner, and he gave up this McMillan guy in the embassy in South Africa. As soon as that guy found an opening, he started shooting, and he wasn't dumb or arrogant enough to think he'd survive the gunfight he started. Essentially, he threw himself on the knife, just like his buddy did the night before."

I listened as he continued.

"All of those things add up to a high-level operation being run in the shadows by people who believe they'll never get caught. This thing is a lot bigger than Teresa Lynn and her best friend holed up in that cabin down there. This is exactly the kind of fire we stomp out all over the world. This time, though, we just happen to have a personal connection."

He paused and took another long look over the breathtaking lake. "Your gut's right, Chase. This thing is a long way from being over, and whatever happens down there tonight isn't going to be the resolution. Trust that gut, boss. It's not wrong very often."

His words washed over me, and I gave him a slap on the back. "If you need Gator, he's yours, but I could use him down there, especially if this thing turns itself inside out."

"I don't need him," he said. "I was just going to take advantage of a teachable moment. It's rare for a young sniper to see a position this good. Heck, it's rare for an old sniper to see a hide like this."

"Take him for half an hour," I said. "I need to brief Clark and pick teams."

Gator joined Singer, and the master brought the student one step closer to snatching the pebbles from his hand.

I installed the final relay station and opened the solar panel toward the sun.

Clark answered as if he'd been waiting by the phone with bated breath. "What's going on out there? I've been trying to reach you for an hour."

"Calm down," I said. "I just got the relay up and running. What's up?"

He said, "The *Lori Danielle* is in striking range, so that helicopter you wanted so badly is all yours."

"That's great news. When they drop anchor offshore, have Gun Bunny sling-load the RHIB and put it in the water at the Naval Prefecture. That'll be our egress plan. We've got good comms up and running on-site, and we plan to make our approach around sundown."

"Sounds solid," he said. "Did you get anything out of the second duo?"

"We did, and I need Skipper to start digging up a Jacob McMillan in the embassy in Johannesburg."

"Which embassy?"

"I assume the American Embassy."

"There's a problem with that assumption . . . aside from it being an assumption. There are about sixty high counsels, consulates, and embassies in Johannesburg, ranging from Australia to Zambia, but guess which one doesn't show up on that list?"

"I have no idea."

He made a buzzing noise. "Wrong, but thanks for playing. The correct answer is the American Embassy. It's located in Arcadia, Pretoria. You'll need to rattle his cage a little harder and narrow down which embassy he's talking about."

"There's a problem with that," I said. "Gator put two in his face after the guy shot Hunter in the hand."

"What? You had the guy trussed up, didn't you?"

"We did, but when we cut him loose, he snatched a throw-down on a string out of his pants and got off a round."

"Is Hunter all right?" he asked.

"Yeah. It was a through-and-through, and Mongo doctored him up."

"Good on the kid for popping the guy. Next time, tell him to search his prisoner before cutting him loose."

"Yeah, Hunter covered that with him."

Clark chuckled. "I'll bet he did."

"Get Skipper on it. Find out which embassy our boy McMillan is in, and do a deep dive."

"You got it," he said. "But next time, try to get a little more specific before you cap a detainee in the brainpan."

"Will do. I'll check in before we launch."

My team was servicing their gear when I stuffed my phone back into my pocket. "Is everybody ready to go?"

Hunter looked up. "We're loaded for bear, but I'm not sure why. Surely, we're not going to shoot at Ms. Bingham, are we?"

"I hope not," I said. "But you never know who might show up and try to get on our dance card."

"How are we pairing up?" he asked.

I said, "I'll take the western draw with Teresa and Gator while you and Mongo take the eastern draw. Singer's on overwatch, and I'm leaving Benicio with him as a second pair of eyes."

Hunter frowned. "Overwatch? Watching for what?"

"Nothing, I hope, but we can't be certain the four guys we put down are the only ones interested in hitting that house. These guys have been well stacked all the way, so I don't want to find ourselves in a fair fight."

Singer said, "If it comes to that, I'll make it as unfair as I possibly can."

"I know you will," I said. "Is everybody ready to move out?"

Chapter 29
Incoming

As the mountain peaks cast their lengthening shadows to the southeast, I called Clark. "We're moving out."

He said, "Roger. Skipper's still working on McMillan, but nothing yet. Be careful out there, and Godspeed. I don't know what that means, but it sure sounds fast."

We descended while there was still enough light to tell the difference between a bush and a teammate and made the valley floors in excellent time. We were using open-channel comms with the relay station overhead working flawlessly. I didn't like not having direct contact with the CIC onboard the ship, but any comms were better than no comms.

I said, "Okay, guys. It's game time. Approach with extreme caution. Remember, we're looking for booby traps, trip wires, reflectors, cameras, and anything else that could serve as a perimeter alarm. Do not approach the cabin. Is everybody good to go?"

Everyone reported ready, and we eased ourselves forward at a painfully slow pace, inspecting every inch of the ground, rocks, rising terrain, and anything else that could hide a sensor. Our night-vision monoculars served to brighten the world enough to continue searching, but without the small amount of light filtering off the lake, we would've been in a tarpit.

An hour into our search, Teresa said, "What's that sound?"

I listened intently but heard nothing.

She said, "It sounds like an electronic hum."

Singer said, "It's a drone, and it looks a lot like one of ours."

Almost before he finished talking, Skipper's voice sounded in my head, "Hey, boys and girls. It's nice to see you again."

"It's nice to be seen," I said. "I assume you're relaying comms through the drone, right?"

"*Drones*, plural," she said. "And I have you loud and clear."

"I hear you the same. Do you have thermal on the drone overhead?"

"IR," she said. "So, yes, I can see heat signatures."

"Please tell me we're alone out here."

She said, "I've got two warm bodies on the peak between the two parties. I assume that's Singer and somebody else on overwatch."

"That's right," I said. "Body number two is Benicio, our mountain guide."

"Oh, interesting," she said.

"Do you see anybody on the lake?"

"Nobody within striking distance. The closest real heat signature is twenty miles to the west, and the chopper and RHIB to the east are, of course, ours. There's a slight signature across the lake from you and the cabin, but it's too small to be a human."

"Who's in the RHIB?"

She said, "Tony's at the helm. I argued, but he won."

"Excellent. It's nice having him in the field with us, even if he's just a driver."

"Yeah, he's not good at being a *former* action guy. Just don't get him hurt again, please."

Teresa jumped in. "Found one!"

She motioned with a flattened palm for me to move closer to the canyon wall. I followed her direction, and she said, "What is it?"

"I don't know yet. I just caught a glimpse. I think it might be a reflector."

"A reflector for what?"

She leaned forward. "It could be a continuous beam system routing a laser to a receiver. You know, like the ones on bank robbery movies where a girl in a spandex bodysuit does a gymnastic routine to get through."

I leaned across her shoulder and shone my infrared floodlight on the device. My night-vision monocular transmitted a perfectly clear image to my eye. "I don't think it's a reflector, but I've never seen anything like it."

Mongo said, "Describe it to me."

"It's about three by three inches with a plastic border around what looks like a screen or a small solar panel."

"Does it have an external wire or a visible antenna?" he asked.

"Yes, there's a short wire hanging from beneath the device, but it's only about four inches long."

"That's all you'd need for close-range transmissions. Is it resting on small wire legs?"

"It is."

He said, "Back away as slowly as you can. It's a mini seismograph —a downsized version of the ones they use to measure the strength of an earthquake. This one is short-range and extremely sensitive. It's designed to detect footsteps or moving vehicles at close range. How did you approach it?"

Teresa said, "We were barely moving. I doubt we made enough vibration to trigger it."

"There's no way to know," Mongo said. "Try backing away as slowly as possible, and don't trip."

"Wait," Teresa said. "If this is a seismograph, I should be able to disturb it seven times and count on Pam to figure out it's me."

Mongo said, "That's Chase's call. I'm just here to tell you what it is. Does it make sense that Pamela would use a device like that?"

Teresa said, "It's exactly in her wheelhouse. She loves her gadgets." She turned to me. "What do you think?"

I backed away two more strides, easing my boots onto the soil as gently as possible. "It's your call. If you want to bump it and take our chances, I'm game. You know her a lot better than we do."

"I think this is our best opportunity," she said. "We've got nice cover here if she shoots, but if we get a chance to talk with her, we're close enough for her to recognize my voice. I'm not going to wait a full minute between taps, though. I think I'll wait fifteen or twenty seconds."

I said, "Does everybody copy what's about to happen?"

Everyone acknowledged, and Teresa took a long, deliberate breath. "Here goes nothing." She slid forward, keeping her body against the slope as much as possible, and I caught myself holding my breath.

She tapped the small device once, and from our perspective, nothing changed. A few seconds later, she gave it another tap, and things started happening. A light that had been on inside the cabin fell dark, and I judged that to be a positive reaction. If Pamela was inside the building, she was making the same moves I would make. Leaving herself backlit inside a confined space was an invitation for a shooter and certain suicide for the hapless victim.

I scanned the window coverings in search of any sign of movement, but nothing budged.

Teresa tapped a third time, and Singer said, "Motion, left side, second window."

I missed it, but a team of wild horses couldn't have pulled my attention away from the window after that moment.

The instant Teresa tapped a fourth time, Singer said, "Motion, same window," but Hunter said, "Motion, second floor, right window."

I asked, "Who else would be in there with her?"

Teresa shrugged.

She tapped a fifth and sixth time, prompting motion in both windows after each tap.

Singer said, "The motion upstairs looks mechanical to me. I think she's got some kind of device shaking the curtains to draw attention away from where she really is. I'd bet she's alone in there."

Teresa took another long breath. "Here comes the money shot."

Instead of tapping the sensor for the seventh time, she wrapped her hand around it and shook it hard enough to jar it loose from its mount on the rocks. Before she released the sensor, a massive explosion of bright white light consumed the rear of the house. I hadn't noticed the high-intensity lights mounted high on the exterior wall, but when they came to life, they were blinding. Instinctually, I threw up an arm to shield my eyes, and I yanked the night-vision monocular from my face.

Light wasn't the only thing filling the air around us. The staccato of full-auto small-arms fire ripped through the formerly dark and silent night, and the hiss and crack of supersonic rounds racing by my head sent me diving for the deck and dragging Teresa Lynn with me. I scrambled across the ground like a scared animal and dragged Teresa around a thin outcropping until we were pinned against the rock wall and gasping for breath.

The most bizarre things happen inside the human mind when death extends her cruel hand through the cosmos and claws at us with hatred and contempt for the living. Things that should be deathly serious become funny, and sounds we'd never otherwise hear sound like trumpets.

Teresa caught her breath and said, "Well, I guess she knows we're here."

Holding back the laughter was impossible, but the moment was fleeting. I called out, "How many shooters are there, Six?"

Singer said, "Only one, but—"

I never heard the rest of his transmission. Everything in the environment was shaken and tortured by the pair of explosions only a second apart, somewhere between my position and the lake.

"What's happening, Skipper?"

"I don't know, but I'm working it. Stand by."

Standing by is rarely a good plan in a shootout, but I wasn't convinced we were in a real gunfight. Rounds were flying in only one direction, and at least for the moment, we were all alive and keeping our blood on the inside, where it belonged.

"I need to know what's going on," I demanded. "Somebody give me a sitrep."

Singer said, "It's mortar fire from across the lake."

"Mortar fire? Who's shooting mortars at us?"

It was Skipper's voice that answered. "Uh, Chase, I don't think they're shooting at us. I think they're assaulting the cabin."

I closed my eyes and tried piecing together the situation. "Six, put some lead on that mortar position."

The thundering concussion of Singer's rifle rang out above the chaos, but three more mortar rounds slammed into their target and shook the foundations of the Earth.

My mind raced, and a thousand decisions came together at once. I ordered, "Six, kill the lights."

Without a word, the best sniper I've ever known sent us back into utter darkness in seconds. He said, "One, Six, the mortar positions are out of range. We've got to get Pamela out of that house before they walk a round in on her."

"That means they've got a spotter. Skipper, find him. Singer, pin Pamela down wherever she is, and hold her there. I'm going in to get her."

To my surprise, Gator grabbed my shoulder and held me down. "No, Chase! We need you in command. Stay here. I'm going in."

Singer's rifle bellowed its awesome report, time after time, and the impact of the massive .338 Lapua rounds crashing through the exterior of the cabin sounded like lightning bolts assaulting a lumberyard.

The open-channel comms filled with Gator's breathing came hard as he accelerated across the open field between our position and the back of the cabin. I threw myself to the ground and low-crawled into position to see him sprinting through the night. A mortar struck the ground thirty feet to his right, knocking the All-American Division 1 safety from K-State off of his feet and sending him sprawling across the ground. His body never stopped moving as he rolled with the momentum and returned to his feet, still in a sprint.

His voice cracked through his body's demand for more oxygen as he continued, undaunted, toward the cabin. "Tell me where she is, Singer!"

The sniper answered immediately. "Right side, three to five yards from the corner."

"Can you see me?" Gator asked.

"Affirmative."

"When I hit the door, bring down the rain so she can't fire on me."

As the scene played out in front of me, I remember thinking I'd never seen greater bravery than what Gator demonstrated with every stride. He was running into a house, under mortar attack, to rescue a woman who'd likely do everything in her power to kill him before he could get to her, but he never slowed down.

His two hundred pounds splintered the door of the cabin, and he disappeared inside. Singer did exactly as Gator ordered and poured lead into the structure as fast as his rifle would cycle, hopefully keeping Pamela's head down so Gator could get close enough to disarm her.

Two seconds after Gator plowed through the door and into the cabin, the mortar crew landed a round on the left front corner of the structure. Splintered wood, stones from the chimney, and debris of every description filled the air, and I said, "Gator, sitrep!"

By way of an answer, he groaned and growled among the sounds of the universe crashing down around him. Nothing he said sounded like words, but he was obviously still alive. The sounds pouring into my head could've been a train wreck or a bull destroying his stall from the inside.

In a last desperate attempt before charging the cabin, I called out. "Gator, report!"

He didn't answer me directly, but what he said told me exactly what was happening inside the cabin.

"Stop fighting me! I'm here to get you out. I'm American, and I'm working with Teresa Lynn."

I heard Pamela's voice for the first time through Gator's comms. "You're lying, and I'm going to kill—"

Another direct hit on the cabin by the mortar team silenced Gator's transmission, but Singer's rifle roared again.

"What are you shooting at?" I demanded.

Singer said, "I found the mortar team's observer. He's finished correcting fire . . . forever."

He didn't need an answer, but reestablishing comms with Gator was crucial.

"Eight, One, say status!"

Nothing.

"Sierra Eight, Sierra One, over."

Countless scenarios ran through my mind, but each one ended with the same conclusion. I said, "We've got to get him out of there. I'm going in. Mongo, you're in command."

I leapt to my feet, pulled my rifle to my shoulder, and took the first running strides toward the cabin that was seconds away from being annihilated by mortar fire. As I drew nearer to the cabin, a new sound pierced the air—a sound no American warrior can mistake.

My eyes flew to the east to see our chopper racing at full speed, only inches above the surface of the lake. The General Electric M134 Minigun poured five thousand rounds per second into the air, reducing everything and everyone north of the lake to lifeless detritus. Although I couldn't see her, I had no doubt who was on that gun. Ronda No-H, the best door gunner in the business, was undoubtedly gripping the weapon with both hands and screaming like a Viking as she mowed down the mortar team and anyone else waiting to join the fight.

With the mortar fire silenced, I refocused on the opening in the back of the cabin, where a door had once been, and I raced toward it and my soldier inside. I prayed I was on a rescue op and not a mission to recover bodies.

As my boot hit the bottom step leading up to the cabin, the empty doorway filled with the silhouette of a true warrior and a woman draped across his shoulder. He staggered across the porch and collapsed down the steps toward me. I lunged forward, planting my shoulder in his chest to steady him, but his body felt like Jell-O against mine.

Flames danced from inside the cabin, threatening to consume everyone and everything in seconds, so I grabbed at Gator and Pamela as I drove my heels into the ground in a desperate effort to drag them away from the fire. My thighs burned, screaming their protest against the task. My breath came in hard gasps as I begged my lungs to claw enough oxygen from the air around me to fuel my body long enough to escape.

When it happened, I could've believed it was the hand of God, but in reality, it was Mongo's enormous meat hook that yanked Gator away from me and into the darkness. With the load lightened by more than half, my legs celebrated the relief, and I repositioned Pamela on my shoulder for the sprint back to cover. I didn't know if her seemingly lifeless body was still breathing or if I was delivering a corpse to Teresa Lynn.

Chapter 30
Shaken, Not Stirred

I laid Pamela Bingham on the ground, well clear of the burning cabin, and looked up hoping to see Gator on his feet, but I was disappointed. Although not standing on his own power, he was sitting relatively erect against the trunk of a tree and drinking from a CamelBak.

Teresa Lynn fell to the earth beside her friend and laid a hand on her chest. Her hand slowly rose and fell with the rhythmic cycle of Pamela's breathing.

Mongo pushed Teresa aside and began Pamela's initial medical assessment. As interested as I was in her condition, duty required that I provide site security and get a picture of our status. "Sierra Six, Sierra One, report."

Singer said, "Mortar position destroyed, forward observer eliminated, house fully involved by fire, chopper is providing high cover. RHIB is en route."

"Roger," I said. "Sierra Eight is shaken, not stirred, and the primary is stable but unconscious. No casualties on this side."

"Sierra Four, report."

Hunter said, "No casualties, and I'm on perimeter security to the east."

I called Skipper. "CIC, Sierra One. Scene secure, primary is stable but unconscious, no team casualties. Put the chopper as close to my position as possible. We need to get Pamela into Dr. Shadrack's hands as quickly as possible."

"Roger, One. Stand by for the chopper."

Gun Bunny flew the Bell 412 with the precision of a surgeon and touched down a hundred yards from my position. With no backboard or C-collar, Mongo hefted Pamela into his arms and made for the helo. Teresa and I trailed in his wake, and as soon as they were aboard, I yelled for them to take off. I stepped away from the skid as Mongo pressed a catheter into Pamela's arm, starting fluids, and they climbed out to the east, over the lake and into the night.

I was surprised to hear Clark's voice. "Sierra One, Sierra Two. We're en route to the Naval Prefecture, and Tony's on his way to you in the RHIB, so don't shoot him."

"Roger, Two. We'll press to the east and meet the RHIB. Have him look for the IR strobe."

I looked up, tracing the line of the cliff to our sniper's position. "Break it down, Singer. We're exfilling to the east."

We moved far enough away from the burning cabin to avoid scorching Tony's eyes when he approached in the RHIB under night-vision goggles. Hunter activated the infrared strobe that would bring Tony to the sloping bank of the lake.

Gator was still wearing his glazed look, so I asked, "How you doing?"

He blinked several times in rapid succession. "I'm okay. I'm not sure what was worse, the second mortar on the house or the haymaker Ms. Bingham landed in my earhole."

"So, you're saying you got your butt whipped by a fifty-year-old woman."

Hunter laughed. "That's what I'm hearing."

Singer joined the rest of us with his massive rifle slung across his back, and I asked, "Where's Benicio?"

The sniper looked over his shoulder at the perch that had been his home for the past several hours. "He's where he belongs. Once we heard Pamela was out of the cabin, he thanked me for the adventure and disappeared back into the mountains."

"We couldn't have done it without him," I said.

Singer nodded. "You're right about that. What do you think happened here tonight?"

I took a seat on a rock. "All I can think of is half of a joint-forces operation. Your idea of assaulting the cabin with mortars sounded crazy when you brought it up a week ago, but I guess the assassins had the same idea."

He said, "I guess so."

Glancing back at the still-burning cabin, I said, "The mortar team was probably poised to strike as soon as either of their two-man elements showed up at the back of the cabin. They had no way to know that both of their teams were dead and we were the ones who set off the powder keg."

"That's a good theory," Singer said, "but it doesn't get us any closer to the man behind the curtain. I'm not sure we got enough intel out of the guy yesterday to find our way to the bottom of the whole thing."

The hum of the RHIB's engines filtered across the lake, and soon we were stepping aboard the boat with R/V *Lori Danielle* stenciled on the sides. Our so-called research vessel may never solve the mysteries of the deep, but she made a fine warship for those of us who spent more time saving the world with grit and muscle than those who tried it with science.

We pulled up to the weathered dock at the Naval Prefecture, where Disco and Clark stood awaiting our arrival. I tossed a line to my handler, and he secured it around a rusty cleat. I took his hand,

and he pulled me out of the boat and onto the wooden planks of the dock that clearly hadn't been used in decades.

A warrior's gun belt is as much a part of his body as his own flesh and blood. Without his belt carrying the tools of his deadly trade, the modern fighter is practically empty-handed. Instead of being fastened solidly around his waist, where he'd carried it since the first day I met him, Clark's belt, with his full complement of gear, lay dangling across his shoulder.

I motioned toward his belt. "What's that about?"

"It's about the new kid. Get him up here."

I'd spent many years having almost no idea what Clark was talking about, and that wasn't going to change in the middle of the night in Patagonia, so I turned back to the RHIB and extended a hand. "Get up here, Gator."

He took my hand and hopped onto the dock with a little more pep in his step than I'd seen just a few minutes before. The fog was gone from his eyes, and he was definitely more sure-footed.

I turned him toward my handler. "Clark's got something to talk about with you."

I leaned close. "If he mumbles and gets confused, just smile and nod. He's getting old."

In typical Clark style, he grabbed Gator's shirt and yanked the quarter-century-younger man to within inches of his face. "I didn't see what you did tonight, but I heard every second of it. Statistically, nobody does what you did out there. Everybody with any sense would agree that it's the stupidest thing a man could do."

Gator's face turned pale. "I don't know what I did, but if I screwed up, I'm sorry, and I'll work on it. Just teach me, and it won't happen again."

Clark released his grip on Gator's shirt and slapped a flat palm against his chest. "Don't ever interrupt me when I'm talking, and don't you dare stop doing it. What you did was, hands down, the most warrior stuff I've ever seen from any man, on any battlefield, anywhere on the planet."

Clark pointed into the distance to the east. "There's a woman on a ship out there who's alive because of you and that gunfighter's heart inside your chest. For nearly twenty years, I've been strapping on my Superman cape and following College Boy into fights all over the world to keep him alive, but he doesn't need me anymore." He snatched the battle belt from his shoulder and shoved it into Gator's gut. "I'm passing the cape down to you, so Chase is your responsibility now. Try not to let him lose any more body parts. Welcome aboard, kid. You earned your keep tonight, and everybody on this team is glad you're here."

Gator stood in awe as he stared down at the worn, weathered collection of gear in his hands that had collected more blood and sweat than most people will ever see. The grips on the Glock 19 were worn smooth, and the tourniquet carrier was stained black with the blood of honorable men. The dump pouch carried dirt and sand from every corner of the globe, and the first aid kit's zipper looked like it had been through a grinder. The magazine pouches sagged beneath the weight of their cargo, and the knife poised on the left side seemed to ooze the blood of countless men who'd fallen victim to its point.

He looked up. "I . . . uh . . . I don't know what to say."

Clark scoffed and pointed at Gator's belt around his waist. "Don't say nothing, kid. Just throw that shiny new thing you're wearing into the lake, and put on a real man's rig."

I caught Gator's hand before he could follow Clark's instructions. "Easy. Let's not get carried away. I'll take your shiny new belt. There's a couple thousand dollars worth of gear on that thing. I'd prefer to keep it out of the lake."

Gun Bunny planted the chopper in the center of what had been a gravel parking lot when the Argentinian Navy still used that piece of ground in years gone by, and we headed her way. With everyone except Tony on board, she brought the machine to a hover over the RHIB, and he rigged the slings to allow the RHIB to soar over the treetops beneath the chopper on her way back to the ship.

Back aboard the *Lori Danielle*, my first stop was in sick bay, and I was relieved to see Pamela Bingham sitting up in bed with a bottle of water in one hand and holding Teresa Lynn's hand in the other.

Teresa said, "Pam, meet Chase Fulton. He was in command of the operation tonight."

Pamela laid her water bottle beside her leg and extended both arms. I hugged her, and she said, "Thank you, Chase. Are you the one who I tried to kill inside the cabin?"

I pulled away and chuckled. "No, ma'am. That would be Gator. He'll be down to check on you in a few minutes."

She smiled. "I look forward to meeting him, but he needs to learn to defend his head a little better. I landed way too many solid punches that he should've blocked."

"He's still learning," I said. "But when you're back on your feet, maybe you can give him a lesson or two."

"Gladly. And thanks again . . . for everything."

"We're not finished yet," I said. "I'm headed to the CIC now, and probably South Africa when the sun comes up."

Chapter 31
Remember Us?

To my surprise, I found the combat information center empty except for the weapons officer, who may have been checking his eyelids for light leaks when I came through the door.

He glanced over his shoulder. "Oh, hey, Chase. Welcome back. Nice work out there tonight."

I made a show of scanning the room. "Thanks. Have you seen my analyst?"

He stretched his arms over his head, and through a massive yawn, said, "Yeah, she's upstairs in the new CIC."

"The new CIC?"

"Oh, yeah. We can't officially move the weapons station up there yet without live-fire sea trials, but everything else is up and running."

I waved him off. "Thanks. Sorry for interrupting. You can carry on."

He stood. "Thanks, but now that you're back aboard, we're secured from general quarters. It's officially peacetime again, and I'm going to bed."

"Sleep well, my friend. I'll see you in the morning."

I stepped through the door into what Weps called the new CIC, and I couldn't believe my eyes. It was a massive version of the closet-sized space that had been our onboard op center since the day we accepted the ship.

"Nice work," I said.

Skipper leapt to her feet and threw her arms around me. "Same to you, big boy. That was quite a night, huh?"

"You could say that." I waved my hand around the space. "What's all this?"

"About that . . . I sort of made an executive decision while you were playing in the mountains."

"Oh, so that's what we're calling it? Playing in the mountains."

She said, "Anyway, I decided the CIC downstairs was way too small, and this space is much better, so we moved everything up here."

"We?"

"Well, you know what I mean."

"What about the weapons control system?"

She pointed to a station in the corner. "It's up here, but until we test it in a live-fire exercise, we're keeping the official function downstairs. Ultimately, though, everything will be run from here when it's all done."

"The scientists aren't going to like their new miniature lab."

She shrugged. "We're not in the science business."

"No, we're not, and I'm thankful for that. I'm not smart enough to live in that world. And I'm extremely happy you moved the CIC up here. I agree that it was way too small downstairs."

"That's a relief," she said. "So, let's get down to business."

I checked my watch. "It's a little after three in the morning, and I'm exhausted. Can whatever you're calling 'business' wait for me to get a few hours of sleep?"

"Can you just give me three minutes?"

I sighed. "Okay, three minutes. Go."

"There's no one named Jacob McMillan working in any embassy in South Africa."

I said, "I'm sure you mean none that you could find."

"Well, yeah, but I'm good at this, and you don't get to use up my three minutes. There *is* a guy named Stefen Foust. His fingerprints were in the diplomatic corps under the U.S. State Department."

"So, he's an American."

She held up a finger. "Again, you're not getting my three minutes, so the clock stops while you're talking. He may not really be an American, but his fingerprints are."

"How can fingerprints have a nationality? What does that mean?"

"Okay, look. The three-minute thing is gone. We're in this now, so buckle up, buttercup. Yes, fingerprints can have citizenship if the country providing the passport includes fingerprint cards as part of the application. This guy, Stefen Foust, has a couple of passports from other places as well."

"So, he's got dual citizenship."

"No. Quadruple citizenship, at least."

"What? I've never heard of that."

She said, "I hadn't, either, but it turns out that it's a thing, and it's not really that rare in the business world."

"But this guy's a diplomat, you said."

Skipper grabbed a folder and flipped it open on her lap. "I didn't say he *is* a diplomat. I said his fingerprints *were* in the diplomatic corps." She spread out several pages on the table. "Here's a list of American citizens with quadruple citizenship or more. The list is pretty short, but their bank statements are not. Most of the names on this list are worth a billion dollars—billion with a B—or more. Other than high net worth, the other thing most of them have in common is ownership or high office in several companies located in several countries. This is considered citizenship by investment. Technically, it's handled by naturalization, but you get to go to the head of the line if you write a big enough check. Imagine that."

"This is fascinating, but is there something eye-opening coming soon?"

"Keep your pants on. I'm getting there. This Stefen Foust guy, whose fingerprints show up in the U.S. State Department diplomatic corps archives, has a left thumbprint that matches the right thumbprint of . . ." She slid a finger across the papers spread on the desk and finally stopped. "This guy."

I followed her fingertip. "Tobias Gjika? Is that how you pronounce it?"

"We're getting warmer. Stick with me here. It's going to get a little curvy, but I need you to keep up. It turns out that Gjika in English is Jacob, and Tobias Gjika's mother is Scottish. Here it comes. Are you ready?"

I threw up my hands. "Send it."

"Jacob's mother's maiden name is Mac Maoláin." She threw down her pen and raised both hands into the air in some sort of victory ceremony. "Bam, Baby! There it is!"

I sat completely lost. "There *what* is?"

"Don't you get it? Mac Maoláin is Gaelic, but anglicized, it's McMillan. Jacob McMillan, aka Stefen Foust, aka Tobias Gjika because of the crossed fingerprint connection."

I leaned back in my chair and squeezed my eyelids closed. "I'm way too tired for this. Explain it to Teresa and Pamela and see if they come to the same conclusion. To me, it's all way too thin, but I'm a knuckle-dragger, not a spy. We'll reconvene after breakfast."

She reclaimed her pen. "No, Chase. It's so simple. Look, it's all right here."

I held up both hands. "Sleep, shower, food, in that order, then we'll start again."

I didn't like leaving her with the impression I wasn't buying her super-sleuth thumbprint idea, but my brain was mush, and I believed sleep was the only option for changing that.

I was right. Sleep was the key, but the pound of bacon and five-egg omelet didn't hurt my brain's computing power, either. As promised, we reconvened in the new-and-improved CIC, but the guest list had obviously grown. The whole team, plus Teresa and Pamela, were waiting—somewhat impatiently—for my arrival.

All three women—Skipper, Pamela, and Teresa—began talking at once, and I felt my frontal lobe melting down again. I said, "Slow down, and please go one at a time."

It didn't work. All three continued, each trying to talk over the other two, so I headed for the door.

Mongo stopped me. "It works, Chase."

I spun on a heel and pointed at the giant. "You—and only you —explain it to me."

It took half an hour for my cranium to conform, but I slowly climbed on board their crazy train of thumbprint bingo. What finally convinced me was an excellent presentation of show-and-tell. Skipper brought up a larger-than-life-sized headshot of a distinguished-looking man with a well-manicured beard and salt-and-pepper hair.

I studied the picture and asked, "Who's that?"

Skipper smirked. "It depends on whom you ask. If you ask Google, his name is Tobias Gjika, an Austrian billionaire businessman with investments all over the world, and five—count 'em, five —legitimate passports."

I said, "Okay. Is there some reason I should doubt Google?"

Skipper held out an open hand toward Teresa, who said, "Google may know him as Tobias Gjika, but Pam and I knew him as Bahadir Kaplan, the Chinese Intelligence case officer from Turkey who ran the two of us for eighteen months."

Skipper jumped back in. "But that's not all. There's one more."

She brought up another picture of the same man sitting on a gorgeous horse and holding a long wooden stick in his hands. "According to the South African Polo Association, his name is Jacob McMillan, one of their most generous patrons."

I squeezed my head between my palms. "This job was so much easier when they just pointed me toward a target and told me to kill it."

Teresa said, "In the world of espionage, this one's pretty simple. In fact, I can't believe no one caught it before now. We've got analysts all over the world working twenty-hour days on this kind of stuff, and apparently, there's no record of a hit of any kind on this guy."

I looked up and finally found Clark hiding in the back with biscuit crumbs all over his shirt. I asked, "So, what do we do now?"

He wiped his mouth with the back of his hand and pointed toward Teresa.

She said, "Let's go get him, Chase."

* * *

We landed in Johannesburg after a short hop from Ushuaia to Mount Pleasant on East Falkland to force every ounce of jet fuel we could get in the tanks of the *Grey Ghost*, then 4,000 nautical miles over the Southern Ocean. I learned that rich people—and especially people who want others to believe they're rich—do a thing called "stomping divots" on the polo field at halftime. It looked ridiculous to me and gave me even more reasons to dislike every member of the equine species. I also learned of another tradition during halftime that didn't involve dodging landmines laid by polo ponies. Some of the players who aren't of the highest moral character rest their horses and spend a few stolen minutes with their concubines while their wives make fools of themselves stomping clumps of dislodged grass back into the ground. Our boy, Jacob McMillan, fell solidly into that group of the morally deficient.

Skipper became quite the actress, putting on her best South African accent and luring good ol' Jacob into her love nest. What he didn't expect to find there was a team of American covert operatives armed to the teeth, four American FBI agents, two officers of the World Court, and one particularly ambitious representative from Scotland Yard. The confusion on his face was more than abundant until the moment American Central Intelligence Agency case officers Pamela Bingham and Teresa Lynn stepped through the door, and each took one of his arms.

Teresa asked, "Remember us?"

Epilogue

The view across my feet—well, across my single real foot and my prosthetic—was spectacular. A roaring fire crackled in the massive stone fireplace of our chalet somewhere outside Vale, Colorado, and the two-story wall of windows gave me the perfect view of the slopes, where skiers and snowboarders of every skill level either crushed the course or crashed and burned. The latter was a lot more fun to watch.

I was sore, still a little cold, and completely certain skiing wasn't for me. Despite Kodiak's excellent instruction, I was out, but the rest of my family seemed to be solidly engrossed in everything about conquering the mountain. I enjoyed watching them enjoy themselves while I enjoyed the fire and the five-thousand-dollar bourbon in my glass.

Once everyone was back inside, dinner was delivered by a team of waiters dressed like penguins and determined to earn every penny of their coming tips. We ate, drank, laughed, and talked about everything except work.

Kodiak said, "I owe you an apology, boss. I didn't think you'd make good on your promise to take all of us skiing, but here we are." I nodded, and he raised a glass. "Here's to keeping promises and making new ones."

A chorus of cheers arose, and we drank.

Singer sipped his tea and turned to Clark. "So, are you really hanging up your boots?"

"I am," he said. "But you're not getting rid of me as easily as you might think. I may have to surrender my sword to a young gun, but I'll still be your handler. You just won't have me in the trenches to help you dodge bullets anymore."

As if we needed another reason to drink, Gator raised his glass. "Here's to gladly accepting a hand-me-down sword from an old guy."

That got a good laugh from everyone except the old guy.

Instead of laughing, the old guy himself raised a glass. "Here's to you, Gator . . . the second-best rookie operator I've ever met."

That almost brought a tear to my eye, and I turned to Clark and mouthed, "Thank you."

He cocked his head in confusion. "You thought I was talking about you? Oh, no. I was talking about a kid named Schwartz from Minnesota. He was really something. At least, I think it was Minnesota."

Laughter abounded, but not from me. I stepped away from the table and onto the deck, where eight inches of newly fallen snow waited on the handrail. I stepped back inside and said, "You may be able to dodge bullets, but how's your snowball game?"

There's never been a more epic snowball fight than what ensued after my initial shot. Everyone, from the world-class Russian ballerina to the retired A-10 driver turned *Grey Ghost* captain, and everyone in between, pelted each other with frozen orbs until we finally collapsed back inside the chalet around the fire. Socks came off, and bare feet hit the hearth for warmth and rejuvenation, and I couldn't stop my eyes from following Tatiana's muscled calves to her tortured feet, bent and shaped exactly like the inside of the pointe shoes in which she'd danced since before she could spell *ballet*. And I couldn't stop thinking about the hearts and souls of the men and women around me, whose scars and tormented forms ran too deep for anyone to see, but just like Tatiana, every one of them welcomed the torment in exchange for the privilege of doing what we were put on Earth to do.

Author's Note

At the time of this writing, it's been six years since *The Opening Chase*, book #1 in this series, began the formal editing process. In those six years, we've created thirty-three full-length novels and a novella. When *Opening* was published in May of 2018, I had an outlandish dream of someday selling three hundred books per month to add a modest royalty check to our retirement income. Now, because of your loyalty and astonishing support of my work, we've sold over a million books and created a catalog of work with tens of thousands of wonderful reviews. I work hard every day to put these stories on paper for you, but I know I'm not the reason the stories have become a commercial success and found homes on bookshelves all over the world. The reason this works is because of you and a few hundred thousand of your reader friends. I could write thirty more books full of nothing but my gratitude for your support and still never scratch the surface of my sincere appreciation for the amazing gift you've given me. I treasure the friendships I've built with so many of you, and I look forward to getting to know so many more of you as time goes by. Ultimately, what I want you to know is that I'm madly in love with the career you've given me, and I'll do my best to keep stacking books on your shelves that fascinate, delight, and captivate you for years to come. I'm having far too much fun to stop now.

268 · CAP DANIELS

Now that we have the thank-yous out of the way, let's have some fun. I'll start by apologizing for the cruel trick I played in the opening chapter of this one. Making the gunfight a paintball event made me laugh. Many of you probably figured it out before I revealed it in the closing paragraph of Chapter 1, but I hope at least a few of you fell for it. Writers, for the most part, are strange people, and we play silly games to amuse ourselves. Keep in mind that most of us spend extended hours completely alone, in quiet places behind a computer, playing with our imaginary friends. That sort of solitary confinement tends to feed our delusion that our characters might actually be real, and that does odd things to our already strange minds. When I write passages that are uniquely for my enjoyment, that is my small effort to drag myself from insanity back into reality. Thankfully, it's not working. Chase and the team are so much fun to play with that I don't care if they're real or not. They're my imaginary friends, and I love them. I hope you feel the same.

While we're talking about insanity versus reality, I feel the need to share a small peek behind the curtain with you. Most of the characters in these stories are based on actual people I've known, worked alongside, and loved through the years. Clark is the first and greatest example. He is absolutely real and one of the best friends I've ever had. I could write millions of words about his exploits alone, but no one would believe them. The reality of Clark is far more fascinating than any fiction I could dream up. He spent a lifetime in service to his country, in and out of uniform. He is the noblest and most sincere person I've ever known, and he's taught me more about myself and the world around us than anyone else in my life. To say I love him like a brother would be an unjust understatement. He's more to me than family. He saved my life one hot, humid night, and almost demolished my sternum doing so. Needless to say, I'll forever be in his debt, but maybe he could be a little gentler next time. For those of you who enjoy his screwed-up sayings, you'll be happy to hear that most of those are direct quotes right out of his mouth. I make up a few of them from time to time, but he provides me with plenty of material on his own. We said goodbye to him in this story, and that broke my heart. I've been cruel to him through the years with injuries and age, so the natural progression of the storyline dictated that it was time for his departure from the battlefield. I believe that's why Gator showed up. I felt like Clark's speech to Gator on the dock at the Argentinian Naval Prefecture was an appropriate hail and farewell. Don't worry, though. Clark isn't going away. He's just going to spend a lot more time in the op center and CIC with Skipper. He might even get some well-deserved time off to lie in the sun on South Beach while Maebelle toils away in the restaurant.

Since we mentioned Gator, let's talk about him for a minute. As you already know, I never write from a plan or outline. I simply sit down every day and write what falls out of my head. I never have any idea how the stories will end or even what will happen on the next page. When Gator showed up, I had a great deal of doubt that I'd be able to work him into a well-developed team and have him accepted by the fictional characters as well as you, the reader. Based on the emails you've sent, my fears were unfounded, and for that, I'm grateful. Gator is fun to write, and he put on a pretty good show in this story. I look forward to watching him grow and develop in the next few years. I hope you enjoy having him along for the ride.

I'm sure you thought I'd lost my mind when I wrote an entire chapter about the ballet. I'll confess without shame that I'm an enormous fan of ballet. The dancers are elite athletes who make an impossibly difficult feat look easy. If you've never seen a live ballet performance, please do yourself a favor and make it happen. By the time it's over, you'll likely be as deeply in love with the spectacle as I am. I realize a full chapter about something so far removed from gunfights and helicopter crashes feels out of character for my writing, but it gave me the opportunity to peel back another layer of Chase's personality and reveal some things about him that aren't obvious when he draws his pistol. While we're talking about it, I have to justify the obsession with the ballerina's feet. If you're not familiar with pointe shoes, they are pieces of silk with a wooden block sewn into the toe on which the ballerina dances for thousands of hours. That tends to do terrible things to their feet. I loved being able to use the analogy of the tortured feet to describe the scarred and tortured soul of the warrior. I may have a head full of imaginary characters, but I don't have a foot fetish.

The helicopter crash hurt my feelings when I wrote it. I didn't understand why it had to happen, and it shined an uncomplimentary light on Clark's skill in the cockpit. I almost cut that scene from the story until the Bell 412 became such an integral part of the mission in the climactic action sequence. The MH-6 Little Bird wouldn't have had the strength to do what the civilianized Huey pulled off. So, I apologize for destroying the Little Bird, but the Huey makes a much more believable piece of aeronautical muscle for the team.

It's time to talk about Tierra del Fuego, the Land of Fire. I didn't realize that magical piece of land at the bottom of the world would become such a character in this story, but I'm so glad it did. I try to turn settings into characters when I'm fascinated with the landscape or people of a location. The tip of South America certainly qualifies as a place worthy of fascination. Literature professors like to talk about symbolism in works of fiction, and I believe I accidentally accomplished a wonderful piece of symbolism in this story, even though nothing I ever write will be considered literature worthy of study. Without intentionally doing so, I believe the character of Benicio, the mountain guide, is the personification of the inanimate mountains. He gave them a voice and used that voice to teach the lessons of the ancient mountains. Benicio's quote concerning the puma is my favorite line of this novel: "Thank you for not shooting her. Sometimes peace requires more courage than war."

I'm not smart enough to understand where those tidbits of wisdom come from, but I love when they drip from my fingertips and onto the page. Singer's wisdom especially fascinates me. When his speeches begin, I type as quickly as my fingers can go, in a desperate effort to keep up, because I never want to miss what he has to say. I made that statement so you wouldn't be fooled into believing such wisdom is somehow embedded in my skull. It's not. I'm a simple man with a small talent for painting pictures with words. When those words present wisdom or something profound, please don't believe me to be a philosopher. I am not. In those moments, I'm merely a typist.

Speaking of typing, I'll share a little piece of my youth with you. When I'm writing well and the story is flowing perfectly in my head, I type around 120 words per minute. I'm pretty proud of that accomplishment, and I recognize that typing is one of the most valuable skills I've ever learned. Without that skill, you would've likely never heard of Cap Daniels. Here's how that skill came to exist in me. Years ago, back in the dark ages, high school students used to stand in line and sign up for classes for the next school year before each year ended. The youth of today will never believe this, but we actually wrote our name on a real piece of paper, with an actual pen, to request the class we wanted for the coming year. Here's a glimpse into fourteen-year-old me. I was standing in line, behind the most beautiful girl in school, waiting to request my future classes. I had an enormous crush on her, and I had no ability to form coherent sentences when she was in the room. When she finished making her selections and stepped away from the table, I looked down to see one glorious, beautiful, blank space remaining beneath her name. It was the last seat available in the class, and I had no idea which class it was. It didn't matter. I scribbled my name in that one remaining space beneath hers. I was so excited about having a class with her in the coming year that I never read the top of the page. To my surprise and enormous delight, she and I both got the class the next year, and it was typing. I never mustered the courage to ask her out or tell her how she made me melt, but I did learn to type, and for that, Cap Daniels is endlessly thankful.

All right. This author's note is running long, and you're probably ready to move on to another book by another author, so in that spirit, I'll wrap this up with one final morsel I think you'll enjoy. When I introduced the character of Teresa Lynn a few books ago, I based her character on my sister, Teri. Fast forward several months, and Teri joined us for a holiday cruise through the Caribbean. My sister has the most delightful and generous personality of anyone I know. She'd rather give away everything she owns to those in need than accumulate anything for herself. The world would be a far better place if there were a few million more Teris on the planet. On the aforementioned cruise, there was a casino where I spent a little time and a lot of money, and in that casino was a dealer with a well-manicured beard, salt-and-pepper hair, and apparently, a great smile. Teri became somewhat enamored with the dealer and would stroll through the casino from time to time to catch a glimpse of him and perhaps swoon a bit. His name was Stefen. I changed his last name in this story to protect the guilty, but that was his given first name, and he was from South Africa. I was determined to work him into the story with Teresa Lynn, but I had no clue how I'd be able to do it. I believe, and I hope you agree, that it came together nicely in the end.

Thank you again for letting me roam around, rent-free, in your head for a few hours while you read this story. I enjoyed the visit, and I hope we get to do it again soon. I promise to put another book in your hands as soon as possible, and I hope you love every page.

—Cap

About the Author

Cap Daniels

Cap Daniels is a former sailing charter captain, scuba and sailing instructor, pilot, Air Force combat veteran, and civil servant of the U.S. Department of Defense. Raised far from the ocean in rural East Tennessee, his early infatuation with salt water was sparked by the fascinating, and sometimes true, sea stories told by his father, a retired Navy Chief Petty Officer. Those stories of adventure on the high seas sent Cap in search of adventure of his own, which eventually landed him on Florida's Gulf Coast where he spends as much time as possible on, in, and under the waters of the Emerald Coast.

With a headful of larger-than-life characters and their thrilling exploits, Cap pours his love of adventure and passion for the ocean onto the pages of the Chase Fulton Novels and the Avenging Angel - Seven Deadly Sins series.

Visit www.CapDaniels.com to join the mailing list to receive newsletter and release updates.

Connect with Cap Daniels:

Facebook: www.Facebook.com/WriterCapDaniels
Instagram: https://www.instagram.com/authorcapdaniels/
BookBub: https://www.bookbub.com/profile/cap-daniels

Also by Cap Daniels

The Chase Fulton Novels Series

Book One: *The Opening Chase*
Book Two: *The Broken Chase*
Book Three: *The Stronger Chase*
Book Four: *The Unending Chase*
Book Five: *The Distant Chase*
Book Six: *The Entangled Chase*
Book Seven: *The Devil's Chase*
Book Eight: *The Angel's Chase*
Book Nine: *The Forgotten Chase*
Book Ten: *The Emerald Chase*
Book Eleven: *The Polar Chase*
Book Twelve: *The Burning Chase*
Book Thirteen: *The Poison Chase*
Book Fourteen: *The Bitter Chase*
Book Fifteen: *The Blind Chase*
Book Sixteen: *The Smuggler's Chase*
Book Seventeen: *The Hollow Chase*
Book Eighteen: *The Sunken Chase*
Book Nineteen: *The Darker Chase*
Book Twenty: *The Abandoned Chase*
Book Twenty-One: *The Gambler's Chase*
Book Twenty-Two: *The Arctic Chase*
Book Twenty-Three: *The Diamond Chase*
Book Twenty-Four: *The Phantom Chase*
Book Twenty-Five: *The Crimson Chase*
Book Twenty-Six: *The Silent Chase*
Book Twenty-Seven: *The Shepherd's Chase*

The Avenging Angel – Seven Deadly Sins Series
Book One: *The Russian's Pride*
Book Two: *The Russian's Greed*
Book Three: *The Russian's Gluttony*
Book Four: *The Russian's Lust*
Book Five: *The Russian's Sloth*
Book Six: *The Russian's Envy* (2024)
Book Seven: *The Russian's Wrath* (TBA)

Stand-Alone Novels
We Were Brave
Singer – Memoir of a Christian Sniper

Novellas
The Chase Is On
I Am Gypsy

Made in the USA
Las Vegas, NV
04 June 2024

90735680R00163